Project Renegade

Samantha Simard

ISBN-13: 978-1-7326392-8-7

Also by Samantha Simard:

Wolfe & Vaughn Mysteries
Stitches
Scar Tissue
Wounded
Shorts Vol 1 (available on Kindle Vella)

For Mom and Dad, always.

And for everyone who supported me throughout my graduate school journey. This is the end result, and it wouldn't have been possible without you!

"Those who can make you believe absurdities can make you commit atrocities."

- Voltaire

"I have come to bring fire to the earth, and how I wish it were already blazing."

- Revelation 20:4

Chapter One

The Chosen One couldn't stop trembling.

It was an involuntary movement, adrenaline dumping into his bloodstream as he realized that the prophecy he'd been preached his entire life was about to come to pass. He stared up at the cross with eyes as blue as cornflower, reaching out tentative fingers to brush against the solid oak. He'd watched from afar as some of the men had cut down trees and hewn the pieces by hand, joining them together before moving it inside the chapel. At only thirteen years old, the Chosen One wasn't large enough for his extremities to reach the ends of the symbol, but he had a feeling that wouldn't matter.

Not to the Reborn, who were fanatical in their belief that his father—*their* Father, as they'd come to call him—was right and just in his belief that God spoke to him directly. Told him that in order for peace to come to Earth, for the sins and blackness of man to be erased, the Chosen One had to be sacrificed. That he would be born again—rise from the dead like Jesus did, on the third day after the crucifixion—and lead the Reborn to glory in the new world after the coming apocalypse. But hearing the fantasy and seeing the reality were two different things, and instead of feeling a sense of calm, or purpose, or even simple resignation, all the Chosen One wanted to do was run screaming out of the chapel.

His eyes slammed shut as the doors behind him wrenched open, squeaking on their rusted hinges.

He wasn't going to get the chance to run.

The Reborn had arrived to lead him to slaughter.

~***~

Chapter Two

Adam "Dev" Devereux jerked awake with a choked-off scream, sitting up straight from where he was slumped over his desk. His breathing came in ragged pants and he squeezed his eyes shut just as quickly as he opened them, adrenaline coursing hot through his limbs. Under his faded gray Army t-shirt the unmarred portion of his back prickled with goosebumps, while the scar that bisected his shoulders and ran the length of his spine in the shape of a cross rippled with tension. It was hardly the first time he'd had the nightmare about the chapel, but trying to convince his body not to react like it was happening in real time was pointless.

A noise from outside Dev's bedroom made him go stock still, gripping the edge of his desk with both hands, blue eyes locking on his closed door. It could've just been the house settling—ancient brick townhomes on Beacon Hill tended to do that—but given the nature of Dev's job, there was always the possibility that a seemingly innocent thing was actually sinister. And if it *wasn't* the house settling, then it was definitely a floorboard creaking underfoot… and he was supposed to be alone in the house.

Quickly Dev's gaze roved over the surface of his desk. It was a bulky metal-bodied find from the SoWa Vintage Market that he'd modified for his purposes, which were twofold: experiments and research. A butcher block top was partially covered by a weathered ink blotter, where his head had been pillowed moments before. Tools of various sizes and shapes were piled up on either side, and a library card catalogue held screws, spark plugs, drill bits, and other odds and ends. His gaze caught on a carpentry hammer and he grabbed it, carefully pushing his rolling chair back and standing up with well-practiced silence.

It took four of Dev's long-legged strides to cross the width of the room, bare feet planted precisely where he knew the joists didn't squeak. He held the hammer in his right hand, near the base of the handle, and took up position on the left side of the door. Just as he reached for the knob with his left hand, the door began to swing inward, so he pivoted his weight on his hip and brought the hammer up and back to strike. The intruder became visible as the hammer began to fall, and he was barely able to stop it from connecting with her face when he realized who it was—not an intruder, but his landlord.

"Fuck me!" Aoife Porter exclaimed, her voice a couple of octaves higher than usual as she took a giant step backward. Hollywood's sweetheart and a North End native, Aoife was supposed to shooting a movie on location in Costa Rica; in fact, yesterday she'd texted Dev a picture of herself with a Macaw on each shoulder. She'd been flushed and happy then, but now she had a hand pressed to her chest, her light brown skin gone pale and clammy. She wore an oversized men's t-shirt and tie-dyed shorts as pajamas, the worn-in clothes hanging off her slender frame. "Jesus, Dev, what the hell? Remind me never to come check on you when I hear you scream again."

"Sorry," Dev said quickly, tossing the hammer on to his bed. It felt like somebody had poured a bucket of cold water over his head—he'd come *way* too close to caving in the skull of one of his closest (only) friends. He braced himself against the doorjamb, holding out an empty hand palm up in Aoife's direction. "Just a nightmare, that's all."

"Just a nightmare, my ass," Aoife muttered, but she took his hand, allowing him to tug her into the room. She sat down heavily in the desk chair he'd just vacated, pushing her tumble of loose black curls out of her face. The ends of her hair were dyed a vibrant pink, presumably for her latest project. "Which one was it this time?"

"An oldie but a goodie: on the verge of being sacrificed by a violent pseudo-Christian cult," Dev replied, sitting down across from her on the end of his bed. Over her shoulder he could see the large bulletin board balanced on top of the card catalogue on his desk. Pinned to the cork was every newspaper article, scholarly journal, and relevant photograph he could locate about the Reborn… and consequently, about his father and himself. Red thread connected potential leads, and black thread was strung between dead ends, like something a police detective used in a movie but not in real life. He'd been building out the board ever since he was told three months prior that the Reborn might be operational again, and it was starting to look as ragged around the edges as he felt. "Why are you here, anyway? Thought you weren't supposed to be back from Costa Rica for another week."

Aoife made a face. "Our illustrious director got stung by a jellyfish in a very… *sensitive* place. He's out of commission for a while, and so are we. The studio's afraid if they try to replace him, he'll have another social media meltdown." She followed Dev's gaze to the board behind her before glancing at him, dark eyes knowing. "Have you talked to—"

A loud buzz interrupted Aoife and had them both turning toward Dev's cell phone, which was plugged into the wall by the bed. It was charging on the nightstand, next to the digital clock that read 5:13 AM. "Must be work," Dev remarked, swinging his body over the corner of the mattress and snatching up the device. He was used to going into work whenever he was needed, but he was perturbed because his team had returned from a grueling field op in Mexico City only about twelve hours ago, and usually they got at least twenty-four hours to recover. Seeing Flynn Walker's caller ID flare to life on the screen would normally be welcome, but not so much now. "I've gotta take this."

"Still not sure why that think-tank of yours is so super-secret," Aoife remarked, her casual words lodging a nettle of guilt in Dev's heart. Despite knowing about his past as the son of Frederick Devereux, notorious cult leader and world-renowned asshole, she had no idea what he *really* did for a living—that when he claimed he was going to a conference or a research lab, he was actually headed out on covert ops. But as usual she respected his need for privacy, standing up with willowy grace and heading out the door. "Goodnight, Dev."

"Goodnight," Dev echoed, knowing full well that his day was just beginning.

He turned his attention to the phone in his hand, but not before catching a glimpse out his window; it looked down on Marlborough Street, its trees and brick-faced townhomes coated in a layer of fresh snow. His gaze caught on his reflection for a second, which showed a towheaded guy with a lanky build and a crooked smile. The picture of Midwestern aw-shucks combined with a dash of Santa Barbara surfer boy, a polite pacifist with a genius level intellect. But on the inside he was a survivalist, and a marksman, and a killer. He could diffuse a bomb as easily as he could make one, and the only reason he hadn't gone down a darker path than the one he'd walked was because he got caught and turned toward the light.

The phone buzzed again, tinny and insistent, snapping Dev out of his thoughts. "Hey, big guy," he said when he answered the call, an unconscious smile slipping across his face. That was the effect Flynn usually had on him, for reasons that Dev never allowed himself to examine too closely. "How are those bruised ribs treating you?"

"About as well as you might expect," Flynn drawled, a strong amount of Texas in his voice thanks to the early hour. He sounded more tired than Dev felt, and with good reason. While Dev had been melting locks off doors to free some trapped migrants, Flynn and Lottie were kicking ass and taking names as per usual, and neither of them had walked away unscathed. "And I'm sure you were wondering whether I forgot it's your turn to bring coffee and donuts to work. The answer is *no*, I did not, so you better be stopping at Kane's on your way over here."

"There's a problem with that, you know." Dev put the call on speaker and tossed the phone on his bed, yanking open the nearest dresser drawer to hunt for clothes. He badly needed to find the time to do laundry. "Kane's doesn't open until seven o'clock. Also, I'm assuming you're not just calling to remind me of my breakfast related duties."

Flynn sighed, and Dev could picture him rubbing at the perpetual salt-and-pepper scruff on his face. It was dark brown when they met, not a hint of gray, and Dev had often wondered how much of the color change had to do with him. The way he operated in the field wasn't exactly traditional, and they'd both had their fair share of near-death experiences as a result. "Afraid not. The boss lady wants us in the war room ASAP. Matter of life and death, national security and some Congressman's wallet is at stake—you know the drill."

"Gotcha." Dev grabbed up a set of boxer-briefs and jeans, glancing only briefly at the bulletin board that displayed a good portion of his life's story. He forced his mind away from it and started calculating the amount of T stops between home and work. "I'll be there in an hour."

~***~

Flynn Walker sat in a leather arm chair in the war room at Project Renegade and contemplated the nature of mornings.

He thought there was something inherently magical about being awake while the majority of people were still tucked away in their beds. He joined the Army right out of high school, and before basic training he hadn't been an early riser. Growing up on a cattle farm should've programmed that into him during his youth age, but that element of their lifestyle had worked its way into all the Walker children *except* him. The Army didn't give him a choice—if he wasn't up at five in the morning when the bugle sounded over the loudspeakers, he was scrubbing toilets with his toothbrush at midnight.

Toilet toothbrushes were a long time ago now, but the lesson to appreciate the quiet stillness of the morning had stuck with him through his transition from Delta Force to the CIA and then back to the Army. He took a moment to practice that appreciation now, watching the sun rise through the huge wall of windows that overlooked Boston Harbor. The Army taught him to eat and sleep when he could because there was no way to know when he would get another opportunity, and he treated absorbing a peaceful atmosphere much the same way.

The war room wasn't a place that most would consider *peaceful*, especially because of its name, but most of the time it served as the calm before the storm. Its features included vaulted ceilings, hardwood floors, and a giant digital screen fronted by an L-shaped couch, a couple of chairs, and a low table for snacks and drinks. Double doors at the top of the stairs leading to the loft closed it off from the rest of the building, framed on either side by computerized glass panels that could frost over if the field team needed privacy.

On paper Project Renegade was a think-tank that did research and advocacy in several fields, including social policy and political strategy. In reality no one without a high-level government clearance ever got past the first two floors of their nine-story blue glass and brick building near the Summer Street Bridge. That was because their "think-tank" was in fact an off-the-books branch of the United States Intelligence Community. More secret than the CIA and Delta Force combined, which was saying something.

Booted footsteps sounded on the stairs leading up to the war room, followed a second later by Charlotte "Lottie" Tran's voice as she pushed the doors open: "Morning, sunshine! How's the ribs?"

"They hurt, but I'll live," Flynn responded, and he traded his view of the light-dappled buildings for one of his coworkers instead. The first female Army Ranger turned super spy, Lottie was the daughter of Vietnamese immigrants and one of Flynn's best friends. Her ochre skin was littered with tattoos, the most eye-catching of which was a red-and-gold dragon that took up most of her right arm. Her jet-black hair hung in a braid down her back, and her dark angular eyes crinkled at the corners when she smiled at him. She was ready for wherever their latest mission would take them in a black t-shirt, biker jacket, and jeans. "You get that cut stitched up?"

Lottie lifted the edge of her shirt, showing him where a bad guy's knife had sliced her abdomen, thankfully not deeply. A gauze dressing covered up the wound and most of her stomach piece, which was a giant colorful Luna moth. Now, unless she chose to get a cover-up, it would be a giant colorful Luna moth with a sick scar. "All better, more or less." She frowned. "Any idea why Kaja called us in so early?"

Before Flynn could respond, the elevator in the back of the room dinged with an arrival. Its doors parted to reveal Tara Byrne, hacker extraordinaire and Project Renegade's resident tech nerd. An old compression fracture in her spine meant Tara split her time between walking and using a wheelchair, and today was a chair day. She was a sharp-jawed blonde with square-framed glasses and a lip ring that gleamed when she spoke. A gray MIT sweatshirt was paired with black Chuck Taylors and a corduroy skirt and tights. "Hey guys. Is it Dev's turn to bring breakfast?"

"Yeah, and that nerd better be picking up Kane's," Lottie said, sitting down on the edge of the coffee table, her elbows on her knees. "Speaking of which… you guys think Dev's doing okay? You know, with the whole 'the narcissistic sociopathic father I thought I killed might actually be alive' thing?"

It never ceased to amaze Flynn that despite having dated for a year after they met, Lottie and Dev were incapable of getting on the same page emotionally. Both of them were dry-witted and somewhat cynical, not so much about the world but about *themselves*, and Flynn thought that was where the disconnect came from. But maybe he was biased, having known Dev for far longer and arguably better than Lottie did, mostly because he paid attention to what Dev *didn't* say. He had joined the rest of the team (plus the office, custodial, and human resources staff) in being equal parts terrified and relieved the day "Delottie" imploded like a dying star, and he liked to think it was because he wanted to see both of his friends be happy. But deep down, he knew that wasn't why. Deep down, he knew had feelings for someone that he knew would never love him back, not in the way he wanted.

He was snapped out of his thoughts by Lottie waving a hand in front of his face and saying, "Earth to Flynn! Come in Sergeant Walker—you alive in there?"

"Yeah, just… never mind." Flynn shook his head, batting away Lottie's hand when she playfully tapped his nose with her index finger. "To answer your question, I think Dev's putting on a brave face. But he's not okay."

"He does seem a little *too* put together, even for him," Tara agreed. She picked up the tablet resting on the table and swiped a few times, bringing the big screen to life. It glowed with Project Renegade's logo, a gold-over-black line art image of a human brain from the side, superimposed over two crossed swords. The agency motto, *scientia sit potentia*, appeared directly below the logo, Latin for *let knowledge be power*. "Are you worried?"

"Of course I am," Flynn said quietly, rubbing a hand over the back of his neck. The thick callous on his trigger finger scratched over his buzzed-down hairline. "I didn't mention this in the debrief last night, but you know how he had to defuse that bomb?" Twin nods from Lottie and Tara, both of them no doubt vividly recalling exactly how wrong their jaunt to Mexico City had gone. "At one point, I looked over at him… and his hands were shaking."

Lottie let out a low whistle, sitting back in her chair. "Seriously? That doesn't sound like Dev."

"It doesn't," Flynn agreed, swallowing hard. Admitting this out loud felt like a betrayal somehow. "When we were over in the Sandbox, he must've disarmed hundreds of bombs. I know there were times when he was scared shitless, because I was too. But no matter what was going on, I *never* saw his hands shake. Until yesterday."

"That's bonkers," Eileen Stanley said from where she was leaning against the doorjamb, accent all South London. No matter how much training Lottie and Flynn had that was meant to prevent getting surprised, Eileen was somehow able to sneak up on them from time to time. Her ginger hair was tucked up under a gray knit hat, hands shoved in the pockets of a matching half-trench coat. Those hands belonged to a thief and a con artist, but also to one of the most loyal friends Flynn had ever known. "You think he's okay to go in the field again?"

"That's not up to us," Tara said, nodding at the woman standing in the doorway behind Eileen. "It's up to her."

"Boo," Kaja Kamienski deadpanned, steering an almost comically surprised Eileen into the room. The sister of a Boston Police detective, Kaja had forged her own path in the NSA, and one particular joint operation with the CIA eventually culminated in the formation of Project Renegade. She shed her winter coat to reveal a smart purple dress that set off her dark hair and eyes, her mouth turning downward in a frown. "And where *is* Dev, anyway?"

The doors swung inward again and Dev entered, arms laden with a big white Kane's Donuts box and coffee stacked on top of it. "Sorry, the fucking Red Line was delayed. Shocking, I know." He aimed a crooked grin in Flynn's direction. "But I made it to Kane's. Clearly."

Flynn's answering smile was carefully friendly as he took the steaming cup Dev offered on his way to put the box of donuts on the table. "All that effort for me? Not sure my black ol' heart can take it."

Lottie snorted. "None of our hearts are black *yet*, but they will be if we keep eating donuts for breakfast." Despite those words, she was the first one with a hand in the box once it was open, extracting a cookies and cream from the dozen assortment. "So what's with the DEFCON one, Kaja?"

Kaja selected a lemon donut. "Well, as you're aware, we're looking for anything and everything we can find related to the

Reborn. Tara built an algorithm specifically for the search, and it's running twenty-four seven." She licked some icing off her thumb, expertly avoiding what looked like a fresh manicure. "But this isn't about that." To Tara: "Bring up the latest uploaded folder."

Tara did as she was asked, flicking her fingers over the tablet until several images, documents, and even a video clip loaded on to the big screen. "What are we looking at, boss?"

"There's a drug manufacturer in Germany that needs our help," Kaja started, somehow managing to make munching on her donut look elegant even as she talked. "A Senator who shall currently remain nameless is trying to get a bill through Congress that would lower the price of certain drugs, and Wohlbefinden Pharmaceuticals is first in line to supply the pills if it passes." She took the tablet from Tara and selected one of the images, blowing it up so they could see it was the inside of a fully-loaded semi-truck trailer. "A large shipment of Dimethyltryptamine—DMT for short, street name Dimitri—will be en route from Wohlbefinden's facility in Hamburg this afternoon, headed for Budapest, Hungary."

Eileen raised one hand from where she'd come to sit on the backrest of Lottie's chair. Her other hand held a strawberry donut. "Why are they using a truck? Couldn't they just put it on a plane?"

"DMT has to stay within a certain temperature range in order to remain stable," Dev said, studying one of the documents, and Kaja made it bigger so everyone could see it. He hadn't taken a seat, only leaned against Flynn's chair. "What is it being used for? The last time I read about DMT was when I went through some old CIA files about abandoned projects."

It was Lottie's turn to raise a hand. "Wasn't that one of the drugs the CIA tried using for mind control?"

"Yes, DMT was utilized during Project MK Ultra, albeit unsuccessfully," Kaja acknowledged, nodding. "But currently it's being looked at as a potential treatment for some mental illnesses—sort of like psilocybin." Otherwise known as magic mushrooms, and from the text on the big screen Flynn parsed out that DMT was also plant based and occurred in nature. "In the wrong hands, however, DMT could do a lot of damage. Anything from being sold on the street to unsuspecting junkies to deliberate torture. Its effects range from euphoria and hallucinations to total depersonalization depending on the individual and circumstances. You can imagine how bad things could be if this shipment gets stolen."

"And you have reason to think it will be?" Tara asked, and when Kaja wordlessly handed back the tablet, expression grim, Tara's eyebrows sprang up to her hairline. "Oh shit." She threw another image on to the screen, of a white wall spray painted black with "YK4" dripping down it in white. "YK4 is a dark web mercenary group out of Europe that basically does whatever as long as the price is high enough. Their financials are always bouncing around, but it looks like they got a big transfer recently. Could be related to some other drug-adjacent thievery that the CIA believes they've been doing for the Russians... but maybe not." She tapped at the screen. "There's a black market auction happening in Budapest the same day the shipment of DMT is due to arrive. Looks like the items on the block include weapons, animals, people... and drugs. Lots of drugs."

"The timing's a little suspect, ain't it?" Flynn remarked, glancing up at Dev. His face was set and grim, brow furrowed, and Flynn forced himself to look away quickly, but not before he noticed that Dev hadn't taken a donut or a coffee. "When do we leave?"

"Right now," Kaja replied. Her tone was more clipped than usual, and Flynn chalked it up to concern. "The jet's waiting to take you to Prague—that's where you and Dev will intercept the shipment, hopefully before YK4 can. Lottie and Eileen will continue on to Budapest and try to find the exact location of the auction." She saluted them with the remainder of her donut. "Good luck."

~***~

Dev had spent so much time on Project Renegade's private jet over the years that it was almost like a second home at this point. The tricked-out Learjet 75 was unmarked on the outside save for a tail number that was changed depending on what country they were pretending to be from. Dark gray carpeting and off-white walls gave the interior something of a homey feel, especially with the lights dimmed, and the big screen along the rear wall allowed them to watch a movie or communicate with HQ if necessary. Dev couldn't count the number of hours he'd spent sleeping in a fully-reclined leather chair, or getting various wounds patched up in the bathroom. He'd been on the other end too, watching one of his teammates snore away after a close call, or scraping blood out from under his nails once he was done applying field dressings.

They were all on their third cups of coffee by the time Dev's phone buzzed with a text message. Unlike a commercial plane, they didn't have to worry about cellular signals interfering with navigation equipment, so he didn't feel bad about checking the screen. It was from Scarlett Vaughn, private eye extraordinaire and work partner to their mutual friend, Jim Wolfe. In the aftermath of a personal crisis the previous autumn, she'd inadvertently informed Dev that his father may not be as dead as previously thought. They had stayed friendly afterwards, and what she wrote made him crack a smile: *Make any progress lately, boy wonder?*

I wish, Dev replied, keenly aware of Flynn's gaze on his face. It was hard not to be, since he was so attuned to everything the older man did, both for work and… other reasons. **Nothing new since the last time we talked. Thank Wolfe again for those maps he found.**

Cartography is like engineering, right? It makes his monkey brain happy. Scarlett had a particular way of speaking that never failed to simultaneously be amusing and accurate. Dev knew that while he was a badass former Army Ranger, Wolfe was secretly also a huge nerd, and sifting through old maps of Montana at the Boston Public Library was probably his idea of a fun afternoon. *Wish there was something else we could do to help. Can't believe I'm saying*

this, but it feels like I killed Raider a little too soon.

He was going to kill you, Dev pointed out. He flashed back to
that October night in his mind's eye, and the fear he felt when he'd
spotted Scarlett floating face down in a bloodied cranberry bog.
Marshall Raider was not only a serial killer, he was a former
member of the Reborn, cast out when Dev was a little boy for killing
a woman outside of the compound and endangering them all. Before
Scarlett had stabbed Raider in the throat, he'd uttered three words in
Latin: *fides in timore*. That translated to *faith over fear*, and it was
the Reborn's motto, which they lived and died by, but it made no
sense for him to use it unless he was back in the fold. And *that*
meant there was something to go back *to*, and Dev couldn't abide
that. **And he killed your mom. I don't blame you for anything.**

"Is that Scarlett?" Flynn asked, and while the sound of his voice
wasn't startling, it was enough to make Dev look up from the screen.
His partner's tone and face were neutral, but his shoulders looked
tense. "How's she doin'? All healed up?" He was referring to the
injuries Scarlett had suffered in her fight with Raider, which had
been serious enough to warrant a hospital stay.

"As far as I know, she's good, yeah," Dev answered, raising an eyebrow and resisting the urge to squirm when he was unable to read the look in Flynn's whiskey-colored eyes. "Why are you staring at me like that?"

"Because he thinks you have a crush," Lottie said from across the aisle, in what Dev privately referred to as her You're a Dumbass Voice. He was all too familiar with it from their romantic relationship, and when he looked over at her, she nodded toward his phone. "On Scarlett. Obviously."

Obviously, Dev echoed mentally, the thought tinged with bitterness. He didn't dare to meet Flynn's gaze, not in that moment. While Scarlett was intelligent, hilarious, and competent at what she did, he didn't have a crush on her. He couldn't, for the same reason his relationship with Lottie hadn't worked—he was already in love with Flynn. Who could never, *ever* find out, because Flynn was as straight as they came and it would ruin their friendship. "Well, sorry to disappoint, but I don't have a crush on Scarlett."

"What about that actress you live with?" Eileen inquired, reclined in her chair. The picture of relaxation, even when they were being sent into the metaphorical lion's den twice in twenty-four hours. "She's quite something. Is she single?"

"I have no idea," Dev said dryly, pocketing his phone. He stretched his arms over his head, the scarring on his back already tight from sitting for too long. "I know she was going out with some producer for a while, but I think they broke things off. But anyway, Aoife and I are friends—that's all." Another glance Lottie's way. "Dating around this job is too hard, anyway."

"I could set you up with my brother," Lottie mused, as though Dev hadn't spoken. She frowned a second later. "Although that might be awkward, and it's got nothing to do with you and me dating before."

"Why's that?" Flynn asked. He was definitely tense now, but why? Dev had never hidden the fact that he was bisexual, except for when they were in the Army and subjected to the parameters of Don't Ask Don't Tell. A comment about Dev going on a potential date with Chase Tran shouldn't have irked him. "I thought he was the golden boy, being a big-time neuroscientist and all."

Lottie chuckled bitterly. "Oh, he is, there's no doubt about that." She shifted in her seat, crossing her legs and studying the toes of her boots. "And God knows, in my parents' eyes I'm a lost cause. Maybe that's why lately they've been so hard on Corrine."

"But Corrine's a good kid," Eileen said, her brow furrowing. "Plus, she's what, fifteen?" A wry smile. "I'd ask how much trouble she could get into, but since I helped plan a museum heist at that age, I'm not sure I've got room to talk."

"That's just it, though: she hasn't done *anything*." Lottie's hair was shiny like an oil slick as she shook her head. "Her grades are flawless, she doesn't smoke or drink—but they won't let her stay over a friend's house, let alone date anyone. She couldn't even go to the harvest dance they had at her school a couple months ago." She made a frustrated sound. "I don't know what they're thinking. Restricting her like this is just going to make her act out."

"You're right about that," Dev told her, a selfish part of him thankful the topic had been successfully changed from his love life (or lack thereof). He levered himself up and opened the nearest overhead bin; inside it was a collection of board games. "One could say my upbringing had some severe punishments attached, and in the end I still did the opposite of what my father wanted." He held up two boxes. "Monopoly or Life?"

"Definitely Monopoly," Flynn said, as he and the girls turned their seats to face the aisle. He pulled open a panel on the nearest wall and turned it until it was horizontal, making a table between the four of them. "I'm never playing Life with Eileen again. We all know she cheats."

"That is a bloody *lie*," Eileen ground out, pointing at Dev. "*He's* the one that cheats."

Dev stuck his tongue out at her, dumping the contents of the box on the table as he sat down. "Am not. Maybe Flynn is just bad at Life."

And if he had a couple hundreds in Monopoly money shoved up the inside of his sleeve, well, his friends would find out soon enough.

~***~

Chapter Three

From the young age of five, Adam Devereux knew he was different.

That kind of self-awareness wasn't common in children before they hit double digits, but Adam was what a teacher might've called *gifted*, if he had gone to school. He had never seen a school, however, let alone been inside one. He also hadn't visited a supermarket, ridden a bus, or worn clothes that weren't hand-me-downs from older children. All he had ever known were the rolling mountains and dense pine trees that surrounded the Reborn's compound, but he knew there was more out there; the new kids talked about the conveniences of the modern world when they first arrived, until they were gradually forgotten.

The compound consisted of five hand-hewn buildings arranged in a rough semi-circle around the fire pit where the Reborn's forty-three members, including Dev, cooked and boiled water for drinking, washing, and bathing. While Dev had never left the compound himself, he had trailed along behind on foot as some of the adults went to the nearest town once a month to fetch supplies. He'd seen the gate at the end of the compound's long, winding driveway, hand operated and made of chain link and barbed wire, just like the fence cutting through the woods at the compound's borders. And unlike any other child who might've tried the same thing, Dev didn't get reprimanded verbally or threatened with a raised hand or a belt. He was the Chosen One, after all, even if he wasn't totally comprehending of what that title meant.

All of the buildings and the fire pit were arranged so they faced the driveway, with the biggest building being the chapel. It sat tall and proud in the middle, flanked on the left by the barn and the mess hall, and on the right by the armory and the only permanent home on the property—the pastor's residence, which belonged to the Devereuxs. The ability to shield oneself from the elements with more than just a tent or a lean-to was highly coveted, and it served to alienate Dev further from his peers. But his mother did her best to close that gap by gathering the younger members of the Reborn around the fire pit after the evening meal for a story before they went to sleep.

While Minnie Devereux was fond of retelling allegories from the Bible in a way that was palatable for children, her favorite story to share was the one about how the Reborn came to be. Dev had heard it so many times he could've recited it in his sleep, but he always took his spot at his mother's right hand, content to listen to the soothing cadence of her voice. Memories of it blurred together now, but certain details prevailed: the twilight of the sky high above them like a bruise, the faces of the other kids hungry with the desire for entertainment and cast orange by dying embers.

"Once upon a time, there was a young man named Frederick," Minnie would begin, her slender arm looped around Dev's bony shoulders. She always smelled of lavender and fertile soil, from working in the gardens all day. Her long blonde hair tickled his cheek, unless she had it up in a scarf, and the gold of her beloved St. Francis medallion necklace glinted in the corner of his vision. "Frederick was very wise and saw things in the world that others did not, including the prophecy of our Lord. He left home as soon as he could to travel the country, spreading His word to all who would listen."

Here she always paused, like she was uncertain of what she wanted to say next even though this was hardly the first time she was telling the tale. While Dev knew it was sinful to doubt his parents, there was a part of him that wondered if she hesitated because she didn't believe the words she was saying. Or maybe it had something to do with Frederick's larger than life presence constantly looming over them, even if he wasn't always there physically.

"One day, Frederick stumbled across a young woman—a girl, really. She had been exiled from her parents' home, and Frederick saw potential in her that they did not. Soon the woman, Minnie, became pregnant." Minnie's arm never failed to tighten around Dev's shoulders at this point, when she began referring to herself in the third person. "And much like Mary and Joseph had to find shelter in order for the first savior to be born, Frederick and Minnie had to do the same in order for the Chosen One to enter the world. So they and several members of Frederick's loyal congregation set forth in search of holy land, and they found it here. And with the birth of the Chosen One—" everyone looked at Adam, why were they always *looking* at him "—the Reborn came to be."

The children all clapped politely, and the smile that graced Minnie's face seemed happy enough, but it never quite reached her eyes. It would be many years before Adam figured out why.

~***~

Chapter Four

After dropping the boys off about fifty miles outside of Prague, Eileen and Lottie continued their journey on the jet until they landed in Budapest. The last time Eileen had been to Hungary, she was newly eighteen and working a con with her ex-girlfriend. To say that particular trip had ended badly would be a kindness; she still felt a stab of guilt, pun sadly intended, whenever she thought about the police officer she'd had to shiv with a nail file in order to evade arrest. Not that anything would've *really* happened to her had she gotten booked, beyond a visit from a very stern, no-nonsense British lawyer flown in on her parents' private plane. Them throwing money at a problem (read: Eileen) to make it go away wasn't a unique solution, and she had no doubt that's what they would've done if she'd wound up behind bars (again).

"Eileen!" Lottie exclaimed, breaking Eileen out of her thoughts. From the indignance in her voice, Eileen could tell it wasn't the first time she'd called her name. "Where'd you go just now?" Tone softening, Lottie maneuvered the nondescript sedan that had been waiting for them at the airport through a particularly narrow intersection in Budapest's Palace District. True to its name, it was an up-and-coming neighborhood known for 19th-century palaces and leafy squares, not to mention the assortment of boutique hotels and trendy art galleries. "You don't usually space out like that."

"Sorry about that, love," Eileen said, sitting up straight in the passenger's seat. She never told anyone the whole truth, but this time she parceled out a slice since Lottie was a friend. "Just recalling the last time I was in this city. It's quite something, isn't it?"

Lottie's nose—which had been broken more than once, not that it detracted from her beauty—wrinkled a little. "I guess," she replied, jerking the wheel and pulling into a parallel spot that had opened up as they approached. They were waiting on some updated intel from HQ, and so far their comms hadn't pinged. "It's pretty, but I haven't seen anything special. Most of Europe kind of looks like this."

"Mhmm, not England." Eileen propped a sneakered foot on the dashboard, rolling the back of her skull against the headrest to try and lose some tension. She glanced over what she could see of the street, but saw nothing of interest as either a spy or a thief. "At least not London, anyway. It's all full of adverts and bullshit now.

Piccadilly Circus looks like the television section at a bloody Best Buy."

"Do you ever miss it?" Lottie asked. Her thumbnail, cut short and practical, was worrying at a loose stitch on the fake leather of the steering wheel cover. "Living there, I mean."

Eileen raised a brow. "Have I made you think I do?"

"The opposite, in fact." One corner of Lottie's mouth rose, and when she looked at Eileen, her dark eyes were studious. "You remind me of me, actually. Not to be super dramatic, but I think I'd drink all the gasoline in this car before I went back to live with my parents in Dorchester."

Chuckling, Eileen let herself hold Lottie's gaze for a moment before she turned her face toward the street again. She feared that if she looked too long, she might give away exactly how painfully attractive she thought the other woman was, and that could only end in disaster. "Why waste the effort drinking it? I realize it's more Dev's thing, but I think between the two of us we could figure out how to make this tin can explode."

Lottie snorted, but before she could respond their comms came alive in their ears. Eileen fully expected to hear Tara's voice, but realized as a different coworker spoke that their favorite hacker was probably busy herding Dev and Flynn, since their mission was currently the more pressing one.

"Hey ladies." Sabene Lyss was in charge of what Flynn liked to refer to as the pointy-head division of Project Renegade. That group of a dozen or so researchers and computer geeks occupied a board room-like space directly below the loft, and spent their time trying to solve problems remotely before they had to be directed upstairs to the field team. "Tara's busy, so the boss asked me to fill you in on what we have so far. I just checked your GPS, and according to what we've been able to find on the dark web we think the auction site isn't too far from your current location."

"Really?" Lottie's eyebrows shot up to her hairline as she exchanged a surprised look with Eileen. "No offense, but this neighborhood doesn't exactly strike me as black market auction material. Can you give us anything else to go on?"

Sabene could be heard tapping against a tablet. "Maybe. The common denominator between all the info we skimmed was that each conversation referenced staying in hotels within a certain radius of each other—that's how we landed on the Palace District in the first place. Let me send you a screenshot of what we have with a map, and you can figure out if anything in the circle looks like a likely spot."

"Sounds good." Eileen tugged her own tablet out of the backpack at her feet, taking a second to connect to WiFi using Project Renegade's ridiculously encrypted hotspot VPN. Tara had crafted it herself during a four-day caffeine binge with her college friend and fellow hacker, Frogger Sampson, and thus it was dubbed the Espresso Express. "How are the boys doing?"

"About as well as they usually do on their own," Sabene replied, their tone wry. They didn't elaborate, only asked, "Did you get it?"

"Yep, just came in." Eileen opened the image and tilted the tablet so Lottie would be able to see it too. She sucked in a breath when Lottie leaned over the center console to get a better look, their forearms brushing. "You were right, Sabene—we aren't far from this radius at all. A couple of blocks, maybe?"

"Just about, yeah." Lottie used two fingers to enlarge the area inside the circle, peering at it intently. When Eileen risked a glance at her, there was a furrow between her brow and a dimple near the top of her left cheek, made when she chewed the inside of her lip.

"Looks like the middle of the circle is in District VII, whatever that means."

"It's another hipster neighborhood," Eileen supplied, hardly recognizing the sound of her own voice. She cleared her throat and ignored the way Lottie's clean, slightly woodsy scent made her pulse pound faster. "Tourists come to see the Grand Synagogue, there's lots of bars…" She trailed off, realization dawning. "And there's a casino."

"Sounds like a good candidate to me," Sabene commented, and now they were typing away on a keyboard. "Vibráló Casino has been around for a while, but it recently changed owners. And it just so happens that the shell corporation that holds the title also has a connection to the corner of the dark web where we found the posting about the auction. Ding ding, I think you've got a winner."

"I do too," Lottie agreed, straightening up and starting the engine. "We'll go check it out. Thanks, Sabene."

"Anytime." There was a smile in their voice. "Ping me if you need me."

The comm line went dead, and Eileen used the tablet to direct Lottie toward the casino. "We doing a drive-by, or taking a closer look?"

"I think we could chance a walkabout," Lottie replied, keeping her eyes on the road and turning where Eileen indicated. "Just depends on what's around it, and if it's one of those casinos that's open during the day or only lets people in at night."

"I'm fairly certain daytime gambling is an American phenomenon," Eileen said wryly, "but I could be wrong."

Miraculously, Lottie found them another parallel parking spot, only about a half a block down from the casino. After killing the engine again, she touched Eileen's shoulder lightly. "You good? Gonna stay with me this time instead of floating off into space?"

Eileen swallowed hard, gripping the door handle and ignoring how that simple touch made her stomach flutter. "I'll do my best. Let's get this done."

~***~

Standing on an overpass, Dev tapped the comm in his ear. "Tara, are you sure this is the right place? We've been on this bridge for a while now and we haven't seen any big rigs, let alone one from Wohlbefinden."

Tara's keyboard clicked in the background of their encrypted frequency. "According to the GPS it's coming right at you," she said, no doubt looking at a highly detailed, real-time satellite feed. The knowledge they were being watched so closely on missions never failed to give Dev the absurd urge to wave at the sky. Instead of being invasive, it was somewhat comforting, to be able to depend on the fact that Tara was always observing them. "Wait, did you say you were *on* the bridge? Over the E55?"

Those words came into Flynn's ear too, and he threw a sharp look Dev's way. They'd already wasted enough time getting there from the nearest airport where Lottie and Eileen had dropped them off; if the intercept point Tara had devised was wrong, they were shit out of luck. "Yeah, he did say that. Why?"

"Because the truck is on the E55, not that surface street!" Tara exclaimed, her normally very collected voice climbing in a way that would've been funny if the situation weren't so serious. "It's going to pass underneath you in sixty seconds! Why are you on that goddamn bridge?"

Dev groaned in disbelief. "Are you kidding me? *You're* the one that dropped the pin here!"

"Shit," Flynn muttered, rubbing a hand over his buzzed hair. He glanced around at the vehicles passing them sedately in either direction, the bridge framed in on one side by a gas station and ramps for the highway on the other. "I don't suppose you can science up a way to get us down there in time?" he asked Dev. "Or stop the truck somehow?"

Dev shook his head, gesturing down at the traffic buzzing along beneath them at eighty miles per hour. "Too much potential for casualties." The cross carved into his back tightened as his brain began calculating relevant vectors, but he needed more information. "Tara? Is the truck's GPS readout one hundred percent accurate, or is there a time delay? It's important."

"Let me check the manufacturer's website." More typing sounds, then: "There's a three second delay between when the position registers with the satellite and when it gets to me."

"Good to know." Dev waited until the semi-truck belonging to Wohlbefinden appeared in the distance, a shiny black cab paired with a white trailer, the company's name emblazoned on the sides.

Then he grabbed the railing with both hands, steel cold as ice under his fingers, and put a boot up on it for good measure. "There's only one way we're stopping that truck, and that's if we're on it."

"*What?*" Flynn grabbed the back of Dev's canvas jacket, seemingly torn between yanking him toward safety and shoving him forward. "I feel like I ask you this at least once a week, but are you crazy?"

"Jury's out on that one," Dev muttered, risking a glance at Flynn before fixing his eyes on the truck again. "You don't have to come with me."

Flynn growled, a low sound that Dev doubted he knew he made. He also let go of Dev's jacket and took up position next to him on the railing. "What did I tell you when you tried to pull that main character bullshit on me back in the Sandbox, huh?"

Dev grinned, unable to help it—adrenaline shot up his spine, the seconds ticking down. He told himself it was because of the danger and not Flynn's proximity. In a poor imitation of Flynn's Texas accent, he parroted, "'Every good main character has a sidekick, Jimmy Neutron.'" Muscles tensed, he prepared to fling himself forward. "Ready? One, two, three—!"

They jumped at the same time, free-falling for a heart-stopping instant before hitting the top of the trailer. Both of them tucked and rolled and in the next second the truck cleared the overpass and they were free to stand. It was easier said than done considering the winds buffeting the truck at that height and speed, but they managed it.

"Now what?" Flynn shouted, putting his arms out to his sides for balance. "Do we get in the back somehow? Can't ride like this into Hungary!"

"That can only be done from the ground!" Dev heard the faintest sound through the roar and glanced over his shoulder. "Uh, Flynn? We've got a problem!"

Problem was probably an understatement, actually. It came in the form of four oversized military-style SUVs approaching on either side of the semi-truck, which was traveling in the middle lane. A fifth vehicle boxed the trailer in from behind, so there was effectively nothing the driver could do to get away. People with guns and body armor were visible through the windows of the SUVs, but they made no move to shoot at Dev and Flynn. It took Dev a second to work out why; they were afraid of a stray bullet piercing the side of the trailer and either destroying the DMT itself or hitting the refrigeration unit keeping the drugs stable.

The passenger's side door on the SUV directly behind the trailer opened, which in and of itself was a risky maneuver given the speed of the vehicle, but then a gigantic bald man clambered out. He had biceps the size of watermelons and a mean scowl on his flat face, and he was decked out in full tactical gear. He hauled himself up on to the roof of the SUV, slid precariously down the windshield, and propelled himself off the hood.

He hit the ladder on the back of the trailer with enough force to make it shake under Dev's feet, and then suddenly he was on top of the trailer with them. From the corner of his eye Dev saw Flynn's hand twitch toward the gun at the small of his back but then think better of it. With the wind gusts and the constant motion of the trailer, there was no telling where—or who—the bullets would hit. He pulled a fixed-blade knife from the top of his boot instead, just in time for the giant man to charge toward them, heedless of the potential for a deadly fall.

There was barely enough room for Flynn and Dev to dodge to either side without splattering on the pavement but they managed, and when their adversary turned around Dev kicked him as hard as he could in the gut. It sent him stumbling back but also only seemed to make him mad, which was less than ideal. One large hand shot out toward Dev but he ducked underneath it, winding up at the big guy's back. He grabbed him, pinning his arms to his side and gritting his teeth as Flynn punched him once, twice before Dev got shaken off like a bothersome fly.

An involuntary scream tore past Dev's lips as he lost his balance near the rear of the trailer and fell, long fingers grasping at the ladder attached to one of the doors at the last possible moment. Just out of Dev's sight Flynn let out an animal roar joined by the distinctive *crack* of bone-on-bone. A spray of blood arced in the air, indicated the giant got his throat slashed, and his corpse flew off the trailer a moment later, nearly taking Dev with it.

Flynn's face appeared, tight and lined with grief… and then he saw Dev and hung his head. "You fucker, I thought—"

"I know what you thought," Dev interjected, his hand numb from gripping the rung so tightly. "Please just help me up!"

Flynn reached down to grab his arm, but before he could the truck swerved violently to the right. Physics being what they were, that meant the trailer swung in the *opposite* direction, and while they lost speed in the process it didn't make it any less dangerous. Dev couldn't see what was in front of the truck, obviously, but a quick glance to either side told him that the SUVs were actively boxing it in from the left and the back, trying to force the driver to pull over on to the shoulder. He felt it the moment the driver over-corrected, the trailer tipping dangerously on one row of wheels, threatening to dump him and Flynn over the guardrail and into the bushes and trees beyond it.

Dev made frantic eye contact with Flynn and overrode every survival instinct he had. "Jump!"

Dev pushed off the back of the trailer and above him he saw Flynn leap away too, and then Dev lost track of him as he fell for what could've been an hour but was really only a second. He hit the bushes behind the guardrail hard and continued to move, rolling through the dirt and underbrush until he smacked into a tree trunk. Wheezing in a breath and clutching at his side, Dev sat up in time to watch the SUVs close in around the semi-truck once more—and promptly threw himself to the dirt to avoid catching a bullet in the face thanks to a parting rifle burst from the follow car.

"Shit shit shit," came from somewhere to Dev's right, and a bolt of relief coursed through him when he saw Flynn pushing himself to his feet, twigs and rocks falling from his leather jacket. "Kid? You okay?"

"I'm good," Dev replied, even though the sting in his ribs told him otherwise. They were bruised, not broken—been there, done that—so he'd live. Didn't stop his heart from pounding a little faster in the face of Flynn's concern, though, and since when was that a thing that happened? Speaking into his comm, he said, "Tara? We lost the truck." He accepted the hand Flynn offered and allowed himself to be pulled to his feet, adding grimly, "Looks like we'll be joining the girls in Budapest after all."

~***~

After making sure Dev and Flynn were on their way to join Lottie and Eileen in Budapest, Tara took her comm out of her ear and stretched her fingers until she felt all ten of her knuckles pop. That'd been a close call with the semi-truck, and while nobody was pleased that the DMT shipment had been captured, she was just happy one or both of her friends wasn't a human pancake on the highway. She knew the team needing to infiltrate the auction meant an even longer day at the office, but that was okay if it meant they got the DMT back in the end.

"Tara?" Kaja's voice sounded from behind her, stern but not demanding. "I need to speak with you." As Tara glanced over her shoulder, she saw Kaja turn her attention to Sabene briefly. "Can you give us a minute, please?"

"Of course," was Sabene's reply, and they set their laptop down on the table before heading for the stairs. "I'll go get us some coffee."

Once Sabene was gone, Kaja flipped the lock on the door to the loft and touched the panel beside it, making all of the clear glass turn an opaque white. Then she sat on the back of the chair nearest to Tara, hands clasped on top of her crossed legs. "I'm going to ask you a question," she began. "And I want you to answer honestly."

"Do you really think I'm dumb enough to try and lie to you?" Tara wondered, holding up her hands in a gesture of supplication when Kaja raised an impetuous brow. "Sorry. What's your question?"

"I know that your algorithm has been looking for any mention of the Reborn online. Has it found anything of substance?"

"I'm assuming that by *substance*, you don't mean Gen Z thirsting over the actor who plays young Frederick in that stupid docudrama that came out last year?"

Kaja's mouth curled wryly. "Good assumption."

"Then the answer is not much." Tara used the tablet that controlled the big screen to pull up her algorithm, which had been running since about a week after Marshall Raider had uttered the Reborn's motto to Scarlett Vaughn before she killed him. "The most I've got is a sighting of a guy named Aleksandr Lichtenson." She brought up his driver's license photo, which showed an albino man in his mid-thirties. He had a severe face that was all angles and hollow cheeks, paired with pale eyes and a thick scar across his forehead that he attempted to conceal by keeping his white-blond hair longer at the top but shaved on the sides. "He was spotted in Bozeman about three weeks ago, right before Christmas. And the reason that's significant is he's the last person Marshall Raider texted before he died back in October."

"And Bozeman is the closest municipality to the Reborn's old stomping ground," Kaja added, studying Lichtenson's visage on the screen. "Did you ever have any luck retrieving the contents of Raider's phone?"

"Unfortunately, no." Tara grimaced at the memory of how she tried and failed to resurrect the cheap device, which hadn't been backed up to the cloud. It had been waterlogged thanks to Raider's tango with Scarlett in a cranberry bog, and there was no way to start it up again. "All I was able to get were the call and text logs from the phone company." She drummed her fingers against the arm of her wheelchair. "We should tell Dev about this. I don't like lying to him."

Kaja digested that for a moment. She was never quick to speak, always taking her time when she chose her words. "It's not lying, because we haven't told him anything that isn't true. And besides, you know he's doing his own research. This is driving him crazy, and we need to figure out a way to help him."

"Yeah," Tara agreed, eyeing Kaja when she looked her way again, gaze heavy. "What?"

"I want to know exactly how far he's gotten in his research." Kaja stood up, the heels of her pumps clicking against the hardwood.

"But right now, I have a meeting. Can you find out what he has and get back to me?"

Tara nodded, feeling slightly hollow as she watched her boss walk away. Then she took a deep breath and got back to work.

~***~

Chapter Five

Adam was eight when his mother left him.

Minnie woke him up in the middle of the night with a shake of his shoulder. She and Frederick had an argument after dinner, and even in the dim moonlight filtering in through the window, he saw her face was puffy and red from crying. He'd been sent off to wash dishes after they ate, and since the clean water was stored some distance away from the bonfire, he had only heard their raised voices and not actual words. But he didn't need words to know they were arguing about him, because he was the subject of the majority of their fights.

"Adam, are you awake?" Minnie asked in a whisper, her voice cracking. Her eyes were the same shade of blue that Adam saw when he looked in the mirror, and they were full of tears. "I need you to listen to me, okay?"

Adam nodded, dread coiling like a snake in his stomach. He knew instinctively that whatever Minnie said next was going to alter the course of his life forever. A part of him wanted to believe that this was just a bad dream, that if he shut his eyes again everything would be fine. But the first thing that died when someone was a part of the Reborn was their sense of naivety, and Adam was no exception to that rule.

"I have to go away for a while," Minnie continued, the words bumping up against each other, like her throat was squeezing them as they came out. Her gaze flicked toward the window briefly, and Adam wanted to look to see what she saw, but her fingers gripped his chin, stopping the motion. "Don't look away, sweetie. Look at me."

"What's going on?" Adam kept his voice low just like hers, barely able to move his jaw with how tightly Minnie held him. He curled his own fingers into the scratchy sheets beneath him. "Mama, you're scaring me."

"There's nothing to be scared of," Minnie assured him, but the way she glanced at the window again betrayed her lie. She tried to smile, the expression stiff and not a match for the desperation in her eyes. "I need you to be a good boy for me while I'm gone, alright? I'll be back before you know it."

"But where are you going?" Adam asked, and sat up the instant his mother let go of him and drew back. He tried to reach for her, but she was still backing up, and now he saw the bag she had slung over her shoulder. "This is about me, isn't it?" His eyes burned. "You and Father are always fighting, and I know it's because of me."

"It is, but not in the way that you think." Minnie's words stung, even though it was more or less what Adam expected to hear. "Like I said... I'll be back soon. I love you."

With that she stepped backward through the door, shutting it right as Adam flung himself out of bed and reached it. He tried the knob and made a hurt sound when he discovered it was locked from the outside. Being stuck in their rooms or tents for hours or days at a time was a common punishment for the children of the Reborn, but his mother had never been the one to use the lock against him until now. Adam turned away, slumping against the door and barely choking back a sob. Crying or throwing a tantrum would get him nothing—or at least nothing he wanted. It was all too likely that someone would overhear him and report it to Frederick, who would give Adam a lecture laden with prophecy before assigning him his punishment for being so weak.

Movement through the gap in the curtains caught Adam's attention and he stilled, then rushed at the glass, pressing his face against it. Outside he saw Minnie being led to a pickup truck that belonged to one of the newer members of the Reborn—Adam was fairly certain his name was Marshall. She got inside, and the brake lights flared to life before the truck began driving away.

In their red glow, Adam just made out the shape of his father, watching him from the tree line.

~***~

Chapter Six

"So which fakey did you guys get?" Lottie asked, using the group's affectionate nickname for their rotating cast of aliases. She tossed a United States passport, a New York driver's license, and a couple credit cards on the table in front of her. "Tara told me to use Cynthia Nguyen."

"I realize this ain't polite to say about a lady—even a made-up gun runner lady—but she's such a *bitch*," Flynn lamented. They were huddled in a semi-circle in the far corner booth of a tapas restaurant, a wicker divider giving them some semblance of privacy. The exposed stone walls were accented by modern art canvases and sweeping palm fronds emanating from the back of the bar. To a casual observer, they looked like a group of American tourists and nothing more. "I got Mickey Doolan. A surprise to no one."

"But you don't have the mustache," Dev said, one leg pressed against Lottie's, the other against Flynn's. Eileen was on Flynn's other side, engrossed in the menu and no doubt plotting what they were going to eat. None of them were bothered by the prolonged closeness, too accustomed to each other's company. Living in each other's pockets was something of a job requirement. "That's Mickey's defining feature, isn't it? You know, besides the nepotism and the games of grab-ass?"

"I think the grab-ass counts as inheritance too, since his daddy's supposed to be a scuzzy CEO," Lottie pointed out, and she found that when her eyes met Dev's and she smiled at him, it was genuine in a way that it hadn't been since their breakup. Each time she looked at him it hurt a little bit less, and it felt a little more like it did when they were only friends, before trying to date muddied the waters. "And let me guess, you're some kind of genius who likes to buy weapons in his spare time?"

"Close," Dev said wryly, which meant she couldn't be more wrong. "Apparently, I'm the ne'er-do-well son of a Romanian crime lord. Sound like anybody we know?"

"Hey, Sebastian's turned things around at his old man's restaurant, from what I hear." Eileen put down the menu and took a sip of her coffee. They were all caffeinating, since this promised to be a long night at Vibráló Casino. Not enough for jitters to set in, but enough to keep them awake. "A little birdie told me he'll be on the cover of *Boston* magazine next month."

"Someday when we ain't working, we should all go over there," Flynn suggested, and there was a part of Lottie that wanted to kick him. Sebastian's Theatre District restaurant, Stela, was very much the type of place you took a date, not a friend group, and Dev was looking at him with puppy dog eyes the size of saucers but he *couldn't see it*. Or he didn't want to, and she wasn't sure which option was worse at this point. "Speaking of work, how much of a clusterfuck do y'all think this auction is gonna be?"

"Total and irrevocable," was Dev's response, before he paused as their waiter returned. They let Eileen order for them, Hungarian rolling flawlessly off her tongue, and Lottie felt a wave of heat down her back, the way she always did when she heard Eileen speak another language. She chalked it up to the restaurant being small and crowded, and didn't think about all the times it'd happened in other situations. Once their waiter had retreated to the kitchen, Dev continued, "And if we had been able to get the truck to its destination, this wouldn't be a problem."

"Fair, but you guys almost got smashed into road paste trying." One of the things that drove Lottie up a wall when she and Dev were dating was his slant toward self-deprecation, even when it was completely undeserved. She had a tendency to engage in that behavior too, albeit less often, and chalked it up to strict (if insanely different) upbringings. "And here's something I don't get—why would these YK4 guys steal the DMT in the first place? If they're known for being hired goons, they're not bringing it to the auction for their own benefit. Somebody has to be pulling the strings… but it's kind of an obscure drug."

"That's true," Eileen agreed, nodding. "Theoretically, it'd be loads easier to snatch a big batch of some other pharmaceuticals, like painkillers or Xanax. They're regulated, sure, but not as closely watched as DMT."

"DMT is rarer, since not as much of it is produced per year," Dev pointed out, frowning. He never met a problem he couldn't solve, after all… and now Flynn was looking at Dev like he hung the moon, except Dev was busy staring into his coffee like it held the secrets of the universe. "Still, Lottie's right. Somebody was willing to pay YK4 to steal the DMT and have them bring it to the auction… but presumably it's going to *sell* at the auction, so whoever is pulling the strings won't get any of it."

"Unless they already took their cut off the top," Flynn said, shifting until he could stretch one arm across the back of the booth behind Dev. "They're bound to make up whatever they paid YK4 once the DMT sells at auction anyway, so what's the harm?"

"Hiring YK4 could also be a smokescreen." Lottie's phone vibrated in her pocket with a few incoming texts, but she ignored them. While she felt a slight pang of guilt knowing they were probably from her sister, she couldn't afford to get distracted on the job. And as it happened, the last puzzle piece just clicked into place. "Think about it: someone hires YK4 to steal the DMT and bring it to the auction, and then whoever did the hiring steals it from the auction themselves. It's convoluted, but we've seen weirder things."

"We don't talk about Tallahassee," Dev, Eileen, and Flynn said in unison.

Lottie winced. As far as missions gone absolutely batshit were concerned, their one and only field trip to Florida was the exception, not the rule. "Yeah, yeah, I know. Tallahassee is at the top of the weird scale, for sure." She shuddered a little, then felt herself brighten as their waiter emerged from the back with a large tray. "Food's coming. And it's not even still moving."

"We *don't* talk about Tallahassee," Dev said again, but there was a glimmer of amusement in his eyes. "It's like Fight Club, only much worse." He pressed his lips together in a frown. "Hopefully Budapest doesn't turn out the same way."

~***~

Kaja considered herself to be a well-traveled person, having circled around the globe several times over thanks to her work at the CIA. She was also the daughter of Polish immigrants, and when you combined those two aspects of her life, she had been exposed to a lot of different foods over the years. But no matter how much gourmet cuisine she consumed, nothing could compare with a good old-fashioned burger at her favorite diner.

Called "Boston's favorite greasy spoon" on more than one internet listicle, Ryan's Diner was as neat as a thimble on the inside despite the crusty Washington Street storefront that made up its exterior. Right in the heart of the South End, it looked every inch like a diner straight from the 1950s, from the chrome edged lunch counter to the cherry-red vinyl booths, the smell of pancakes ripe in the air no matter the time of day. Across the street was the Burying

Ground, and one could draw a straight if morbid line from the historic tourist destination to the restaurant's success.

"Sorry I'm late," was the first thing her lunch date said as he slid into the booth across from Kaja, shaking some stray flurries from his canvas coat. A tall man with a crooked nose and strong jaw, David Wolfe was an old friend of Kaja's from their shared days at the CIA academy and one half of the duo that had assembled the team that became Project Renegade. He was about ten years her senior, but he'd come into the spy game later in life after being recruited out of Army Special Forces. He'd been forced to fake his death after a mission gone wrong, and had only reunited with his ex-wife and sons in the past year. That... hadn't exactly gone to plan, to put it mildly. "What is it with winter that makes everybody in this town forget how to fuckin' drive?"

Kaja smiled, both hands wrapped around a hot mug of coffee. "I have no idea, but that's why I took the T over." She took in the dusky shadows below his green eyes and hummed contemplatively. "How are you?"

"Well, I think I've finally managed to make peace with the whole 'my eldest son was a sociopathic serial killer and my younger son had to shoot him in the head in order to stop him from killing my pseudo-son that my ex-wife had with another man when she thought I was dead' thing." David let out a snort when he was done speaking, turning his mug over so the waitress would know to fill it with coffee when she came in their direction. "Or at least I've processed it. Not sure *that's* something you ever really get over. The brass keeps trying to get me to see a shrink… but anyway, none of that is why I wanted to talk to you."

"I didn't figure it was," Kaja replied, pressing pause on the conversation while they ordered food—the aforementioned greasy burger for her, and a lumberjack special for David. Once their waitress made herself scarce again, she continued, "So what's up?"

David sighed, taking a long swig of his freshly poured coffee. "Very special asshole agent in charge Dwight Whitney doesn't want me back in the field with my partner, that's what."

Kaja raised an eyebrow, disappointed but not surprised. At the same time that David's eldest son Josh was terrorizing the community for the second time as the Mass Art Murderer, David's partner and newly-minted girlfriend, Diana Johnson, had been thoroughly traumatized during an undercover operation gone bad.

And while Diana had spent the past three months mending her body and mind, evidently Very Special Agent Dwight Whitney didn't feel as though she should be operational. "What's his reasoning? And how long does he want to keep her benched?"

"That's the part that's pissing me off," David said. "He doesn't have a reason, not really. Physically, D is fine. Mentally, she passed all of her psych evals with flying colors. Whitney says he doesn't think she should come back before her six months of optional leave are up, she deserves the time off, blah blah… but between you and me, I think he's trying to force her out of her job."

"He's never been fond of either one of you," Kaja mused. She tapped her nails against the boomerang-patterned laminate of the tabletop. Her own encounters with Whitney had been few and far between, but her general understanding of the man was that he was a massive shitheel. "He knows damn well that Diana would never last at riding a desk. And if she quits—"

"Then I'll quit with her, yeah," David interjected, finishing the thought. "And you're right, that wouldn't exactly break Whitney's heart either. I refuse to play politics to please him, and Diana's too much of a loose cannon in his eyes." He rubbed at the red stubble on his jaw. "But she also *loves* this job, and losing it right now, especially like this… she would never admit it, but that would hurt her." He paused meaningfully. "That's where you come in, I hope."

"You know I love Diana," Kaja started, smiling wryly at him. "Maybe not as much as you, but still. What do you need from me?"

David's fair skin flushed at those words, betraying their accuracy, but he forged ahead: "I want to prove to Whitney that D can handle being in the field, but since he won't let her near a CIA op… I thought maybe she could hang out at Project Renegade for a bit? Work with you guys, and maybe get both feet back on the ground?"

Kaja waited to answer until their respective plates were set down in front of them, tamping down the urge to drool when she saw her burger and fries. "Of course she can. You know you're both welcome at Renegade whenever you want to visit. It wouldn't exist without you, so it would be a little ridiculous if I tried to keep you away." She pointed at him with a fry. "*But* I have a condition."

"Name it," David said immediately. He poked his sunny side up eggs with his fork, the yolks running in a fashion that Kaja found truly disgusting—but she liked her eggs with tomatoes, so to each their own. "Whatever you want."

Kaja knew what she had to say would be far from a deal breaker—and that David had probably already thought of it—but she felt compelled to verbalize it anyway. "You have to tag along too. I'm fine with Diana coming to play in our sandbox, so to speak, but since she's still on probation with the CIA, she's your responsibility." She made a face as soon as those words were out. "Please, never tell her I said that. I'd rather not wake up with a decapitated horse head in my bed."

"I was planning on joining you anyway, so we have a deal." David winked at her, offering a tiny salute with his toast corner. "And your secret's safe with me."

~***~

Back before her days at MIT, Tara had been something of a troublemaker. Nothing *too* nefarious—a couple of petty thefts, maybe some light carjacking—but enough to make her parents worry, and for her to catch the eye of her local police department. And being that she grew up in a small town in Vermont, it wasn't long until she built up a reputation. Looking back on it after a lot of years and therapy bills, Tara had to wonder if she'd done so much acting out because she felt trapped inside a body that didn't match her mind. First because she was assigned male at birth but a part of her knew that was wrong, and *then* because her injury reduced her mobility, but her mind continued to work on overdrive.

"This is a terrible idea," Tara muttered to herself, reaching inside her fuzzy sherpa coat for the lock-picking set she'd brought with her to Dev's place. Left behind was her wheelchair, folded up in the back of her Jeep. She knew just by walking up Marlborough from where she'd parked on Clarendon that Aoife wasn't home, her modest looking yet incredibly expensive Acura nowhere in sight. "Dev is going to *hate* you."

Would he hate her, though? That was the question that had plagued Tara the whole way over from Project Renegade. Dev valued honesty above all else, and to say he didn't trust easily was the understatement of the century. But Kaja had given Tara an order wrapped in the guise of a friendly conversation, and in order to know what Dev knew, she had to see his research firsthand. While he could use a smartphone or a computer just fine, Tara knew Dev much preferred evidence that he could hold in his hands. Which was why she was here, about to pick open Aoife's front door and disable

her fancy alarm system, except…

Except the door was already open.

Tara noticed as she reached for the knob and paused, then drew

her hands back, replacing the lock pick and torque wrench in their

leather case. There was a gap of about a half inch between the door

and the jamb, and it looked to her that someone had picked it ahead

of her rather than forcing it open. Only a couple of scratches graced

the metal, meaning whoever did it was at least as good at petty crime

as Tara, but she had the distinct feeling Aoife's house wasn't a

random target for a burglary.

Swearing under her breath, Tara reached under her coat again.

This time she produced a matte black SIG Sauer P226, which she'd

hemmed and hawed over leaving in her glove box before ultimately

deciding to bring it just in case. Now the nine-mil's weight was

comforting in her hands as she nudged the door open, wincing

internally when it creaked on its hinges. Her lower back ached with

tension amplified by her injury, and as her gaze swept over the foyer

and living room, she saw nothing amiss. Aoife's effortless Gothic

yet chic style permeated the entire space, from the antique floor-to-ceiling mirror propped in one corner to the green velvet couch and leather coffee table.

Tara listened hard and heard the faintest sound: a floorboard creaking almost directly over her head. That put the (other) intruder on the second floor, probably in Dev's room. Heart pounding double time in her chest, Tara mounted the stairs, taking care to stick to the side near the wall to avoid making any creaks of her own. Soon she was at the top of the staircase, facing the hall that led to Dev's portion of the house. The door to his room was closed, but the way the hair stood up on the back of Tara's neck told her danger lurked behind it.

She made sure she was shielded by the jut of the nearest corner, gun held in front of her body. Then she spoke loudly and clearly to make sure she was heard through the wood and plaster: "If you come out now, I won't call the cops. Let's talk about this."

There was a beat of silence, followed by words in a man's voice that she was shocked to recognize: "Tara? Is that you?"

"*Wolfe?*" That single word echoed Tara's disbelief, her mind racing with questions. She was quick to slip her weapon back into her coat as she hurried to the door, which was already opening. "What the hell are you doing here?"

"I could ask you the same thing," Jim Wolfe pointed out, his broad shoulders filling the entry to Dev's room. He cut an intimidating figure, but his grayish-green eyes were kind, crinkling at the corners as he smiled. Short reddish-blond hair and matching stubble was paired with a fair Irish complexion, a heavy Carhartt coat layered over a thermal shirt and jeans. His large hands were busy holstering a gun of his own. "Although I guess since you work with Dev, you'd have a better excuse than us."

"Not really—wait, us?" Tara came into Dev's room when Wolfe stepped aside, and immediately spotted Wolfe's partner, Scarlett Vaughn, sitting on the rolling chair in front of Dev's desk. "Oh, hey."

"Howdy," was Scarlett's response as she spun slowly in place. She had on a dark blue toggle coat that went to her knees, and extracted her hand from her pocket where a gun was no doubt concealed. Her wavy blonde hair hung past her shoulders, and what she lacked in stature she more than made up for in sarcasm and smarts. Her pale blue eyes flickered over Tara's form before her eyebrows arched. "Well, *somebody* looks awfully fucking guilty. I'm guessing Dev doesn't know you're here?"

Tara sighed, slumping against the doorjamb. Her back ached, and she knew a muscle relaxer was in her near future. "No, he doesn't. I was actually going to lock pick the front door, but then I noticed someone beat me to it." She looked from Scarlett to Wolfe curiously. "But you two were the last people I expected to find... so why are you here?"

The two PIs exchanged a glance, and in that single interaction Tara could tell they had a whole conversation. It reminded her a little of the way Dev and Flynn worked together—seamlessly, even when they didn't say a word. It was Wolfe who spoke, after a moment of consideration: "When we got to the office this morning, we found this on the floor." He reached inside his coat and pulled out a medium-sized manila envelope, holding it out in Tara's direction. "Somebody pushed it in through the mail slot. Take a look."

Tara took the envelope and immediately noticed that it was heavier than it looked. She inspected the outside briefly, seeing nothing remarkable; there was no writing on the yellow-orange paper, and other than some blemishes where Wolfe or Scarlett had torn open one end, it seemed brand new. Peering inside at the contents, she let out a low whistle—it was full of cash. "Wow. How much is in here?"

"A thousand bucks," Scarlett replied, planting her low-heeled boots on the floor to stop the motion of the chair. "There's a note, too."

Tara thumbed some of the money aside and retrieved a piece of printer paper. The message typed on it started by listing Aoife's address in bold font, then continued: **RETRIEVE ANYTHING RELATED TO THE REBORN AND BRING IT TO CASTLE ISLAND TONIGHT AT MIDNIGHT. MORE WHERE THIS CAME FROM.**

"First of all, who the hell picks *Castle Island* as their clandestine meeting spot?" Wolfe wondered, shaking his head in disbelief. "Second, this is insulting. Barring the fact that whoever this is probably doesn't know Dev is our friend, assuming we'd take a job like this even if he were a stranger is pretty shitty." He hooked a thumb over his shoulder at a large bulletin board propped against the wall on top of Dev's desk. "We found what this asshole is looking for, and we were going to take it with us in case they decided to send along somebody less savory than us if we don't do what they want."

"I tried getting ahold of Dev, but my call went to voicemail and he's not answering his texts," Scarlett added, frowning. "Is he on a mission?"

"Yeah, he and the team are out of the country," Tara said, mindful as always of exactly how much information she revealed when it came to work. She pushed off the doorjamb and handed the envelope full of cash back to Wolfe on her way past him. Stopping next to Scarlett at Dev's desk, she leaned in to inspect the bulletin board. "This is impressive." She noted that Dev had found the same information she had on Aleksandr Lichtenson, the pin holding his DMV photo to the board stabbed straight through his forehead. "And while I agree with you guys that it shouldn't just be lying around here, I can't let you take it either. This has to come back to Project Renegade with me."

Wolfe frowned and looked like he was about to protest, but then his eyes caught on something out the window. "Get down!" he exclaimed, grabbing Tara by the shoulder and throwing her to the floor, hooking an arm around Scarlett and knocking her down too.

He landed on top of both of them, his weight squeezing the breath from Tara's lungs as pain lanced up her spine. Before she could do more than register the discomfort the window exploded inward under a spray of bullets, glass shattering and furniture splintering from the assault. Her first panicked thought was of the bulletin board and if it had been damaged, and evidently Scarlett had the same fear because she slid out from under Wolfe and belly-crawled until she could reach up and snatch it.

"We've gotta go!" Tara shouted over the cacophony of sound, grabbing Wolfe's shirt in case he tried to do something logical but stupid, like try to sneak a peek at whoever was shooting at them. "I'll check the cameras later!" Her mind raced through options for their escape. "I parked on Clarendon!"

"You're closer than us!" Scarlett foisted the bulletin board on her partner and drew her gun, leading their progress toward the door. "Let's get the fuck out of here!"

~***~

Chapter Seven

By the time he was ten years old, Adam had exactly one friend: Theodore "Teddy" Vasquez, an older boy who had joined the Reborn with his mother, Rosa.

Adam wasn't precisely sure why Teddy had a mom and no dad, but the word around the compound was that Teddy's father had abandoned Rosa and Teddy because Rosa couldn't have more children. To Adam, that seemed like a silly reason to leave someone you were supposed to love, especially since Teddy was intelligent and kindhearted. With his tan skin and chestnut hair, Teddy stood out from the crowd, and for whatever reason he preferred hanging out with Adam over the boys his own age.

Not that Adam was complaining, mind you. He'd spent much of his time alone after Minnie left the Reborn two years prior, and no matter how many times he asked, Frederick refused to tell him where she went or how she was doing. He always insisted that if it was the Lord's will, Adam would be reunited with his mother after the End of Days, but Adam had no desire to wait around for that. There was something about the way Minnie just disappeared that night that didn't sit right with him, yet he was kept so busy with training, schooling, and scripture that there simply wasn't enough time in the day to contemplate it much.

Speaking of training, Adam was in the thick of it. He sat huddled in the pitch black of night with Teddy, the two boys curled into the forked roots of a tree. It was cold enough for them to see their breath each time they exhaled, and the press of Teddy's shivering body against his own was the only thing keeping Adam grounded. His mind threatened to float away any minute, wondering if they were hidden well enough, how they would be punished if they were the first ones to be found—

"Hey," Teddy whispered, right against Adam's ear to keep the sound to a minimum. But after being silent for over an hour, the sound of his voice was like a gunshot. "You doing okay?"

Adam nodded shakily, not trusting himself to speak. His eyes had long adjusted to the darkness, the lights of the compound nowhere in sight, and he saw nothing to indicate that another team was nearby. His ears fed him the same information, but no matter how many times they did this, any comfort he found in these woods during the daytime was long gone. Now the forest and everything in it was a potential threat… except for Teddy. He trusted Teddy with his life, because unlike the other children, Teddy didn't take every word that fell from Frederick's lips as gospel. He held the same doubts in his heart that Adam did, only he was brave enough to voice them. Yet the so-called Chosen One couldn't bring himself to question anything in front of the others—and wasn't that just pathetic?

"I can hear you thinking," Teddy commented, the words low. He nudged Adam lightly with his shoulder, mindful of the bones that had begun protruding more from Adam's skin as of late. The adults were cagey about many things, including how much food was stockpiled and when everyone ate. "This is dumb, right? Is Dani even looking for us?"

Dani Torrence was on the younger side compared to Frederick and some of the others, which made her a little more relatable to the kids. Rumor had it she'd been a Marine until she got dishonorably discharged for beating the shit out of her superior officer, who'd tried to rape her. Shortly after being taken in by the Reborn, Frederick had directed her to start training the kids for the hell on earth he believed they'd endure after Dev's "death" and resurrection.

For whatever it was worth, Dev got the sense that much like Teddy, Dani didn't buy into everything Frederick preached, but she didn't speak out against him, either. And she certainly didn't turn down the opportunity or the power trip of whipping a bunch of mailable children into shape.

"I bet she is," Dev murmured, but before either of them could say more, a twig snapped somewhere far off to their left. "Shhh."

They fell silent once more, even after whoever was stalking them gave up their search. It was companionable, not uncomfortable… and Dev had no idea then how much he would miss Teddy's silences once he was gone.

~***~

Chapter Eight

After extracting a promise from David that he would put in for an extension to his leave from the CIA, Kaja parted ways with him and headed up to Charlestown. When she had asked David how Diana was keeping herself busy during her leave from the CIA, she honestly didn't expect to hear that the other woman was teaching a self-defense course at a gym a few times a week. Diana was many things, but a sufferer of fools wasn't one of them… then again, maybe sharing her immense knowledge of martial arts with those who were vulnerable was therapeutic somehow.

Ginger's Gym sat on Main Street, squatting low to the ground between a Starbucks and a CVS Pharmacy. It was a brick building with window frontage, so if you were running on a treadmill or using a stationary bike, you could people-watch at the same time. The outside was covered with spray-painted artwork, depicting the city's skyline in almost cartoonish format. When Kaja walked through the front door she was immediately hit by the dueling smells of cleaning products and body odor, but to her surprise it wasn't nearly as unpleasant as it should've been. Maybe that was because she could

tell the patrons of the gym were working on bettering themselves…
or maybe it was because she'd grown up with an older brother and
had therefore smelled much, *much* worse.

She spotted Diana nearly instantaneously inside the boxing ring,
in the midst of demonstrating a counterattack to a group of a half-
dozen women of various ages, skin colors, and types of workout
clothing. Diana herself was a vision similar to the goddess whose
name she bore, with her long raven-black hair in a ponytail and her
fair skin covered in a sheen of sweat. Her eyes were as pale and icy
as the clear winter sky outside the gym, and they scanned over her
opponent—a man twice her size and easily a hundred pounds
heavier—with calculating precision. She ducked when he reached
for her with both hands, turning as if she were going to flee, only to
be jerked backward when he grabbed her by her ponytail. Instead of
allowing this to debilitate her, she leaned into it, slamming her heel
into his shin and twisting her body at the same time. He was forced
to let go, and the assemblage of women clapped politely.

"We'll go through that one more slowly in a moment," Diana
declared, spotting Kaja near the weight racks. A hint of her native
Bulgarian pulled at the words, which made Kaja glad—she wasn't

hiding so much of who she was anymore, now that she wasn't spying on her adoptive father while also maintaining a day job as a spy. "Let's take ten." Her tone brokered no argument, and her students dispersed along with her guinea pig. She hopped down out of the ring and grabbed a bottle of water before loping over to Kaja. "Hello, *skŭpa*. I take it David got to you."

"You make it sound so sinister," Kaja said, unable to stop a smile from forming on her face at being called *dear*. "But yes, he did. Asked me to bring you on a field trip to Project Renegade. You up for it?"

"Do I have a choice?" Diana wondered, voice dry. She drank half of her water in one go, then wiped her face off with a nearby towel. "More importantly, how do *you* feel about this?" Her top lip curled in a sneer, an expression filled with such vehemence it would've caused an individual with a weaker constitution than Kaja to step back. "Afraid I'm going to snap and start maiming people again?"

She was referring to a time back in October, when her undercover operation inside Blakely Manor had gone sideways and resulted in a dormant and much more vicious part of her emerging.

That version of Diana had an unfortunate meeting with Lottie and Eileen that resulted in both of Kaja's agents returning to the war room bruised and bloody. Since then apologies had been exchanged, and for Eileen and Lottie, Kaja knew it was water under the bridge. But the same couldn't be said for Diana, evidently.

"If I was afraid of that, we wouldn't be having this conversation at all," Kaja pointed out, putting a hand on Diana's shoulder and squeezing lightly. "And for the record, no, I don't think you'll lose yourself like that again. You've worked too hard to win back control." She gestured around the gym with her free hand. "I'll admit, I didn't expect this, though."

"Neither did I." Diana glanced around at her scattered class of trainees and smiled, just a little. "I have been coming here for a long time to work out, and when one of Ginger's trainers quit... one thing sort of led to another, you know? But I'm sure she won't mind if I take some time away." She turns her gaze to Kaja. "Give me five minutes to shower and change, and we can get out of here."

"Sounds good," Kaja said, taking a seat on a nearby bench to wait. She glanced at her phone but saw no new messages, and had to wonder if that was a good thing... or a very bad one.

Once they were in Tara's Jeep and away from the shooter, it didn't take long for Tara, Wolfe, and Scarlett to formulate a plan of action. They all agreed that it was a little too convenient that Wolfe and Scarlett had been "hired" the same day that someone did a drive-by of Aoife's house—more likely than not, the person who slid the fat stack through their mail slot was the same individual who had just shot at them, or had retained a hired gun to clean up their mess (and get their money back). That meant there was something on Dev's bulletin board that was extremely valuable (read: incriminating), and it made protecting said bulletin board their collective number one priority.

"But where do we go?" Tara wondered aloud, from the passenger's seat of her own damn vehicle. Wolfe was a little bit of a control freak when it came to driving, and she had to admit that he'd done a very thorough job of making sure they weren't being followed. "I don't want to take this thing back to Renegade—for all I know, this could be an inside job. And we can't bring it to your office, or any of our homes."

"I've got an idea," Scarlett said from the backseat, the bulletin board cradled between her knees, her gun resting in her lap. "Jimmy, make a left up here. You think our intern will mind if we pay him a visit?"

"Intern?" Tara echoed, confused until she remembered that Wolfe's boyfriend, Sebastian Codreanu, was still working for Wolfe & Vaughn Investigations on paper as part of an operation they'd conducted the previous year. She glanced over their surroundings quickly and realized Scarlett was directing them into the heart of the Theatre District. "Are we going to Stela?"

"Yep," Wolfe replied, navigating the convoluted one-way streets with the ease of a native. That made sense, seeing as he grew up in nearby Somerville and drove these roads nearly every day for work. "They don't open for dinner until five o'clock, so we've got a couple hours to figure out our next move." He took a parallel spot on Stuart Street and killed the engine. "Come on, let's get inside."

The three of them exited the Jeep, with Scarlett carrying the bulletin board turned inward against her chest. As soon as her feet hit the pavement, Tara couldn't help but wince, pain lancing up her back and making her teeth ache. She tried to breathe through it but found herself wavering on her feet… until Wolfe laced his arm through hers, keeping her upright.

"I've got you," he said, and there was a distinct lack of pity in his voice. When Tara glanced up at him, his eyes were full of understanding. Looking down at his hand where it was touching her elbow, she noted the scars that crisscrossed the back of it and recalled Frogger telling her he'd been the sole survivor of an IED detonation. That kind of trauma could've easily turned him bitter, but instead it had only made him kind. "I know how it feels to not be able to trust your own body."

"Thanks," Tara muttered, forcing her legs to work and shuffling forward on the icy pavement. She took a moment to gawk at the building Stela occupied, the dining room of the Romanian-American restaurant visible through its glass front. Red cloth napkins stood out starkly against white linen tablecloths, gold-rimmed plates with matching silverware lined up with precision for every setting. It was the kind of establishment where you not only needed a reservation, but a suit jacket or a very expensive dress. "Wow. This place is… really something."

"I will take that as a compliment," Sebastian Codreanu said from the doorway to the restaurant, a wry smile belying the amusement in the words. He was runway-model handsome, with bright blue eyes and cheekbones that could cut glass. Golden skin and dark hair paired well with the black of his dress shirt, and when Tara got close enough she could smell hints of expensive cologne. "Were you followed?"

Wolfe placed a hand over his heart in mock-offense. "Bash, give me some credit. This isn't my first time getting tailed." He let go of Tara to grasp his boyfriend by the waist for a half-second, pressing a kiss to his cheek before walking inside. "I take it Scarlett told you?"

"Duh," was Scarlett's response, freeing up one hand from the bulletin board to tug at the front of Sebastian's shirt, probably in place of ruffling his hair. "Honestly, I'm just glad he understood whatever I sent. Texting and running for your life ain't as easy as it sounds."

"It does not sound easy." Sebastian shook his head a little, then turned his attention back to Tara. He smiled again, polite but just a touch wary; Tara recognized the expression from her time around Dev, when he was confronted with someone he didn't know very well. "Please, come in." He picked up on the stiffness in Tara's posture and his brow creased. "Were you injured?"

"Not today," Tara replied, pasting her own smile over a wince. Once the door to Stela was closed and locked behind her, she added, "I've never had the chance to eat here, but I've always wanted to. I hear it's only gotten better since you took it over."

"You'll have to come back on a day when you are not being pursued by armed miscreants," Sebastian said, offering his arm much like Wolfe had. His smile widened when she took it, losing some of its earlier hesitancy. "As far as I'm concerned, you now have a permanent reservation. Would you like some ibuprofen? Or a hot compress?"

"I wouldn't say no to either of those things." Tara allowed Sebastian to lead her through the expansive dining room to a back corridor, where Wolfe and Scarlett had already gone. They passed the kitchen, which was bustling with people in white chef's attire doing prep work for the evening's patrons. "So what exactly did Scarlett tell you?"

"That you retrieved something of great import from Dev's apartment and needed a place to lay low after getting shot at."

Sebastian sounded completely unbothered by the idea, and Tara had

to remind herself that he was much more than just a pretty face; he'd

been involved in Boston's criminal underbelly since he was a

teenager. "I have learned not to ask too many questions when it

comes to a Wolfe and Vaughn investigation."

"Probably for the best, honestly," Tara said as they entered an

office at the end of the hall, past the bathrooms. It was a small but

comfortable space, real wood paneling on the walls and a glass-

topped desk acting as the focal point. On it was a laptop, a Tiffany

lamp that Tara had no doubt was real, and some tastefully organized

stationary. There was a rolling chair behind the desk, along with two

leather chairs for visitors in front and a dark green velvet couch

along one wall. Sitting on the couch and trimming his nails with a

penknife was Sebastian's bodyguard and friend, Constantin Ionesco.

"Hi, Constantin."

Constantin nodded at her in greeting. A bulky guy in his mid-

fifties, nary a strand of slicked-back black hair was out of place on

his head, and his clothes were flawless from the pinstripes in his suit

to the shine on his steel-toed loafers. "Miss Byrne, it is good to see

you again. Do you require medical attention?"

"Get one of the sous chefs to heat up a bag of rice," Sebastian instructed, helping Tara sit down on the couch while Constantin exited the room. He held up a hand and caught the bottle of ibuprofen that Wolfe threw him, which appeared to have come from one of Sebastian's desk drawers. "Thank you, Jim."

"No problem." Wolfe crouched down and opened a miniature refrigerator that was artfully concealed by some potted plants in one corner. He retrieved a bottle of water and sidestepped around Scarlett, who was placing Dev's bulletin board on Sebastian's desk. "Here, Tara, have something to drink."

Tara took three brown tablets with a huge slug of water, doing her best to relax into the plush softness of the couch. Her back throbbed, but she ignored it, choosing instead to focus on Sebastian. "So how's legitimizing your dad's cooked books going?"

"About as well as you might think," Sebastian replied dryly, sitting on the edge of the coffee table in front of the couch and pushing a hand through his hair. "I finally located an accountant that wasn't either a criminal in their own right or more interested in my father's crimes than in helping me. I am just thankful the FBI allowed me to keep Stela and the house on Beacon Hill as assets while we awaiting my father's trial."

"Apparently they were the only two things of Anton's they determined he acquired legitimately," Wolfe added, taking the seat next to Tara on the couch. He stayed at a respectful distance and was careful not to jostle her, which she appreciated. "Big surprise there."

"Be more sarcastic, I don't think they heard you all the way in Saugus," Scarlett said, stepping back to look at the bulletin board and crossing her arms over her chest. "Okay, so which part of this *A Beautiful Mind* bullshit is the part worth paying or killing for?"

"Perhaps the portion with the man who looks like he would happily chew out someone's jugular with his teeth?" Constantin suggested as he returned to the office, shutting the door behind himself and offering Tara a cloth bag full of rice that was warm to the touch. "In my experience, the people who look like they could be the villain of the story often are."

"You mean Aleksandr?" Tara guessed, frowning. "I guess he could be behind this. But if that were the case, why not break into Aoife's house and steal the board himself?"

"If he's a part of the Reborn, that seems like it'd be more his style," Wolfe said, able to read the information about Lichtenson on the bulletin board even while seated thanks to his overall height. "But maybe he's trying to keep this as far away from himself and the cult as he can."

"Maybe," Sebastian echoed, rubbing at his chin in thought. He was painfully attractive, and if she hadn't known he was very much taken, Tara would've been sweating lightly in his presence. He glanced at Constantin. "Who do we know that would take a shooting job that was not gang related?"

"Terry Berry," Constantin said immediately, with the complete confidence of someone who was positive they were correct. "Of course. Who else would it be?"

"What now?" Scarlett tilted her head, blonde waves shifting with the movement. "The fuck is a Terry Berry? Are they related to Mary Berry?" When she received several blank looks, her eyebrows shot up. "Seriously? Nobody watches *The Great British Baking Show*?"

Sebastian stared at her for a moment longer, then shook his head. "Terry Berry is a nutcase, even amongst those with less than legitimate occupations. And since I know you are going to ask where you can find him, I'll tell you: when he isn't sticking up the elderly for their last dollar, he frequents a bar in the South End."

"Lotta bars in South End, Bash," Wolfe said, dry but not unkind. "You're gonna have to narrow it down for us."

"It is one with which you are already familiar," Constantin said, pulling a face. "The Hole."

"No shit?" Scarlett looked surprised, and clarified for Tara's benefit, "Sebastian used to spend a lot of time there playing piano, before we poached him for gumshoeing."

"Well, let's hope Terry Berry hasn't moved on to greener pastures too." Grimacing, Tara tucked the warm bag of rice into the back of her waistband, then stood up. "Come on, let's get moving. I'd rather not have to explain this colossal fuckup to my boss."

~***~

When Lottie and Eileen had informed Dev and Flynn that the site of the black market auction was a casino, they had both been a little skeptical. Even with the security team under a mobster's thumb, it seemed like a high traffic and therefore high-risk place to host an event that was supposed to be on the down-low. But now that he'd breezed past the bouncer in his tuxedo and had Lottie on his arm in a burgundy velvet dress, Dev could admit he saw the appeal.

Unlike casinos in the States, which were all about flash and glitz, Vibráló Casino was set on a quiet narrow street in District VII, not far from a sprawling park. The outside was tall and stately, with a mansard roof and plain coloring that spoke to the building's age. An arched doorway opened into the lobby, reminding Dev a little of a library, just with less books and more gambling. Dark wood paneling lined the walls, and antique amber glass globes provided illumination.

Plush black carpeting cushioned their footsteps, and while a doorman took their snow-dusted coats, Dev and Lottie pulled out their phones and waved them over a computer terminal. Tara had sent over pre-purchased entry passes linked to their aliases, so when their fake IDs were checked everything matched up perfectly. A quick stroll through a metal detector was the last step, and then they were allowed on to the casino floor.

"This is... surprisingly nice," Lottie commented quietly, taking Dev's elbow once again. They stood on the steps for a moment, surveying the space. It was big and filled with everything from slot machines to card tables, but... tastefully so, somehow. There was separation between the different sections, and again unlike in the States there weren't drunks stumbling around spilling overpriced cocktails, or coked-up airheads clinging on to guys who were having the time of their life... until they weren't. "Weird how quiet it is, though."

"Weirder that it doesn't smell like a bottle of Colt 45," was Dev's response as they descended the stairs. He wasn't kidding about the smell being livable, as they also weren't surrounded by the stench of fried food and flop sweat. Instead, it was just... air, albeit fairly warm air from all the bodies playing various games, plus the heat output from the machines themselves. "Everybody's comms working okay?"

"Hear you loud and clear," Flynn said, laying his Texas drawl on thick to fit his assigned persona. When Dev did a second scan of the casino floor, he spotted Flynn and Eileen by a craps table; he was painfully handsome in a pinstriped suit adorned with a bolo tie, and she looked elegant in a floor-length creme colored gown. "Lookin' sharp, stud."

"You too." Dev heard the faintest trace of longing in his voice and squashed it in his next breath. He didn't miss the side-eye Lottie gave him, and wondered not for the first time if she knew how he really felt about Flynn. "Anybody got eyes on a back room? I sincerely doubt they're going to have the auction out here."

"I'm checking the camera feeds now," Sabene's said in their ears, and Dev frowned. He liked Sabene well enough and they were good at their job, but walking the field team through an op seemed to be a bit above their pay grade. He fully expected Tara to be the one talking instead. "Although if there is a back room where they plan on selling illicit goods, they probably don't have security cameras in it."

"You'd be surprised," Lottie said dryly, meeting Dev's gaze for a moment as they made their way over to the bar. "A lot of career criminals are super paranoid. Kinda comes with the territory." A weighted pause. "Sabene, where's Tara?"

"On assignment," was their response, as if they had been expecting the question, and it would be an insult to Sabene's intelligence to assume otherwise. "Kaja had something she needed Tara to take care of, so I'm what you've got. I'm sure that won't be a problem, will it?"

"Not at all," Eileen cut in, always ready to smooth things over. She was the opposite of Dev in that respect, inherently able to diffuse tension where he naturally created it. "We're just a bit of a change adverse bunch. I think I speak for all of us when I say when we get surprised, it's usually bad news."

"I understand." Sabene's tone was kind, any trace of frostiness gone. "Now, where were we?" They typed for a bit, keys clacking as Dev and Lottie ordered their drinks and received them, beginning a slow walk around the casino floor; to anyone who didn't know better, they looked like a couple of honeymooners checking out the different ways to lose their life savings. "Ah, I think I've got something. On the back wall of the casino floor, there's a corridor that leads to the bathrooms. Beyond that is another door that *looks* like it should be a maintenance closet… but the blueprints submitted when they retrofitted the place suggest otherwise."

"That sounds like exactly what we're lookin' for," Flynn said, and when Dev glanced his way, it was just in time to see him win his game. He made a show of celebrating with Eileen, twirling her around and shouting, and once that was done they collected their chips and moved on to another table closer to the back. "We can't all head that way at the same time, though."

"We'll go first." Lottie pretended to sip the neat bourbon in her free hand, the other one still hooked around Dev's elbow. The silver shadow on her eyelids glimmered under the soft-focused lighting. "You guys follow us in about five minutes."

"You won't be alone," Sabene warned. "I ran the footage back, and about two dozen people have gone through that door so far tonight. There's a bouncer directly on the other side. When he asks you for the password, make sure you tell him it's *gazdagság*."

"Riches, huh?" Eileen muttered, touching a hand to her chignon like she was checking for loose hair; in reality, Dev knew she had ceramic chopsticks in it that could be used as weapons. "That's a bit on the nose, don't you think?"

"Maybe a little," Dev agreed, wandering with Lottie down the corridor that led to the bathrooms. It was quieter and more shadowed than the casino floor, and while it was still opulent there was far less drama. He spotted the gilded doors for the bathrooms first, and beyond that was a plain wooden door set into the furthest wall. "Found it."

"My fakey carries more weight in a place like this than yours does," Lottie said quietly, squeezing his bicep. "Let me do the talking." She squared her shoulders and downed the rest of her bourbon in one slug, setting the empty glass on a credenza before rapping her knuckles on the door. "I know you're back there!" she called haughtily. "The password is *gazdagság*." She completely butchered the pronunciation, like any good American would. My... *friend* and I would like to come in now."

There was a long pause, and then the sound of multiple locks snapping open reached their ears. The door swung inward and an imposing man in a black suit and tie filled the entrance to a utilitarian-looking hallway. He didn't say anything, simply moved aside so they could pass, and Dev clocked the bulge of a handgun under his left arm. Then they were walking down the hall, Lottie's stiletto heels clicking against the linoleum floor, and Dev had the grim thought that it would be much easier to clean blood off a floor like this than it would the carpet in the casino proper.

The hallway opened up into a much larger room, and it took Dev a second to work out where they were: a church. The casino must've occupied what used to be a rectory, and a false wall had been built between the two to offer separation for the black market auctions. What was once most likely a beautiful place of worship full of ornate woodwork and stained glass windows was now stark and barren, stripped back to the studs in the walls. There was a small circular dais in the middle of the space, and surrounding it were swathes of metal folding chairs, each with a numbered paddle taped to the back; the numbers appeared to correspond to their invitations.

Dev did a quick count and estimated there were a hundred chairs, with the church about half full of criminals already. "We're in," he muttered into his comm. "Sabene, do you have a visual?"

"Wherever you are, there's no cameras," they replied. "I lost you as soon as you went through that door. Any sign of the DMT?"

"It's probably back there," Lottie said, nodding toward where the altar should've been. In its place were several tall wooden dividers that acted as a screen between the guests and the merchandise. "They must bring the lots up for bid out one at a time."

"That would make sense," Flynn agreed, and when Dev glanced back toward the door, he saw him and Eileen making their entrance. "Means we might have to wait for a while, though."

"The longer we have to wait, the more likely it is that someone will figure out we don't belong here," Eileen pointed out, her expression remaining serene despite her tense words. "We better hope that DMT is an exciting enough prospect to terrorists and mercenaries that it gets put on the block first."

Lottie, always the optimist: "Conversely, that's why they might save it for last." She tugged at Dev's arm and they took their seats, which were almost directly across the dais from Flynn and Eileen. "Thankfully none of the crooks here are ones we've personally offended."

"Yeah, that would make things awkward." Dev curled his fingers around his paddle and scanned the growing crowd, trying to block out the low hubbub of conversation and study faces. He didn't see any of the men who had helped steal the truck full of DMT back in Prague, but that didn't mean members of YK4 weren't around. He turned his attention to Lottie, not wanting to get caught staring by anyone who might shoot him for it. He frowned when he saw the look on her face. "Hey… are you okay?"

"What? Yeah, I'm fine," Lottie said, in a tone that wasn't convincing at all. When Dev simply raised an eyebrow in response, she sighed. "No, not really. I'm worried that something is going on with my parents beyond just being strict with Corrine. I know this is the last place we should be having this conversation, but…" She trailed off, hesitating. "Do you think they'd tell me if they were having money problems?"

Dev frowned. "I'm… not sure," he admitted, thinking back to the times he'd been a guest of the Trans. Lottie's mother, Mai, was a fantastic chef and the brains behind the family business, an authentic Vietnamese restaurant called Saigon Special in Boston's Dorchester neighborhood. Her father, Hao, managed front of house and finances. But that was before last fall, when Dorchester fell victim to the dumping of a toxic street drug called Rapture into its water supply by the leader of the Red Dynasty gang, Danh Sang. "I know they were shut down until the city came in and cleaned everything up—didn't they just reopen?"

Lottie was about to answer but the lights went down, dimming almost like they would in a movie theater. A hush fell over the crowd of miscreants, and any who were still standing moved quickly to their seats. A short bald man in a tailed tuxedo emerged from behind the dividers near the remnants of the altar, and Dev figured he had to be the auctioneer. He was proven correct a second later when the man climbed on to the dais, a spotlight shining down on the raised segment of the floor to direct attention.

"Good evening, esteemed guests," the bald man said, his voice carrying thanks to a lavalier microphone on his lapel. He gestured toward the dividers, which parted to allow two burly suited men to drag a third man to the center of the room, clad in nothing but a pair of dirty underwear. A fourth man followed, pushing a rolling cart holding what appeared to be a large temperature-controlled container. "We'll be starting the evening off with a demonstration of the first product up for bid." He reached inside his tuxedo jacket and produced a syringe, uncapping it swiftly before making his way to the barely-conscious man in between the pair of guards. "We'll start the bidding at five hundred thousand dollars for one thousand doses of Dimethyltryptamine... but please, witness its potential before you raise your paddles."

"Shit, this is bad," Flynn ground out through Dev's comm. "They're opening the auction with the DMT *and* they're about to dose this poor sap?"

"We can't let that happen," Dev declared, getting to his feet. Time seemed to slow down around him as it often did in these situations. He glanced at the mostly-full drink in his hand, then at a particularly mean-looking, tattooed man seated across the aisle from him. Before he could think better of it, he tossed the drink at the man's head, dousing him in alcohol. "Lottie, can you get that for me?"

"Oh fuck *you*, Devereux!" Lottie exclaimed, standing too as the tattooed man let out an almighty roar and rose. Despite her words, she grabbed the skirt of her dress and yanked hard, the fabric splitting and allowing her to move more easily. She kicked off her heels and climbed on Dev's vacated chair, vaulting off of it and wrapping her legs around the guy's neck in a flying scissor takedown as he tried to get to Dev. "Go!"

Dev ran for the dais, not needing to be told twice. By now chaos had taken over, with nearly every paranoid criminal in the building involved in some kind of fight, since no one was quite sure who had kicked things off. He pushed and shoved his way to the front, body-checking the guy in his underwear out of the way in his haste to get to the rolling cart of DMT.

A hand clutched at Dev's shoulder and he reached back without a second thought, grabbing on to the person's forearm and dipping forward at the same time, throwing them over his body and expecting them to hit the floor hard. To his surprise, they twisted in midair and landed on their feet, and when they straightened up Dev swore he felt his heart stop.

"Hello, Adam," Teddy Vasquez said, as if he weren't an apparition, a dream, but a real-life, solid person. He was older and taller, eyes flat and void. "It's been a while." He bared his teeth. "I think we have some catching up to do."

~***~

Chapter Nine

The day that everything changed, Adam had eleven years to his name. He also had scars on his knuckles from fighting barehanded, muscles more developed than the average boy, and an unruly mop of flaxen hair. Finally, and perhaps most important, he'd learned to walk silently and listen well.

He and Teddy were thick as thieves, despite the urgent mania thrumming through Frederick's sermons and the invisible ticking clock hanging over Adam's head. In less than one year, he would be sacrificed and reborn for the greater good of humanity. That was no small thing, but Teddy acted as though it didn't matter. He was the only person who could make Adam forget his fate, even for a little while, and he made the hunger pangs and the bitter cold a bit more bearable.

But like all good things in Adam's life, Teddy came to an end.

They'd finished up Dani's training regime for the day—a grueling combination of agility, climbing, and shooting of both guns and bows that left Adam's joints sore and his ears ringing—and after washing off in the creek they loped back to the compound together in thin t-shirts and scratchy shorts. The late July sun was just beginning to slip past the trees, casting everything in its red-orange glow. That fading light was the only reason Adam spotted Frederick having a hushed, tense conversation with Marshall Raider behind the chapel.

He should've kept his mouth shut, should've known better, but instead he elbowed Teddy and asked, "What do you think Raider did wrong this time?"

Teddy snorted. "Hard to say, the guy's such a fuckup." At this point in their friendship, Adam had stopped flinching when Teddy swore; as long as he didn't do it in front of the adults or the other kids, he'd avoid getting his mouth scrubbed out with soap. "Let's find out."

Before Adam could think to protest, Teddy grabbed him by the arm and led him half-crouched over to the side of the chapel. They pressed themselves up flat against the rough-hewn planks, and while Adam could've easily bailed then, he didn't. He couldn't, not once the roaring of his pulse calmed enough to hear what his father was saying.

"—can't believe you were so *sloppy*." Frederick had his back to them, but the *crack* of the backhand he delivered to Raider's face was as loud as a gunshot. "I thought I could trust you, Marshall, but I can see I was wrong."

"I'm sorry, Father," Raider mumbled, bowing his head in supplication. He didn't move to wipe the blood away when it dripped from his mouth, the inside of his cheek no doubt cut by his teeth. "I thought the truck would burn completely if I added enough gas. And even if it didn't, it was so deep in the woods... I never thought anyone would find it."

Adam frowned, exchanging a look of confusion with Teddy. One of the pickup trucks used for supply runs and transporting big game like bucks and elk back to the compound had gone missing a few years ago. Raider's story at the time was that he was hunting solo and left the truck parked on a fire road; when he came back, it was gone. The theory was it had been stolen by some sort of vagrant, but considering how far away they were from Bozeman, that didn't make much sense. Adam had been so preoccupied with Minnie leaving the Reborn that he hadn't given the thinness of Raider's story a second thought until that moment.

"And now that they have?" Frederick prompted, his baritone voice crackling with barely-controlled anger. "When they realize who that truck belongs to, they'll come here." A heaving breath. "They'll come looking for Minnie, and what will they find?"

"Nothing," Raider said quickly. Too quickly. "She's buried deep, Father. The worms'll have her by now."

The earth seemed to tilt beneath Adam's feet, his whip-quick mind processing the words but not really understanding them. He lurched forward, an animal noise wrenched from his throat, dimly aware of Teddy trying to hold him back and failing miserably. Frederick turned to face them as Adam approached, his silvery hair and beard glinting in the fading sunlight. He wasn't physically imposing—in fact, he was shorter and less muscular than most of the other men at the compound—but there was something in his presence that gave people pause.

There were words being said, and it took Adam a moment to realize they were falling from his lips, over and over: "You killed her, you killed her, you *killed*—"

Frederick grabbed him by the throat, cutting off the stream of sound. "She was not loyal, to me or to you," he said, voice flinty and eyes void. "She would've told the outsiders of the prophecy, of our plans." He seemed unphased when Adam scrabbled at his arm, desperately seeking oxygen he wasn't getting. He had that blank stare locked on Teddy. "And she was far from our only Judas. Isn't that right, Theodore?"

"What?" Teddy's face was pale as two of the border guards appeared from nowhere, yanking his arms behind his back and dragging him away, back toward the woods. "No, I didn't—Adam, help me—"

His cries were the last thing Adam heard as his world faded and went dark.

~***~

Chapter Ten

"Teddy?" Dev whispered, barely audible to his own ears over the chaos of sound that had enveloped the former church. He took a stumbling step backward, his training failing him as he struggled to make sense of what he was seeing. "How—"

The question died on Dev's lips as Teddy rushed him like a linebacker, tackling him directly into the cart holding the DMT. It toppled over, glass breaking and skittering, but Dev was too busy trying not to get his face caved in by a dead man to care. He got an arm up in time to block the hammer blow Teddy aimed at his nose, bringing a knee up into his gut at the same time. He grunted but didn't relent, grabbing Dev's arm and yanking it down, his other hand flickering as a thin plastic blade slid into his palm from inside his sleeve.

"I've waited so long for this," Teddy hissed, his breath warm and alarmingly alive on Dev's face, but the sound of his voice was all wrong, nothing like the kind soul Dev once knew. "Goodbye, Adam."

Right before Teddy could slip his knife between Dev's ribs, there was a blur of motion behind him and he was struck on the back of the head. He collapsed on top of Dev, his unconscious body weight nearly suffocating until Flynn pushed him aside with his leg and grabbed Dev by his lapels, hauling him to his feet.

"Are you okay?" It was nearly impossible to hear Flynn over the roar of the fight around them, but Dev was adept at looking at his partner's mouth (without being noticed) and saw the shape of the words. "Who is this fuckhead?"

"We have to take him with us!" Dev exclaimed, and it was his turn to dig his fingers into Flynn's jacket, yanking him down before either of them could be hit by a spray of stray bullets. The wreckage of the DMT cart provided shelter, at least for the moment. When he was faced by Flynn's skeptical down-turned brow, Dev tacked on: "Just trust me!"

"I'm with you," Flynn said, and while it was far from the first time he'd said something like that, the sentiment still made Dev's heart lurch pleasantly. "We takin' any DMT with us?"

"As much as you can carry," was Dev's response, gaze bouncing around the room, seeking out Lottie and Eileen. "Sabene, you there? Do we have an escape route?"

"Head for the altar," they said through his comm. Their voice was carefully controlled, and Dev realized absently that this was the first time Sabene had been on comms with them as a mission went sideways. "There's a door back there that leads to the next street. I'll find you a place to rabbit to from there."

Dev and Flynn both scooped up the vials of DMT that hadn't been broken, which amounted to around a dozen, and stuffed them into the inner pockets of their jackets. From everything Dev understood about the drug, it would be enough to send a small army on the psychedelic adventure of a lifetime. He was careful not to touch anything that had been contaminated by DMT, and was gratified to see Flynn doing the same without being told. He glanced up from their business in time to see Lottie grab a notorious Iranian arms dealer by the elbow and twist, smashing her forehead into one of his bodyguard's faces. Meanwhile, Eileen had scampered to the back of the church, behind the altar, and a second later the lights cut out—she must've found a breaker box.

"Now's our chance," Flynn said, moving in the shadows to grab Teddy and haul him into a fireman's carry. He grunted with the effort, ribs no doubt aching under the strain. "You sure we need to take this asshole with us? He was gonna kill you."

"A long time ago, that asshole was my only friend," Dev replied, leading his partner in a crouched run toward the altar. Grunting and crunching and the occasional gunshot told him Lottie was still beating the shit out of people, but he knew she'd bug out before any potential reinforcements could arrive. Then, because he also knew Flynn wouldn't let it go unless he had more information, he added, "That's Teddy."

"*This* is Teddy?" Flynn knew the bones of what Dev had been through with the Reborn, though he lacked some of the connective tissue; there were things Dev had experienced that he couldn't repeat to anyone, because he was afraid he would have to relive them. "I thought he was dead."

"So did I," Dev muttered, straightening up and tapping Eileen on the shoulder when they got close enough. "Hey, don't stab me."

"Wouldn't dream of it, love," Eileen said breezily, her fiery hair fallen from its updo. She clutched a bloodied chopstick in one hand, the other one most likely buried deep in a corpse. She spotted Flynn's motionless cargo and raised a perfect brow. "Who's the stiff?"

"Teddy, and surprisingly, he ain't dead," Flynn replied before Dev could. Behind them the last two men standing in Lottie's way fell to the floor, their heads smashed together like coconuts. "Nguyen! You coming or what?"

"No, asshole, I'm just breathing hard," Lottie sniped, practically shoving them out the back door that Sabene had promised. "We need a place to lay low, like, yesterday."

"Coming right up," Sabene said, more confident now. Probably a side effect of the team reuniting. "Get to the car, and I'll guide you the rest of the way."

~***~

As soon as Kaja came up the stairs to the loft at Project Renegade with Diana, she could tell something had gone FUBAR. Sabene was pacing the width of the room in front of the big screen, staring down at their tablet and speaking in a hushed voice to someone through the comm in their ear. When Kaja cleared her throat, Sabene jumped like they'd been stuck with a cattle prod and swore, almost dropping the tablet in the process.

"You look like you're having fun," Diana commented, the words as dry as dust. She looked up at the big screen, which displayed a satellite map of Boston and a blinking GPS dot tagged as TARA. The dot was moving at a slow but steady pace that meant its owner was in a vehicle, unless Tara had taken to rolling herself downhill very fast in her wheelchair. "Why don't you transfer the call to video?"

Sabene looked as though they wanted to protest, but one glance from Kaja had them doing exactly as Diana asked. The video call came up and showed a slightly frazzled Tara holding her phone in front of her face, in the passenger's seat of an SUV that Kaja belatedly recognized as Tara's Jeep. "Hey, boss lady," she said, mustering up a grin that could only mean bad things. "How was your meeting?"

"Splendid," Kaja deadpanned. She put her hands on her hips. "What the hell happened to you? And if that's your Jeep, who's driving?"

Tara tilted the phone slightly to her left, showing Scarlett Vaughn in the back seat and Jim Wolfe behind the wheel. They both waved. Beside Kaja, Diana smacked herself in the forehead with the heel of her hand and muttered something impolite in Bulgarian.

"Hey," Wolfe said, not sheepish in the slightest. His eyes stayed on the road, but he must've glimpsed Diana from the corner of his vision, because he asked, "Where's my dad?"

"Getting more leave time from the CIA," Diana told him, taking in a long breath through her nose. She and Wolfe were exes with a somewhat messy history, made no less complicated by the fact that Diana was now going steady with David. "Who are desperate to dump my ass in the nearest ditch, by the way. Hence why I am here, proving I am not crazy."

"Well, let's not set our expectations *too* high," Scarlett said, looking pleased with herself when the remark made Diana snort out a laugh. "And by the time we get done telling you what we're doing, you might lose your last marble after all."

Between Tara, Wolfe, and Scarlett, they recounted everything that had happened since Kaja left for her meeting with David, including what was currently going down with the field team. When they were done, Kaja felt the distinct edge of a migraine between her brows. "So let me make sure I have this right," she started, ticking off the salient points on the fingers of one hand. "You three were sent to locate Dev's information on The Reborn for *very* different reasons and almost died retrieving it, and now you're on your way to talk to some hired gun that may or may not know who paid Wolfe and Scarlett to steal the bulletin board. Meanwhile, the field team wound up in a firefight at the black market auction and came away with a handful of DMT and a dead man as a reward." She rubbed at her forehead. "Okay. This is officially a clusterfuck."

Diana turned to Sabene. "What's the status of the field team?"

Sabene winced. "They're on their way to a warehouse outside of Budapest. The plan is to hole up there until morning and interrogate Teddy Vasquez in the meantime, since he's most likely still affiliated with the Reborn." They pulled up another satellite map on the big screen, next to the video call. This one showed the suburb of Üllő, which Kaja was pleased to see had both an industrial park and a straight path on the highway to the airport. "It was the best I could do on short notice."

"It's good," Kaja told them, noting the cluster of GPS signals over the northeast corner of the industrial park, which represented the team. "What do you have for background on Vasquez?"

It was Tara who answered: "Not much. He isn't mentioned in any of Dev's notes, and all they say in that stupid docudrama is that he and Dev were friendly, rather than at each other's throats like the rest of the kids." She paused. "I assumed he died, since the info on him is scarce. But I guess not."

Diana shot Kaja a look. "Can Devereux handle this?"

Kaja felt her mouth settle into a grim line. "Let's hope so. Because if he can't, we might be fucked."

~***~

"I don't believe this," Lottie said for the third time since they'd arrived at the warehouse Sabene had led them to. Her dress was torn ragged at the knees, her feet were bare, and she'd retrieved her gun from their getaway car and had it strapped to her thigh. "And I don't get it, either. If this guy used to be your best friend, why does he want to kill you?"

"I don't know," Dev replied, blue eyes luminous in the moonlight filtering in through the building's high windows. As far as

Flynn could tell, it was a medium-sized industrial space that was once used to store concrete blocks of various shapes and sizes, probably for construction work. There were a couple of big forklifts near the cargo bay where they'd left the car, but everything was covered in a fine layer of dust, suggesting no one had worked there for some time. "Maybe... maybe he thinks I abandoned him."

"How could you abandon somebody you thought was *dead*?" Flynn wondered. The three of them stood partially concealed behind a pallet of blocks, and he glanced over at where Eileen was keeping an eye on Teddy. He was secured to a metal chair with some loose chain wrapped around his arms and legs, and Eileen had a shoulder propped against a support pillar, gun in hand. "This ain't your fault, Dev. You can't honestly tell me you believe that."

"I believe that I fucked up tonight," Dev said, loosening the bowtie at his throat. "I got distracted, and the rest of the DMT is probably on a plane back to the States by now." He tossed the tie aside but didn't remove his ruined jacket, since he was carrying vials of DMT just like Flynn was. "There's no way that what got broken and what we stole was all of it."

"Okay, you're right about that part," Lottie admitted with a frown. She grabbed Dev's arm, squeezing lightly, and that simple gesture did *not* make jealousy burn behind Flynn's sternum. No way. "But Flynn's right too. Whatever's happened to Teddy since the last time you saw him... you aren't responsible for it."

Dev looked like he was about to argue, but before he could, Teddy's voice floated over to them from the chair. "Are you *ever* going to get on with this interrogation? I've done you the courtesy of not screaming my head off—I would think that would earn me an expedited torture session."

"I'm not going to torture you, Teddy," Dev said, walking over to stand a few feet away from his not so dead childhood companion. He folded his arms, and Flynn knew it was partly a defensive gesture, but also concealed the bumps from the vials of DMT. "I would like to know why you want to kill me, though."

"Isn't it obvious?" Teddy tried to gesture around them, but the chains kept him immobile. Still, he wasn't deterred. "You *let* them take me away, *Adam*." Dev couldn't conceal a flinch at the emphasis on his real name, and Flynn's knuckles ached with the desire to hit something—Teddy's face, preferably. "All it took for the so-called

Chosen One to fly off the handle was finding out his daddy had his mommy dearest killed by that scumbag, Raider. And yet somehow, *I* was the one that paid the price for it."

"You know as well as I do that I had no power over Frederick." Dev's voice was tight, and he didn't look away from Teddy even as Flynn and Lottie flanked him. "Or any of the other adults, for that matter. I could've begged them to leave you alone and it wouldn't have made a difference."

"But you didn't even *try*," Teddy implored, and while his expression had been eerily flat up until this point, now he looked almost manic. "You didn't—" All of a sudden he gave a full-body twitch, twisting under the pressure of the chains, his head snapping so hard to one side that Flynn heard his neck crack. When he turned it to look at Dev again, a vein was bulging in his forehead with strain. "Adam," he wheezed out, and now Flynn could tell what the strain was from—Teddy was fighting for control. "Adam, you... please, help me. They d-did something to me, and I—I can't s-stop *listening*—"

Dev didn't hesitate to go up closer to his old friend, and Flynn tensed, right hand twitching toward the gun he'd returned to its usual spot in the small of his back. Next to him, Lottie's fingers jerked similarly by her thigh, but neither of them actually drew their weapons for two reasons. First, Eileen was already holding a gun, and she was in a better position to shoot Teddy if something went wrong, and second, they all trusted Dev's judgement, even in an intensely personal situation like this one.

"Teddy," Dev started, calm and even. He crouched down in front of Teddy and put a hand on his knee. "I don't know exactly what's going on with you, but I suspect you've been dosed with DMT— probably a lot of it. Then you were conditioned to believe you wanted to kill me. But I don't think that's really what you want." A pause, his shoulders tensing. "Is it?"

"No," Teddy whispered, wide eyes staring down at Dev's face. "But I d-don't know how to stop."

"Keep looking at me," Dev instructed. "And keep talking." Another pause, this one thoughtful, then, "You remember those biscuits your mom used to make?" When Teddy nodded, Dev continued, "They were the best damn biscuits I've ever had. Better than anything my mom or any of the other parents made. Remember that one time on my birthday, when she put pecans in them? And we all lost our collective shit?"

"They were glazed. And sweet," Teddy said, his voice gone soft and slow with recollection. He wasn't fighting the restraints anymore, and when Flynn looked closer, he saw tears in his eyes. "She's dead, Adam. Got trampled to death the night you became Judas. And b-between that and what they did to me after they took me away… I think that's why I wanted to hurt you."

Dev went very still, his free hand clenching into a fist against his thigh. "I'm sorry about Gloria," he said quietly. "But killing me won't bring her back, and it won't change what happened to you. Whatever Aleksandr told you—"

"Aleksandr?" Teddy repeated, brow furrowing. "He didn't do this to me, it was Frederick, and—"

An explosion rocked the building, chunks of concrete and clouds of dust flying haphazardly as the loading dock wall was obliterated. Flynn started moving as soon as it happened, pulling his gun with one hand and grabbing Dev by the back of the jacket with the other. He ignored the way his partner screamed Teddy's name, manhandling him behind a nearby industrial-sized cement mixer.

Thankfully, while Flynn dragged Dev backward, Lottie threw herself forward, yanking Teddy behind a pillar by the chair he was chained to, Eileen following her a split second later. There was no shooting, at least not right away, which meant the men in tactical gear that had followed the lead of their Semtex charges were sweeping the building.

"F-Flynn, did you hear him? He said my father—" Dev broke off, taking a deep breath. He was good at assimilating information quickly, even the life-altering stuff. His long fingers dug hard into Flynn's arm. "How many are there?"

"At least a dozen," Flynn murmured, heart flying with adrenaline as he took a peek at the flashlights moving around the warehouse. He couldn't feel any pain where Dev touched him, even though he knew his grip was tight enough to leave bruises—there was only the warmth from his hand and the sound of combat boots scuffing across the floor. "They're stacked with body armor and AKs."

"Shit," Dev whispered, his gaze locking on something over Flynn's shoulder. "Teddy? What are you doing?"

"Your friend with the tattoos and the short temper let me go," Teddy replied, finishing his low-crawl through the shadows on

Dev's other side. His face was pale in the darkness, but his eyes were clear. "Let me help."

No was on the tip of Flynn's tongue, but Dev's hand squeezed his arm again, causing Flynn to sigh. He eyed Teddy for a long moment, then reached for the second gun he kept strapped to his ankle for the unlikely scenario in which his main weapon jammed, but also for situations like these. He held the snub-nosed .38 out to Teddy, but kept it in his grip for a second when the other man's hand closed around the barrel. "Fuck this up, and escaping from the Reborn will be the least of your worries."

"Understood," Teddy murmured, taking the gun once Flynn released his death-grip. He checked the load, then snuck a look around the pile of cinderblocks, much like Flynn had. "What's the plan?"

Flynn snorted. "Bold of you to assume we have one." He felt Dev's hand leave his arm, right before fingers snuck into his back pocket, and he barely stifled a groan. "Seriously, dude? Why is it always *my* phone you have to destroy?"

"Because I love you so much," was Dev's snarky response, and the words made Flynn's poor old heart trip in his chest even though he knew Dev didn't mean them that way. "Keep them distracted. I need... five minutes?" He successfully pried the case off, along with the back of the phone. "No, three."

"Wonderful," Flynn muttered, glancing toward where Teddy came from. He could barely make out the shapes of Lottie and Eileen in the darkness, but he flashed them a quick set of hand signals to indicate where they should go, and he got a thumbs-up from Lottie as confirmation. Then he looked at Teddy. "You take left, I'll take right?"

"Works for me." Teddy scurried over to the next pile of concrete blocks and let out a shrill whistle. "Come and get me, fuckers!"

A cacophony of gunfire erupted, and Flynn swore he saw Dev grinning from the corner of his eye. Jealousy churning sour and ugly in his stomach, Flynn made himself a target too, trying hard not to think about why exactly he felt that way.

~***~

Chapter Eleven

When Adam had a dozen years to his name, things were bad at the compound.

Calling it *bad* was a kindness, Adam thought as he watched their cattle pasture from the crotch of an old ponderosa pine. *Horrendous* was more apt. It was early spring, the snow beginning to melt, and climbing high up into trees was just about the only privacy Adam could get. Thankfully, nobody wanted to come out to the pasture anyway; the amount of feed the milk cows and goats received had dwindled to half of what it should've been. It left the animals listless and glassy-eyed, not unlike some of the humans, who were also suffering from malnutrition.

Adam wasn't, of course. He was Frederick's son, the *Chosen One*, and so he always got first pick of whatever the women had whipped up at chow time. And each time he filled his plate, he felt the burning glares of the other children, those who hadn't already succumbed to disease or training accidents. He was still thin, but not as thin as them. If Teddy had been there, it might've bothered him less, but... Teddy was gone. After that day behind the chapel, Adam had never seen his friend again. It haunted him, but there was little he could do about it without risking Frederick's wrath.

Sighing, Adam forced himself into motion, climbing down the limbs of the tree and dropping the last few feet to the ground. Any remaining faith he'd had in God or his father's prophecy had vanished when Teddy did. He was a good person, and so was Minnie. Surely there was no way a just and understanding God would allow people like that to have such horrible things done to them, while people like Marshall Raider got kicked out of the Reborn and allowed to roam free. Adam didn't have all the details on that situation, but apparently Raider had killed a woman in town after sleeping with her, and the other adults were afraid his carelessness would be their downfall.

"Focus," he muttered to himself, digging his fingernails into his palms on his walk back into the main portion of the compound. Arms straight, shoulders back, every step regimented. "If you don't, you'll get your ass handed to you in training."

"There he is," Dani drawled when Adam emerged from the woods a few minutes later, her arms crossed over her chest. She looked decidedly unamused, not that Adam had ever seen her be particularly cheerful. Her black skin shone with moisture in the morning light, probably from sunscreen—much like Adam, she was afforded some luxuries because of her position. "About time you showed up, Chosen One. I should give you a demerit for tardiness."

"Wouldn't matter," one of the older boys, Aleksandr, said under his breath, glaring at Dev with his pale eyes. His words caused the children near him to scowl, because they all knew it was true. "He could *kill* one of us and it wouldn't matter."

Adam felt those words like a physical blow, but he forced himself to remain aloof. He met Dani's steely stare with one of his own. "What's on the agenda for today?"

"Live fire," was Dani's response, causing both Adam and the other kids to freeze; the one who shot off his mouth about Dev not being punished for hypothetically killing one of them going paler than milk. "You'll get a five minute head start, and then I'll be coming after you, along with Tyler and Brandon." She drew the handgun she kept in a holster in the back of her waistband. "The bullets are real, and so are the blades. If you want to survive, you'll have to use every bit of training I've given you."

"This is crazy!" a girl exclaimed, beginning to back toward the tree line. Several other kids followed. "You can't do this!"

Dani's flat face turned sympathetic for a brief moment. "Unfortunately, I can," she said, raising her pistol to the sky. She fired off a single shot, deafening and terrifying. "Father's orders. Your five minutes starts now."

~***~

Chapter Twelve

One haphazard getaway and a debrief from a very miffed Kaja later, and Eileen found herself watching her friends interact with their new charge—or in Dev's case, his old friend, Teddy.

Growing up in a wealthy family full of socialites and politicians meant that Eileen had learned the correct way to observe people unobtrusively at a young age. She could watch someone she didn't know for five minutes and learn what made them tick—or at least figure out how to lift their Rolex without them noticing. By that logic, it was entirely possible that her sordid life of crime had developed *vis a vie* boredom; nevertheless, it was a useful skill to have, being a spy and all.

Eileen went around the plane clockwise and started her observations with Lottie. She forced herself not to notice the little wisps of hair at her temples or the purple bruise that had erupted on her jaw; instead, she deduced from the tilt of Lottie's head and her fingers drumming against her armrest that she didn't trust Teddy at all. Not surprising, considering how little they really knew about him, beyond the fact that he was from Dev's old life. Hell, Eileen was still amazed that the four of them plus Tara didn't kill each other over perceived slights when they first started working together as a team.

Next up was Flynn—poor, angsty, downtrodden man that he was. He couldn't see the depth or nature of Dev's regard for him, even when it was obvious to just about everyone else. But by the same token, Dev had to be blind to not know that Flynn's protective nature extended far beyond friendship or the familial sort of tie Eileen felt toward Dev. Either way, she thought, it was a little amusing to watch Flynn glowering in Teddy's direction—especially since their charge seemed to have no idea it was happening, or he just didn't care.

Speaking of Teddy, he was busy talking to Dev near the rear of the plane, their heads leaned so close together they almost touched. Since reading people was her bread and butter, it was easy for Eileen to see that there was a brotherly affection between them, which hadn't been dulled by their time apart. It was in the way Dev brushed Teddy's arm or his knee occasionally with his fingers as they conversed, like he was reminding himself that he was really there. Or in the way Teddy's sallow face brightened when Dev said something funny, only for him to elbow Dev a second later in playful reproach.

"Hey," Lottie said, cutting through Eileen's concentration. She didn't mind, turning her gaze back to the other woman as she took the seat next to Eileen's. The former Ranger looked uncharacteristically nervous all of a sudden, picking at her cuticles. "Can I ask you something?"

"Of course, love," Eileen replied, resting her elbow on the armrest between them and putting her chin in her palm. "What's up?"

"I've decided I need to go and talk with my parents when this is over." Lottie gestured vaguely toward Dev and Teddy to indicate what she meant by *this*, then rubbed at an eyelid that was already smeared with mascara and the remains of glittery shadow. "See what's really up with Corrine, all of that. Would you mind coming to the restaurant with me?"

Eileen offered Lottie what she hoped was a reassuring smile. "I'd be happy to, although it's not often I get asked to be moral support."

"I know, but… you're so good at talking to people, in a way that I'm not." Lottie smiled back, and Eileen's heart didn't beat a little faster, it *couldn't*. This was her friend, her coworker, who by all accounts was straight—she'd dated Dev, for Christ's sake. "Thank you, Eileen. I appreciate it."

"Okay," Dev announced suddenly, the single word traveling easily within the confines of the plane. "We've got a plan to go after the DMT... and the Reborn. But none of you are going to like it."

"*We* don't even like it," Teddy added, scratching at his jaw. It looked as though he usually shaved religiously—probably had something to do with Frederick's concept of the ideal male—and now that hair was starting to grow in. "That being said, it's also the only thing either of us can come up with that seems like it might be remotely effective, so..."

Flynn's mouth was set in a grim line. "How bad are we talking, exactly?"

"According to Teddy, the Reborn are not only still operational, they've started recruiting again," Dev began, folding his arms over his stomach in a self-hug; considering the circumstances, Eileen was surprised he wasn't pulling into himself more. "My father... my father is alive, and he's started spouting off some kind of new prophecy."

"One that doesn't involve you dying and coming back to life, then making everyone else immortal?" Lottie's tone was effortlessly caustic. They all knew enough of Dev's history to know that Frederick Devereux was nine different kinds of fucked up. "Color me shocked."

"Frederick… isn't well," Teddy said, seeming to select his words with care. "No one except maybe Aleksandr knows exactly what's wrong with him, but I suspect it's something terminal. It's almost like he's trying to prepare the Reborn to continue operating after he's dead. Even when I was under their… mind control, or whatever, I never got close enough to find out what was really going on." He paused. "That's why we've decided the easiest way to get more information is for me to give Frederick and Aleksandr what they want."

Eileen's gut clenched, a bad feeling brewing. "And that would be?"

"Me," Dev answered simply, holding up his hands in supplication when Eileen, Lottie, and Flynn all erupted in protests that were mostly swearing. "Hey, cool it! Do one of you have a better idea?"

"No, but—" Flynn cut himself off with a frustrated sound. "Dev, you're the smartest person I know, but that's a fucking *stupid* plan. How would that even work?"

"I go back to Montana, with Dev as a prisoner." Teddy flinched when all of their gazes focused in on him at once, but recovered quickly; Eileen was impressed. "When they ask what happened to my men, I tell them a version of the truth—they died in the firefight at the auction. Then you all took me, and I pretended to go along with you so I could get close enough to Dev to kidnap him once we landed in the States."

Lottie stared at Teddy for a long moment before she made a frustrated sound. "Shit. As much as I hate to admit it, I don't see another option. At least not right now."

"And we don't have much time to debate it," Dev said. His voice was steady, but Eileen saw a hint of fear playing around his eyes. "My father and Aleksandr are planning on doing *something* with the rest of the DMT, and soon. We need to get it back before that happens."

"Here's a question." Eileen debated how to phrase it for a second, then threw caution to the wind: "How did Frederick survive being shot point-blank in the chest?"

It was Dev's turn to flinch. "I don't know, Eileen. And neither does Teddy, because he wasn't there."

"Yeah, that's something that doesn't make a whole lotta sense," Flynn pointed out, narrowing his eyes in Teddy's direction. He stood up and jabbed a finger in Teddy's face. "Actually, why'd they keep *you* alive, huh? Just to make you a puppet?"

"Does it really matter to you?" Teddy countered, and oh, he had some balls after all. He rose to his feet, just a touch shorter than Flynn but all muscle. "Or are you looking for an excuse to kill me?"

"Enough!" Dev got up and put himself between the two men, a hand on both of their chests. "We *are* on the same side, whether you guys want to see that or not." He looked at Lottie and Eileen. "You two are acting rational. What do you think?"

"I think Teddy making such a miraculous mental recovery is a bit fishy, and that's why Flynn is suspicious," Eileen started, rolling her eyes when Dev immediately frowned at her. "*But...* at the same time, clearly you two have quite the bond. It makes sense that he would be able to see reason if it came from you. Which is probably why the Reborn did their level best to keep you apart for as long as they did."

"As much as I hate your 'plan'—" Lottie's air quotes were like no other, big and exaggerated "—it *does* make sense, from a tactical perspective." She eyed Flynn. "Take your personal connection to Dev out of it for a second. If it were anybody else, would you say okay?"

Flynn faltered, dragging a hand over his face and turning away. He took a deep breath, then slowly nodded his head. "You know I would."

"Then you need to trust me," Dev implored, his hand hovering in the air momentarily before landing on Flynn's shoulder and squeezing. "We can work out the details once we're back at HQ."

Eileen snorted. "Oh boy. Have fun explaining this to Kaja." She chuckled when Dev got a shade paler. "Didn't think of that, huh?" She glanced at her watch, estimating their remaining flight time in her head, then stood up and reached for the overhead bin. "I think this would be a *great* time for some Parcheesi, don't you?"

~***~

The Hole, Tara thought, was a very apt name for the bar that Terry Berry frequented, since it was little more than an actual hole-in-the-wall. A blood-red door led into the basement of a battered brick walk-up near the Northeastern University campus, and a crudely lettered whiteboard near the entrance advertised live music on Friday and Saturday night. The walls were splattered with neon paint, the floors were sticky, and the drinks were overpriced—in other words, exactly what one might expect from a place that boasted Fireball as a top-shelf bottle.

"You know, when I came here looking for Sebastian, I never noticed exactly how badly this place stinks," Wolfe commented as soon as they were inside, stomping the snow off his boots. One booth near the back of the establishment was occupied by a pair of off-duty hookers, and a man who bore an eerie resemblance to Mr. Clean sat at the bar; other than that, The Hole was painfully empty. "But what does it stink *like*?"

"Eau de asshole?" Scarlett suggested, wandering up to the bar and offering the androgynous bartender a bright smile. "Three of your strongest Diet Cokes. In cans, bottles, or literally anything but a glass." The bartender grunted and clicked their tongue ring against their top teeth, complying with the request. "Thanks so much." She took the seat on Mr. Clean's left side, leaning her elbow on the bar as Wolfe circled around to the one on his right. "Terry Berry, I presume?"

"Depends on who's askin'," the bald man replied, looking and sounding as if the White Russian in his hand wasn't his first of the day. The smell that hung in the air, Tara realized as she got closer, was coming from Terry Berry, a highly unpleasant combination of vodka and old fish. "And how much you're payin'."

"Not a dime," Wolfe said, clamping a hand down on the place where Berry's neck met his shoulder when he tried to get up. "We're just really, *really* pissed off about getting shot at earlier today. You wouldn't happen to know anything about that, would you?"

"And before you bother trying to lie, be aware that we really, *really* don't like liars." Scarlett's smile from earlier had changed to bared teeth, and she slid a hundred dollar bill to the bartender without looking. "Please keep the change."

The bartender set down their obviously warm and flat Diet Cokes and pocketed the money, heading into the back room without a word.

"Look, I don't know nothing, okay?" Berry tried moving again, making a distressed sound when Wolfe's grip tightened, thumb digging into the soft place where Berry's collarbone connected to a tendon. "*Ow*, stop that!"

"Not until you tell us what we want to know," Tara said, darting her hand out and grabbing the revolver stuck in the back of Berry's pants. "And you're not gonna be using this, by the way."

"Okay, God, fine!" Berry flailed a little, trying to get enough leverage to ram his elbow into Wolfe's side; sensing this, Wolfe threw Berry forward on the bar, so his face was mashed into the disgusting surface and his ribs pressed painfully against the edge. "Yeah, okay, somebody hired me to shoot up that broad's house— but I don't know who, or why! The only thing they told me was to make sure I didn't kill anyone."

"Bit of an odd request, considering the amount of bullets you used," Scarlett observed, straightening up to drag a fingernail down the back of Berry's head and neck, just hard enough to draw blood. She bypassed his back and went for the phone sticking out of the rear pocket of his jeans, sticking it in front of his face to get it to unlock before handing it off to Tara. "How'd you get paid?"

Berry grunted with discomfort. "It was real high-tech shit, some fancy encrypted app that deleted itself off my phone. You can look all you want, but it won't be there."

"Here's the thing about technology," Tara said, removing her laptop from her bag and setting it on the bar. She plugged the phone into it, then began hacking her way into the backend of the device. "Nothing ever *really* gets deleted, even by the biggest tech nerds on the planet. There's always a little trace left behind." Several dozen lines of code and some creativity paid off. "Like the cell tower triangulation where the payment was sent from." She read it again, just to make sure she wasn't seeing things. "Shit. I think I know who's behind this."

"Seriously?" When Berry finally broke free of Wolfe's grip and twisted around to run, Scarlett just stuck out her leg so he'd trip. Her voice didn't change in pitch or register even as Berry crashed face-first into more than one table. "Who?"

"She's tall, blonde, and very mean," Tara replied, packing up her things and heading for the door. "She also happens to be an assassin, and Flynn's ex. We've gotta regroup and handle this carefully, or we'll all be dead."

Wolfe let out a little laugh and bumped Scarlett's shoulder with his own as they followed her out of the bar. "Just another day at the office, huh?"

~***~

"You didn't have to come with us, you know," David said to Kaja as they and Diana stepped off the Green Line at the Copley T stop on Boylston Street. "It was my idea to look through CCTV footage around Jimmy and Scarlett's office. Questioning a homeless dude who may or may not have seen something isn't exactly director-level stuff."

"Sabene didn't need me breathing down their neck while they check up on Aoife," was Kaja's response, shoving her hands in her coat pockets to ward off the chill. "And while Diana's working for Renegade, she's my responsibility. So technically, even if I didn't *want* to be here, I'd *have* to be."

"Now it's *that* kind of sentiment that warms the cockles of my cold dead heart." Diana's tone couldn't have been drier if she were actively burning. Her breath fogged the air as they waited to cross the street. "What is this man's name again?"

"Clark Griswold," David replied, shrugging his shoulders when both women shot him an incredulous look. "What? I didn't name him. If it helps, he doesn't look a thing like Chevy Chase."

"That doesn't help at all," Kaja muttered, slowing her pace once they reached the other sidewalk. They were on the same side of the street as the building where Wolfe & Vaughn Investigations made its home, but they hadn't quite reached it yet; inside the nearest alley was a tent, tucked away neatly to one side so pedestrians could pass it. "Is this the place?"

"Certainly looks that way." Diana approached the tent, which had its flap partially unzipped, and a vaguely human shape in a sleeping bag was visible inside. "Clark? We'd like to speak with you for a moment." She pulled a gift card from her pocket. "There's a meal at Panera Bread in it for you."

The shape moved, rolling out of its enclosure, and resolved itself into a haggard-looking man around the age his fictional namesake was when he had a particularly terrible Christmas. His hair and beard were unkempt and overgrown, sticking out from under a bright orange hunting cap and tangling in the collar of his stained jacket.

When he spoke, it was with a lisp caused by a few missing teeth. "What you wanna know?"

David brought out his phone, thumbing it open to a still from the CCTV video that had started their field trip. In it was the clearest image they had of the vehicle they believed belonged to whomever had slid the money under Wolfe and Scarlett's office door the previous night, parked illegally in front of a fire hydrant. It was a tan panel van with the windows tinted, and only the last two digits of its Massachusetts license plate were visible. In the furthest corner of the shot, Clark Griswold's alley and tent were present, albeit very out of focus. "Did you see the person who was driving this van?"

Griswold squinted at the screen, then went eerily still. "Where'd you get this?" he rasped out, shooting to his feet so suddenly that Diana took a step back, her hand quickly trading the gift card for the end of the collapsable baton she had concealed in her jacket sleeve. "I swear I didn't do nothin' but what they told me—they wanted to know when those two detectives left the office, that's it!" His eyes grew impossibly wide, cheeks reddening. "Are you... I'm going to miss it, aren't I? The rebirth?"

Kaja's blood ran cold when she heard that last word, and the next few seconds seemed to happen in slow motion. She reached out her hand to try and stop Griswold when he burst into motion, shoving Diana in the chest with his shoulder, but her fingers couldn't catch a grip on the slick material of his coat. He managed to dodge David as well, who looked as shocked as Kaja felt, and bolted straight into traffic. The pedestrian signal at the intersection with Dartmouth must've just expired, because there was a split-second instant where Griswold turned to face them, hands held out from his body in supplication.

"*Fides en timore!*" he exalted, and was unceremoniously run over by a commuter bus.

~***~

Chapter Thirteen

Adam ran.

He ran like he'd never run before, arms and legs pumping as he dodged around trees and hopped over fallen branches and cresting roots. He could barely hear above the pounding of his feet on the ground and his pulse clanging in his head, but what snatches of noise he did process weren't good. More than one of his fellow trainees let out a cry of pain as they either tripped and fell or were struck by *something*—a bullet, a knife? Adam had no way of knowing, and he wasn't about to stop and find out.

He relied solely on instincts and Dani's relentless training to guide his path, knowing the most important thing at the moment was to put as much distance between himself and his pursuers as possible. His next priority would be to find something, anything he could use as a weapon beyond the small multi-tool all of the trainees carried. While the knife attached to it was useful for things like cutting rope or sharpening sticks, it wouldn't make for an effective defense against someone with a gun, or even a bigger knife.

It's not the size of the weapon that matters, Dani's voice said in his head, but it was an echo of Teddy who finished, *it's how you use it.*

Easy advice to dispense on a training field. Not so much now.

More screams reached Adam's ears and his heart ached. No matter how the other children had treated him as of late, he didn't want to see them dead. He had to find a way to help them, but *how?* His mind raced, examining options and discarding them, and that distraction was enough to make him step wrong. His ankle rolled underneath his weight and he fell hard, palms and cheek scraping the dirt. He was in a hole, he realized quickly, a grave that had been dug up by scavengers, and there was... *something* underneath him, not dirt, not rocks, what—

Bones. He was lying on bones.

Adam knew where the livestock keepers buried the animal carcasses, and it wasn't the part of the forest he was in now. With a trembling hand, he reached for the closest shadow and bit back a scream when he felt the shape of a human face, worn down to nothing but waxy crust and skull. His hand dragged downward instinctively, trying to get away, and his fingers caught on a chain.

He ran his nails down it, heart in his throat, and when he felt the familiar coin shape of his mother's St. Francis medallion, he started to shake. He'd known she was dead, of course, but this… the indignity of a pauper's grave, of being mutilated at Marshall Raider's filthy hands, it was too much to bear.

And Frederick Devereux was to blame.

Adam sprang to his feet with energy he didn't know he possessed, rage a living thing clawing at his ribcage, demanding to be set free. The way he felt in that moment, he could have run all the way back to the compound and torn each and every lying, hypocritical adult there apart with his bare hands. And he would've done it, too, except he got something heavy and metallic smashed into the back of his head, and down into the darkness he went.

~***~

Chapter Fourteen

"Absolutely not," was the first thing Kaja said in the dining room at Stela the following morning, as soon as she heard what Dev and Teddy were planning. Her arms were crossed firmly over her chest, wrinkling the material of her dark blue dress. "There's no way in hell I'm going to agree to send you back to that place, Devereux."

Dev sighed. He'd fully expected her reaction, along with the immediate protests from the others gathered in the closed restaurant. Tara, Wolfe, Scarlett, Sebastian, Constantin, David, and Diana were all present, having been roped into the situation either directly or by circumstance. They'd decided not to have this meeting at Project Renegade after Kaja, David, and Diana's encounter with Clark Griswold the day before; that kind of indoctrination by the Reborn meant there were very few people they could trust. It wasn't worth the risk, even if sitting around tables in Stela with the blinds lowered and the lights off was kind of creepy.

"All due respect, ma'am, but we've already had this conversation with these two knuckleheads," Flynn said, one arm draped casually over the back of Dev's chair. He held a to-go cup from Dunkin in his other hand, courtesy of a delivery order facilitated by Sebastian. "And as much as I fuckin' hate it, we don't have any other good options."

"A brute force attack against an organization like the Reborn won't work," Lottie added, chomping on a blueberry muffin. "They know the area where they live like the backs of their hands—better than Dev at this point, probably—and they've gotta have at least one contingency plan. Plus, we've got no way of knowing how much armament they have or how much training they've done over the past decade or so."

"So striking from the inside out is the only way," Wolfe mused. His arm was hooked over the back of Sebastian's chair, coffee held in a similar manner to Flynn's, and Dev tried desperately not to read too much into that. "Is there anybody we could send in with Teddy and Dev?"

"No one that would be believable," Teddy replied, not unkindly. To say Dev was relieved that he seemed to be stable was an understatement; he never realized how valuable it would be to have someone in his life that understood the Reborn experience from a firsthand perspective. "Eileen could maybe lie her way inside initially, but any reason we could come up with for her being there would be looked at under a microscope. Aleksandr will cut his losses and kill us all if he even suspects something is wrong."

"There's a few things we need to take care of here before we can send you out to Montana, anyway," David pointed out, not appearing to be phased by the venomous glance Kaja shot him. "First thing is, we've gotta figure out if there's a mole inside Renegade. At this point, my money's on yes, but where? And how much information have they transmitted to the Reborn?"

"That shouldn't be too hard to do," Tara said. "I'll probably need to bring in Frogger to help me, since trusting Sabene isn't on the table right now. But all I really need to do is search our employee database. I'll start by looking for anyone with problems at home or extreme political views, and narrow it down from there."

"And once we have a list, we'll need to manufacture a situation in which we can get the mole to incriminate themself," Diana added, her booted feet propped on a fancy wooden bench that looked like it cost more than Dev's monthly salary. She was Sebastian's adopted sister, though, so he supposed she could get away with more than the rest of them. "Next?"

"Valeriya Sidorova," Eileen said grimly, reflecting exactly what Dev felt about Flynn's ex… minus a little extra jealousy. "To say that woman is temperamental would be an understatement, and she wants to kill Flynn more often than not."

"True, *but* if she's as much of a badass as you say, she could've done a lot more damage than a drive-by if she wanted to," Scarlett said, busy making a tower of Munchkins on her plate, probably fully intending to eat them all in one go. "So apparently she's capable of restraint."

"If she wanted to get *your* attention, why'd she strafe *my* place?" Dev wondered aloud, glancing at Flynn, who shrugged. "I mean, it's Aoife's place, technically, but still. It's not like you live there."

"She wouldn't risk that," Kaja said, and while she didn't sound thrilled, some of her hostility seemed to have faded. "Rambo lives with Flynn, remember? Valeriya might hate Flynn's guts, but she loves that damn dog."

"You have a dog?" Constantin asked, his serious demeanor brightening suddenly. "What kind?"

"She's a Rottweiler," Lottie said, grinning widely. "Tough on the outside, but a big softie on the inside. Just like her dad."

"Oi," Eileen muttered, rolling her eyes. "So what do we do, then? Use the dog-child as leverage in the divorce?"

"Something like that," David mused, glancing around the room. "We've got about twenty-four hours to get everything ready, or Teddy and Dev turning up at the Reborn's compound is going to look fishy. Anybody that doesn't get a paycheck from the government, this is your chance to back out if you want to." Unsurprisingly, no one took the out. "Okay then. Here's the plan..."

~***~

Until he started dating Valeriya Sidorova, Flynn hadn't known much about the Boston gang scene. Sure, he'd picked up on some stuff here and there over his years of living in the city—his kind of training didn't have an off switch, even when he wanted it to—but Valeriya... in the time they were together, she'd opened his eyes to something much darker lurking in Boston's underbelly. That knowledge hadn't left Flynn, even if they'd stopped going out two years ago. Her father was Grigoriy Sidorov, leader of an arms-dealing run-and-gun gang called the призраки, or the Spectres in English. And as dirty as his dealings were, there was a bigger and more notorious Russian gang roaming the streets called the пачка, or the Pack, under the watchful eye of Mikael Ivanov, known to many as the Wolf of Moscow.

Back in Russia, Ivanov and Sidorov had actually been friends, insofar as any Russians had friends. At the very least, they weren't rivals, but that all changed once they moved their operations to the States after the Cold War. Now Ivanov's gang had shot to notoriety for helping Anton Codreanu make Rapture, a drug that had wreaked havoc on thousands of people in the city over the past eight months or so. Meanwhile, as far as Flynn knew, Sidorov's people were barely scraping by, crippled by the Pack's control of Boston's ports. While Flynn had little to no interest in what the gangs did on a daily basis, he *did* care what happened to Valeriya. She was strong-willed and stubborn, which made them butt heads a lot, but she was also smart, and—huh.

Maybe he had a type.

"Flynn?" Dev's fingers snapped in front of Flynn's face, causing him to jerk back a step on the sidewalk. They were in Brookline, a sprawling town famous for bordering six of Boston's most eclectic neighborhoods: Brighton, Allston, Fenway-Kenmore, Mission Hill, Jamaica Plain, and West Roxbury. Specifically, they were standing on Harvard Street not far from Coolidge Corner, within spitting distance of a bookstore, a Starbucks, and a Trader Joe's that were swarming with MIT nerds. Nestled in the center of the brick-sided strip across from them was an unassuming little business: a Russian tea room, decreed by the plain Cyrillic and English sign that labeled it simply as *Val's*. "You good?"

"Not even close," Flynn replied, exhaling harshly. He put his hands on his hips, pistol grip digging into the skin at the small of his back. That little bite of pain was grounding, as was Dev's ever-bright presence next to him. "What are the odds she's even here?"

"Pretty good, from what I could tell on Yelp," Lottie offered, shoulder braced against the nearest telephone pole. Snowflakes caught in her pigtail braids, the top of her head covered with a tan beanie that had to be Army surplus. "Lots of five-star reviews, most of them mentioning the owner by name." The crosswalk signal changed and they moved across the road, coming to stand three-abreast before the tea room's front windows. "You know, for a murderous psychopath, I always thought Valeriya had her charms. Why'd you two break up again?"

"Can we not talk about this?" Flynn asked, hearing the pleading note in his voice and not giving a shit. "I realize it's an ironic request, since we've literally talked your breakup to death, but—"

"Flynn," Dev interjected, arching an eyebrow as Flynn reluctantly met his gaze. "You were *really* vague about the breakup when it happened, and we let it go then because we're your friends and you clearly didn't want us to pry. But we're more or less walking into a lion's den, here—I'd rather not be blindfolded."

A bell above the door to the tea room tinkled, followed by a sonorous voice wrapped in the broad intonations and rolling *r*s of a Russian accent: "Then perhaps you should come inside and ask me. I am positively *titillated* at the idea of informing an interested party about *all* of Flynn Walker's shortcomings."

Flynn squeezed his eyes shut, just for a moment. "Hello, Valeriya." When he opened them again, it was to Valeriya Mikaelovna Sidorova's strong shoulders and cutting, full-lipped smile. Her blonde hair hung down her back in a double-layered fishtail, a black turtleneck and corduroy pants expertly tailored to hide the numerous weapons Flynn knew she carried. She wore no jewelry save for a nest of piercings in both ears, glimmering like tiny stars. "You look… good."

"I look flawless," Valeriya corrected, indigo eyes ticking over the three of them briefly before she swept an arm toward the tea room. "Please, join me. I just had Inessa put on a fresh pot of oolong. And since you very clearly want something, you may as well beg for it over a hot beverage, like civilized people."

"Nice to see you again too," Flynn muttered, glancing around as they stepped inside. There was a smattering of patrons seated at plush red booths and gold-edged tables, sipping from bone china cups and admiring the collection of art on the forest green walls. Soft yellow lighting gave the impression that the space was much smaller than it was in reality, although it did contract as they followed Valeriya to the back, past the kitchen and the bathrooms. "A tea room, huh? Doesn't exactly seem like your thing."

"And what *is* my thing, Flynn?" Valeriya wondered aloud, ushering them into a private room, filled with a big conference-style table that was made from mahogany and must've cost a small fortune. Standing beyond the table against the wall were two very stoic-looking men who were obviously bodyguards, which Flynn found hilarious; Valeriya was the last woman in the world that needed a man's protection, except maybe Lottie. "Gutting men like fish and stringing them up in my bedroom like trophies? Is that what you've told your friends what I do?"

"That sounds like a fun Tuesday night," Dev commented, taking a seat once Valeriya did, opting for the one across from her. He offered her a smile, but Flynn could see how tense it was. "I know we only met once or twice when you guys were dating, but it is nice to see you again."

"Oh, so polite." Valeriya crossed her legs, leaning her elbows on the table and putting her chin in her hands. "Your hair, your eyes—you remind me of a puppy." Her own eyes glittered as she watched Flynn take a seat on Dev's right. "It only makes sense that you have a mutt to protect you."

Dev's expression shuttered. "Careful. This puppy has fangs." He mirrored Valeriya's positioning, and Flynn felt a spark of pride—he wasn't intimidated by her in the slightest. "And I don't want to bite you, but I will."

Valeriya studied him for a moment… and then tipped her head back and laughed, clapping her hands together once like an amused child. "Oh, I *love* him, Flynn! I can see why you were so determined to keep us apart." She turned her attention to Lottie. "And what about you, hmm? Tell me you are more than just a pretty face."

"That depends," Lottie drawled, kicking her boots up on the table with enough force to make one of the men behind Valeriya flinch. "Are you more than just a hundred-megawatt bitch? Because that's all I see right about now."

"Ballsy," Valeriya observed, lips curling into a satisfied smile. "I like it." She spread her hands. "What is it that I can do for you, then? I doubt this is about Rambo's latest veterinary bill."

"You paid a very weird guy a lot of money to shoot up my landlord's house," Dev said, never one to beat around the bush. "And you didn't really bother to hide the fact that it was you, which makes me think you wanted us to come here. The question I can't answer is why."

"Oh, that's easy," Valeriya replied, waving over the woman who appeared in the doorway bearing a tray ladened with a steaming teapot and four cups and saucers, plus a sugar bowl, a jar of honey, and a plate piled with Russian tea cakes. "I needed to speak with you, and no one was answering their fucking phone."

Flynn rubbed a hand over his face. He wasn't one for migraines, but he felt pain building behind his eyes. "So... you couldn't reach me or the rest of the team by phone... and you decided *shooting up Aoife's house* was the next best method of contact?" *This,* he thought to himself, *is* exactly *the reason we broke up... beyond me having a stupid crush on the guy sitting next to me.*

Valeriya waved a hand around as she poured them all tea, passing out cups and dismissing the woman and her bodyguards with a few curt words in her native tongue. "It worked, did it not? But I apologize for the inconvenience, and I will send a contractor at once to repair the damage. I wanted to speak with you because I have some information to pass along." She tipped her chin at Dev. "To you, specifically."

"Me?" Dev didn't bother concealing his surprise. "Why?"

"When we were together, Flynn often..." Valeriya actually paused to choose her words, glancing at Flynn for a half-second before refocusing on Dev. "He spoke fondly of you, and may have mentioned you have a past. One that you do not like to revisit." She reached behind her, and for a moment Flynn feared she was retrieving a weapon—but no, only a folded piece of paper from her back pocket. She set it on the table and pushed it across the shiny wood to Dev. "Take a look at that."

Dev grabbed the paper and unfolded it. It was a flyer, and judging from the jagged tear at the top it was most likely stripped from a telephone pole. An upside-down cross took up the majority of the page, bold and black and a near-perfect replica of the one carved into Dev's back. Arranged in a column of text below it was *fides en timore,* REVELATION 20:5, two dates and times that had passed, and one that was yet to happen, about three hours from the current time. There was another line that was most likely an address, but it had been blacked out with permanent marker.

"You must forgive me," Valeriya continued, once they had all had a moment to absorb the information. "My Latin is quite good, but I am not a Biblical scholar."

"'The rest of the dead did not come to life until the thousand years were ended'," Dev murmured, quoting the verse like he had a copy in front of him. "'This is the first resurrection.'" His eyes shut briefly, a muscle in his jaw working. "That wasn't chosen at random. It means something."

"There used to be an address on that poster, and I sent some men to it yesterday," Valeriya said, relaxing back in her chair. "It is an office building in the South End. And while they arrived too late to observe anything of note, they believe it was some kind of recruitment event for the Reborn. They appeared to be targeting the… feebler among us. The desperate."

"Like the homeless guy," Lottie said, frowning as she looked from the paper to Valeriya. "Let me guess, you won't give us the address unless we do something for you?"

Valeriya snapped her fingers in Lottie's direction. "*Definitely* more than just a pretty face." She took a sip of her tea, holding the cup as delicately as a flower. "I have a small problem with a client who refuses to pay me what I am owed for my services. The issue is, he is a very paranoid individual, and he will see me or my men coming from a mile away. But you—" now she pointed a finger-gun at Lottie "—should be able to get close enough to twist his arm. Literally, if necessary." She stood up, tea cup still in hand, and walked around the table to the door. "I will give you a moment to discuss your options. But the clock is ticking."

As soon as the door shut behind her, Flynn swore. "*Fuck*. She's got us over a barrel and she knows it."

"We could try to find another one of these," Lottie suggested, tapping the flyer clutched by Dev's hands. "But it might take a while, and I'd bet money that Valeriya's men tore down as many as they could find before they went to that address yesterday."

Dev breathed in through his nose and out through his mouth, then crushed the paper into a ball and tossed it aside. "I don't see where we have a choice but to play along." He looked at Lottie. "But it's your call, since she clearly wants you to stick your neck out for her."

"I've done worse for less," Lottie said grimly. "Let's get this over with."

~***~

"Are you sure this is going to work?" Eileen asked, folding her arms across her chest. She stood next to Wolfe in a plain room that was no bigger than an oversized closet, looking through a one-way window into Project Renegade's rarely-used conference room. "Because I've heard of some harebrained schemes in my day, but this one might take the cake."

"I've always wondered where that saying came from," Wolfe commented. His tone was casual enough, but his gaze was fixed squarely on the dozen or so employees gathered around the big glass-topped table in the next room. They all looked some shade of nervous, talking amongst themselves in voices too low to hear or tapping maniacally at their phones. "Isn't cake supposed to be a good thing?"

"Touche." Eileen watched him for a moment. "You know, you're a lot like your father... but you're also very different from him."

Wolfe's mouth twitched into a smile. "I'm going to take that as a compliment, Eileen. You're not the first person to make that observation." He tensed as the door in the other room opened, and Kaja stepped inside holding a tablet. "Here we go."

"Thank you all for coming," Kaja said to the group of Renegade workers, walking over to stand at the head of the table with her back to Wolfe and Eileen. Her posture was relaxed and she gave no indication she knew she was being watched. "I'm sure you're wondering why you're here."

"Are we fired?" a particularly sweaty young woman asked, her eyes wide, nails chewed down to nubs. "Oh god, you're firing us, aren't you?"

"*Patricia*!" another woman hissed, elbowing the sweaty one. "Be quiet!"

"I'm not firing anyone." Kaja's voice was mild but louder than the others, and she began to swipe at the tablet. "I need to show you something… and then I need a volunteer." She pulled up a live video feed, which was visible over her shoulder for a few seconds before she turned the tablet toward her audience; Eileen was just able to make out a disheveled-looking Scarlett, sitting at the table in their interrogation room. "This is Sandra Lee." *Always pick a first name that starts with the same letter as your own*, had been Diana's advice, and given that she had even more aliases than Eileen, she knew what she was talking about. "We've detained her because we have reason to believe that she's doing recruitment work for the Reborn—I'm sure you all know by now that they're a fanatical cult that has ties to Agent Devereux. We think she was pretending to be his friend, probably to catch him unawares and bring him back to the Reborn. We have to assume their operatives are familiar with Agent

Devereux's real friends and won't respond positively to being questioned by them. Which is why I need one of you to do it instead."

"I still can't believe Scarlett based her alias on that woman from the Food Network that put vodka in everything," Eileen said during the stunned silence that followed Kaja's words, nodding toward the tablet. "And I don't know what the opposite of cleaning up well is, but she gets a gold star."

"I guess that's what happens when you roll around in alleyway snow for ten minutes." Whenever Wolfe spoke of Scarlett, it was with the pride of a brother, and it was obvious to anyone with functioning ears and eyes that he was just as fond of her as he was of Sebastian—in vastly different ways, of course. "Oh look, Patricia's raising her hand."

If it were possible for a person to sweat a waterfall, Patricia would've been doing it, but her voice was steady when she spoke: "I'll do it." Her colleagues looked at her in surprise, and she stood up. "What? *Somebody* has to do *something* about these people. Dev has been nothing but kind, to all of us. If there's a way to help him with this, I want to do it."

"That's what I like to hear," Kaja said, shutting off the tablet and tucking it under her arm. She gestured for Patricia to follow her. "Let's not keep Sandra waiting."

~***~

Chapter Fifteen

Consciousness returned to Adam in pieces, and at first he had no idea what to make of the sensory input. His head throbbed with pain, which wasn't all that odd since the last thing he remembered was being struck. What *was* strange was that he was lying face down on something cold and smooth. It took prying his eyes open a quarter inch to realize it was the marble of the altar, and that he was in the chapel. He tried to move his limbs and couldn't, and for a panicked second, he wondered if he was paralyzed, but no—thick coils of rope were wrapped around the backs of his knees and just below his shoulders, pinning his legs down and his arms to his sides. The ropes were wound underneath the overhanging marble at either end of the altar, so there was no way for him to wriggle loose.

Once his initial panic dropped to a dull roar, he recognized Frederick's voice, booming over the congregation from somewhere beyond the bloodied back of Adam's head: "—and *that*, my children, is precisely why we cannot let a blatant shirking of our traditions stand. My poor misguided wife, and Theodore Vasquez, they were sinful without remorse, unworthy of the blessings that the Chosen

One will bring upon us when he is sacrificed!" His hand came down suddenly on Dev's back, hard and stinging like a slap. "We must act now to cement his holy status along with our own."

Movement in his peripherals caught Adam's attention, and he tensed when he saw several of the adults leaving the crowded pews to join Frederick on the dais. His breathing quickened, and when he tried moving again there were hands on him, and now he realized he wasn't wearing clothes, he was *naked*, why—

A metallic flash in the candlelight made Adam freeze once more, his usually tireless mind taking several heartbeats to process that Frederick held a blade. Not just any blade, but some kind of ceremonial dagger with a gilded handle, wicked and sharp. It moved toward him quickly, and for a moment after the first slice across his shoulders, he didn't feel a thing but disbelief. The pain arrived with the blood, and when he was cut a second time, a third, a channel being carved down his back now as well, snuggled up to his spine, he began to scream.

And with those screams, Adam died on the inside... and Dev was born.

~***~

Chapter Sixteen

"The chances that this was a coincidence are slim to none and I am *pissed*," Lottie ground out, pacing the sidewalk next to Flynn's black Toyota 4Runner. She glanced up at the building across the street, then tore her gaze away again and tried to stifle the snarl building in her chest. She failed. "I'm going to strangle that Russian bitch with her own goddamn *hair* the next time I see her."

They were in Dorchester on its eponymous avenue, just steps away from a restaurant called Saigon Special—which was owned by a pair of Vietnamese refugees turned citizens named Tuân and Cai Tran, also known as Lottie's father and mother. It was a staple for *pho* and *bánh mi* in the city, occupying a brick storefront and surrounded by a tire shop and a walk-in clinic. The restaurant had suffered some damage a few months prior during a riot, which was caused by Danh Sang dumping his inherited reserve of Rapture into the water supply. People had lost their minds for a while, smashing the windows and tearing down the awnings, not to mention wreaking havoc on the interior; thankfully insurance had paid for most of the repairs and the citizens who caused the mess had put up the rest.

"You don't have to do this," Dev said for what had to be the tenth time since they left Valeriya's tea room, reaching out to grab Lottie's elbow. He was one of very few people who could get away with unauthorized touching without losing his teeth. "Lottie, this is… not what any of us expected. We can find the information on the recruitment event another way."

Flynn sighed. "Wish we could, hoss, but you know as well as I do that Val had her goons take down every one of those posters they could find. And she ain't gonna tell us what she knows unless Lottie scares the crap outta this guy."

Lottie took a deep breath through her nose and let it out via her mouth, resisting the very strong urge to dent Flynn's car with her boot. "Okay. I guess I'm going to have to explain to my parents that I don't actually work security at a think-tank. That's gonna go over like a fart in a spacesuit."

"Unfortunately, I don't see how to get around it." Dev let out a snort. "And here I thought the most awkward part of this would be visiting the Trans for the first time after our breakup."

"Didn't think anything could make my situation worse, but you always find a way to surprise me," Lottie said wryly, lingering on the sidewalk for a moment longer before she forced herself to cross the street. A yuppie on an electric bicycle nearly ran her down, and she gave him the finger when he yelled an obscenity. "This city really knows how to put you in the mood for a brawl with your parents."

"Seems like every time I call my old man, we get into a fight," Flynn agreed, holding the door for her and Dev, the picture of a gentleman. A bell jangled over their heads as they walked inside. "And he ain't even here. It must be contagious."

"What is?" a girl's voice asked from a booth near the entryway, and Lottie nearly tripped over her own feet—it was her fifteen-year-old sister, Corrine, who had spoken. She had several textbooks and a laptop spread out on the table, along with a notebook, mechanical pencils, and a very large Vietnamese iced coffee. Before Lottie could formulate a response, Corrine was up and hugging her, the top of her head almost to Lottie's nose—had she grown since the last time they saw each other? "I didn't know you were coming to visit today. You didn't bring, like… SARS or MRSA with you, right?"

"Wrong kind of contagious," Dev said kindly, letting out a grunt when Corrine grabbed on to him next. She had always had a bit of a crush on him, and since she was blushing when she pulled away, Lottie doubted that had changed. "So, working hard or hardly working?"

"More like trying not to fail AP Calculus," Corrine grumbled, giving Flynn a hug too and squealing when he lifted her off her feet for a moment. While until this point Lottie had avoided mixing her family up in her work, Corrine had been her plus-one to just about every non-government party or event since she was in middle school, and that meant she'd had a lot of face time with the boys, plus Eileen, Tara, and Kaja. "Can one of you quiz me?"

"Sure," Dev replied, glancing at Lottie and tipping his head subtly toward the kitchen. There were a couple of patrons scattered around the dining room, but nobody that matched the description Valeriya had given them of her errant client. If Lottie was going to let her parents in on her real life, this was the time to do it. "I think Flynn and I can handle that. Right, Flynn?"

"I can handle flipping the index cards," Flynn drawled, sliding into the booth and shuffling said index cards like he was getting ready to play poker. "The nerdy talk is all you, stud."

Rolling her eyes and wondering if either of them realized they were constantly flirting with each other (the answer was most likely no), Lottie traipsed to the kitchen, pushing the double doors open. As luck would have it, Tuân and Cai were both inside, with her mother dropping beef knuckles into a super-sized pot to make broth, and her father slicing a tremendous number of French baguettes in half lengthwise. Both black-haired and dark-eyed like their daughter, Tuân was the taller of the two but not by much, his shoulders rolled forward from years of chopping ingredients. Before they came to America as Vietnam War refugees, Tuân had been a cook in the South Vietnamese Army, and Cai was a nurse. Their story was the classic immigrant tale of success after years of hard work, and sometimes it was the only thing that made Lottie believe she'd done the right thing, becoming a Ranger and then continuing to protect her inherited country as a spy.

"*Mẹ, Bố,*" Lottie began, steamrolling right over their shock, both at her sudden appearance and how she addressed them as *Mom* and *Dad* in Vietnamese, not in English. "There's something I have to tell you, and I'm not sure how much time I have. So I need you to wait until I'm done to ask me any questions, okay? Please?" To her own surprise, neither of them moved to interject, so she plowed forward in a rush: "I'm not a security guard at a think-tank—I'm a spy, and so are Dev, Flynn, and the rest of my friends. What Project Renegade does is so secret that even most people in the government don't know about us. I'm telling you this because there's a man that's supposed to come here that I need to… intimidate, in exchange for some information. When I agreed to do it, I didn't realize the restaurant we were coming to was yours, but now that I'm here I don't have a choice."

Her parents exchanged a glance, and then Cai said, "We thought you were never going to tell us."

Lottie blinked, sure she'd misheard, but then Tuân spoke: "Charlotte, did you really think we were stupid, or just deliberately ignorant? Going from your position in the military to being a security guard would be a downgrade. We knew that was something you would never accept. Besides, your friends all have… unique traits. Ones that do not lend themselves to a think-tank." He scratched his chin with the hand that still held a very large chef's knife. "Hmm. The man you're talking about—describe him."

Still in something of a stupor, Lottie repeated what Valeriya had told them back at the tea room: "Around five-ten, heavyset, with a bad comb-over and suits that don't fit him well. He's an accountant, apparently one that didn't want a client of his snitching about some of his less than legal business practices, so he had them killed. The... person who has the information I need, she wants the money he owes her."

"I think that's Ed," Cai mused, stepping over to the sink to wash her hands. "He comes in every weekday afternoon around five—in fact, he should be here soon. I didn't know he was an accountant, but he mentioned he works in the area."

"That tracks," Lottie said, swallowing hard. "Thank you. Both of you." She hesitated. "Can I ask... why have you been so hard on Corrine lately?"

"She didn't tell you?" Tuân asked, then shook his head. "Of course she didn't. Probably made us out to be monsters who won't let her do anything fun."

"Your sister was almost kidnapped." Cai delivered the news with a solemn expression, and Lottie felt the world tilt under her feet. "It happened a few months ago, and luckily she got away unhurt… but you can imagine why we would want to keep her close."

"We're talking about this later, all of us," was Lottie's response, as the bell above the door jingled. She peeked through the pass-through window and saw a man that matched Valeriya's description almost perfectly. "That's him. I need to go take care of this."

She was barely two steps out of the kitchen before Ed spotted her, bleary eyes going round with panic. He froze halfway to the bar, and Lottie knew he was going to rabbit before he actually did, turning and making a beeline for the door. He promptly tripped over Dev's foot, which he'd stuck out from under Corrine's table without looking, and landed in an inelegant heap on the floor. Smiling to herself, Lottie strode over and grabbed Ed by his collar, hauling him up and back and using his tie to restrict his airway.

"Hello, asshole," she said, smacking him upside the head when he tried in vain to claw at the loop of fabric around his throat. "Behave, and you might make it out of this with all your fingers and toes." She drew the fixed-blade dagger she kept in the side of her left boot, flipping it by the handle and making sure Ed could see the matte black blade from the corner of his eye. "You owe something to a friend of mine. She wants it, and she wants it yesterday. With *interest*. Understand?"

When Lottie loosened her grip enough for Ed to speak, he wheezed out, "I… I'll get it to her tonight, okay? The money's in my car, I just… I kept putting it off, that's all! Jesus H, who *are* you?"

"Someone who would make one hell of an enforcer," Valeriya said, striding into Saigon Special like she owned the place. She was trailed by the two goons from earlier, who both perked up slightly at the smells coming from the kitchen. "If only I could convince her to give up the self-righteous shtick."

"Pretty sure that's Dev's thing, not mine," Lottie said wryly, allowing Ed to fall back to the floor like a sack of potatoes. She sheathed her knife and put her hands on her hips. "I did what you wanted, and you know where your money is. The address, Valeriya. Now."

"It's an office building in Brookline, near the high school." Valeriya snapped her fingers, and one of her men grabbed Ed, relieving him of his keys before heading outside, ostensibly to check for the money. The other one dug inside his jacket pocket and produced a piece of paper—another flyer, only all of the text on this one was intact. She took it from him, holding it out to Lottie. "I was serious, by the way. You ever get tired of being a… what is it you Americans say? Goody-two-shoes? Come and find me."

Lottie tried not to show exactly how much that thought repulsed her. She took the flyer, looking into Valeriya's snake-flat eyes all the while. "I'll keep that in mind."

~***~

From behind another one-way mirror, Kaja watched with Wolfe and Eileen as Patricia sat down across from Scarlett in the interrogation room. She was still perspiring, sweat marks visible on her clothes, and Kaja—who spent much of her time reading tells, as any good spy did—found herself wondering how much of the sweat was due to nerves about her situation, and how much was due to hiding something.

Scarlett sneered at Patricia, looking her up and down before glancing away dismissively. "Who the hell are you? Did you just get back from the YMCA? Or was it an onion farm?"

"Ouch," Eileen said with a wince. "She can be brutal when she wants to, eh?"

"She stabbed a guy in the throat *after* he stabbed her in the gut," was Wolfe's response, hands shoved into the front pockets of his jeans; Kaja would've bet money his fingernails were digging into his thighs. "Brutal is an understatement, but in this case it's not real." He nodded toward Patricia. "She just needs to believe it."

If the way Patricia's posture changed was any indication, she did. "I need to know something," she said, putting her hands flat on the table and leaning over in a way that was probably meant to be intimidating. "What were you planning for the—for Dev?"

The slip-up was painfully obvious, and Scarlett smiled with all of her teeth... then slipped out of the cuffs like it was nothing, standing abruptly and shoving Patricia back into the nearest wall. "I don't know, peaches. Why don't *you* tell *me* what you had planned for the Chosen One?" She pinned Patricia with a forearm across her chest, pulling a folding knife from inside her bra with her other hand and flicking it open. The entire motion was fluid, like a dance, and Kaja absently wondered how often she and Wolfe sparred. "After all, it's just us gals in here."

"I d-don't know what you—" Patricia cut off with a yelp when Scarlett pressed the knife blade to her cheek. It left behind a red welt that began dribbling blood. "Okay, okay! I was sent here by Aleksandr to observe and report, but I swear that was it! He didn't tell me why, or even what I was really looking for."

Kaja pressed a button below the one-way glass, which activated the intercom. "That's enough, Scarlett. We'll be in there shortly." She led Wolfe and Eileen out of the observation room and into the interrogation space. "What did you report back to Aleksandr? What did he want to know?"

"I *told* you, he just…" Patricia made a frustrated sound, still held against the wall by Scarlett. "I grew up in the Reborn, okay? I was one of the ones who survived, and I got hand-picked for this mission." She took a deep breath, something settling behind her eyes, nervous sweat cooling on her skin. "He wanted to know everything he could. Not about the Chosen One, but about the people closest to him." She glanced between Kaja and Eileen. "Including the two of you."

"Oh yeah?" Eileen put her hands on her hips, cocking her head. "And what exactly did you tell him?"

Patricia smiled, a plastic, caustic expression. "Everything."

As soon as she uttered that single word, she reared back and bashed her forehead into Scarlett's face, causing the other woman to swear and stumble away, clutching her bloodied nose. She dropped her knife in the process and Patricia lunged for it, no doubt intent on ending her own life the way Clark Griswold had. Thankfully Wolfe got there first, flipping the knife shut and tossing it to Kaja, then snapping Scarlett's abandoned handcuffs around Patricia's wrists.

"God*damn* it!" Patricia all but wailed, yanking fruitlessly at her restraints. She looked nothing like the uneasy girl from the conference room, or even the one who'd walked in to talk to Scarlett—she was practically feral. "You'll burn, do you hear me?" she screamed as they left the room, Kaja already reaching for her phone to get a medic for Scarlett. "You'll all *fucking* burn!"

~***~

After a surprisingly frank discussion with the Trans—in which it was decided that Cai and Tuân needed to let Corrine have some of her freedom back as long as she promised to be cautious with it— Dev, Flynn, and Lottie headed over to the address Valeriya had shared with them. It did indeed belong to an office in Brookline near the high school, across from a baseball diamond teeming with kids and parents. The building was a converted center chimney Cape, nondescript in that it was exactly like a ton of others in the area. But as soon as he spotted the large FOR LEASE signs in the front windows, Dev got a sinking feeling in the pit of his stomach that they were too late.

"Shit," Flynn said as they piled out of his car, echoing Dev's thoughts. He drew his gun, holding it down along his thigh, and started forward. "Looks like we missed the party."

"We wouldn't have if Valeriya hadn't insisted on playing tit-for-tat," Lottie grumbled, flanking Flynn on his left with her weapon out, with Dev bringing up the rear. It was a typical formation for them, and it worked well. "Would it kill you to date somebody nice for once?"

Flynn glanced back at Dev, which—what? That didn't make any sense. Especially when he let out an almost pained chuckle and replied, "At this point? It probably would." He reached out with his free hand and tried the door, which swung inward with ease. "Ah, always a good sign."

They made their way inside as a unit, boots noiseless on the cheap industrial carpeting. Almost immediately they were confronted with a staircase, so Lottie went to clear the second floor while Flynn and Dev inspected the first. They found nothing other than some fast food wrappers and the smell of flop sweat and burned hair.

"Taser," Dev muttered to himself, noting that there were filaments from such a weapon left behind on one of the desks. "So much for Frederick's gospel being enough to change minds."

Other than that, there was nothing of note in the space at all... except for the large corkboard at the back of the building, in what used to be a kitchen. Someone had left it where it was deliberately, two desk lamps pointing at it like makeshift spotlights. It bore eerie similarities to the corkboard Dev had kept in his bedroom, except instead of string connecting places and people related to the Reborn, these threads came together around his friends. Flynn, Lottie, Eileen, Tara, and Kaja seemed to be the main focus, but Aoife and even Wolfe and Scarlett also had their pictures pinned up... along with photos of their homes, their cars, and other personal information.

"What the hell?" Lottie was indignant as she came to stand beside him, holstering her weapon. "They've been watching us?"

"They've been trying to figure out how to get to me through you guys," Dev said, feeling as though he was hearing himself talk from a great distance. The edges of his vision danced red, and his hands curled into fists. "They've been *using* you." He moved without conscious thought, punching the whiteboard so hard that it cracked, a streak of blood left behind where the skin over his knuckles tore. "Fucking Aleksandr. He's behind this."

"That's a pretty good bet, yeah." Flynn's voice was soft to Dev's ears, but maybe that was just because his pulse was roaring inside his head. His hand landed on Dev's shoulder and squeezed, gently tugging him back. "Lottie, can you call in a team to come and get rid of this stuff? We can't leave it here, but we're on the clock."

"Yeah, no problem," Lottie replied, already pulling out her phone. "Go get some air."

Dev allowed Flynn to guide him back out the front door, but as soon as they were outside he broke away from his partner's hold, shoving both hands into his hair and pacing a few steps down the sidewalk. The one he'd used to hit the whiteboard throbbed with pain in time with his heart. He was so angry he couldn't speak, breath catching inside his chest and hunkering down, keeping the words at bay.

"I know you're mad," Flynn started, then corrected, "Scratch that, I know you're pissed the hell off. But breakin' your fingers isn't gonna get us anywhere except the ER."

When Dev found his voice, it was dull and hollow. "They're not broken." He dropped his hands from his hair, but couldn't bring himself to face Flynn. "I know what that feels like, remember?" He didn't expect Flynn's hand to wrap around his wrist, tugging gently until he turned around.

"Lemme see," Flynn murmured, drawing Dev closer, until he could use his thumbs to check each of Dev's fingers for fractures. "This hurt?"

It was excruciating, but not in the way Flynn meant—no, it was hideously intimate, and Dev found himself fascinated by the smile lines at the corners of Flynn's eyes even though he had seen them thousands of times before. The smells of leather and gunpowder filled his nose, achingly familiar, and Dev swayed forward, drawn in like a moth to flame. "No," he whispered, and when Flynn's eyes snapped up to his, no doubt taking in the lack of distance, Dev's

throat went dry. "Not much. I told you, they're not broken."

"Good." Flynn stared at him, an entire universe flickering in the

depths of his coffee-colored eyes. "Dev... *Adam*, I—"

Dev didn't think.

That was rare for him, but in this momentary lapse of reason, his

brain just... stopped. He grabbed the lapels of Flynn's leather jacket

in both fists and yanked him forward, their teeth clacking together

accidentally as their lips met in a bruising kiss. It lasted only a few

seconds that felt like hours, fire racing up and down his spine. For an

instant, he could've sworn he felt the pressure against his mouth

being returned, but it was so fleeting there was no way to be sure.

A tinny chime interrupted them, breaking Dev out of his trance

and filling him with a syrupy sense of horror. The look on Flynn's

face—absolute shock—confirmed what Dev already knew, that

instead of defusing bombs he set them now, blowing up the

relationship that had been a constant for him since he left the

Sandbox. He tore his eyes away from Flynn, forcing his hands to

unclench from his jacket. Then Dev dug around in his pocket until he could grasp his phone, staring down at the message on the screen like it held the secrets to the universe.

"They found the mole." When Dev heard his own voice, he barely recognized it. Behind him, the door to the office slammed shut—Lottie was coming, and he was certain neither of them wanted to drag her into whatever the hell had just happened. He turned toward Flynn's car, resigned to his fate in a way he'd never been before, not even at thirteen. "It's safe to go back to Renegade. Which means we need to get to Montana. Now."

~***~

Chapter Seventeen

After he got the cross carved into his back, Dev was never the same.

It had little to do with his change in preferred name, and everything to do with the pulling. The wounds were deep and took forever to heal, but even once they were closed up, it felt like there were sets of claws buried in his flesh, yanking it in different directions each time he moved. It was almost as if his battered body was telling him to get out, to run as far and as fast from the Reborn as he possibly could. But for some reason, he couldn't get his feet to move. Perhaps he was afraid of the unknown, of the vast and cruel world which Frederick had been describing to him since he was small… or maybe he was afraid that his punishment for rabbiting would be worse somehow than the crucifixion he could expect in just a few months' time.

Speaking of time, it was ticking down both slower and faster than Dev could comprehend. Training for him and his peers—the ones that didn't fall down dead on that awful night, anyway—had only intensified, and much like Dev knew the sky was blue and the dirt was brown, he knew he would be sacrificed on his thirteenth birthday. On the same day Christ was born, to cement the idea that Dev would die on the cross and rise again, granting eternal life to all of Frederick's believers. That way they would be able to survive the coming end of days that the outside world was allegedly working so hard to initiate.

But getting carved up like one of his birthday meals left Dev wondering if Frederick's way was the only way. He thought he could glimpse similar ideas on Dani's face now and then, when she believed no one else was looking, but he was afraid to say anything. After all, the last time someone spoke up it was Teddy, and look where that got him—dead in the ground with Minnie and so many others. Still, there was a part of Dev that wanted to subvert his fate, and he knew deep down that there was only one way he could accomplish that goal. Only one turn of events his father's fanatical followers would take as gospel.

He would have to kill Frederick.

But could he do it?

~***~

Chapter Eighteen

By the time they got back to Project Renegade and began packing up their gear, Flynn barely knew which way was up. Of all the things that could've happened outside that office building in Brookline, the last fucking one he'd ever expected was for Dev to *kiss* him. And it wasn't *just* a kiss, no—it was a life-altering, mind-bending clash of their mouths that made him sweat.

The problem? They'd had exactly zero time to talk about it.

Lottie had seemed unaware of the metaphorical elephant in the car on the drive over, or she was a good enough friend to both of them to not say anything. Flynn would've bet money it was the latter, since he doubted very much that she would've missed the way his hands were white-knuckled around the steering wheel, or how Dev kept glancing over at him from the passenger's seat. Their eyes had met accidentally, and the look on Dev's face... Flynn hadn't seen him so closed off since they first met. It was almost like he was overcompensating for his earlier flagrant display of emotion.

But *which* emotion was behind that kiss, anyway? Flynn had no clue what to make of it. Dev was obviously in a pretty shitty headspace considering the whole mess with the Reborn, but Flynn couldn't believe that would make him act out in that way at random. Dev never did anything without at least considering it first, which meant he'd thought about kissing Flynn before he actually did it, even if it was only in passing. And *that* was a hard concept for Flynn to wrap his head around, considering he'd spent so much time telling himself he was too old and broken for *anyone* to love him, let alone someone like Dev.

"Is it always this quiet in here?" he heard Teddy ask in a stage whisper, and when Flynn glanced over he observed him leaning against the locker next to Eileen's like they were having a friendly chat. "I feel like locker rooms are supposed to be loud. Although everything I know about that came from direct-to-video movies, so... maybe not."

"No, it's a bit like a mausoleum at the moment," Eileen agreed, throwing a change of clothes and a heavy parka into her duffle bag, because if things were cold and snowy in Boston, they were most likely that times a hundred outside of Bozeman. "Something happened at that office that nobody's too eager to share, would be my guess."

"You know we can hear you, right?" Dev snapped, slamming his locker door shut. He had the one next to Flynn's, and it made the entire row of metal boxes rattle ominously. When Eileen merely looked over at him and raised her eyebrows, Dev blew out a breath and pinched the bridge of his nose with his free hand; the other one held the straps of his bag. "Sorry. But you sound like a couple of car salesmen at a water cooler."

"Holy outdated reference, Batman," Lottie teased from over by the weapons rack on the opposite wall. She appeared to be debating between bringing a pump-action or semi-auto shotgun; with a nod to herself, she put the semi-auto into her duffle, along with two boxes of shells. "Do people even use water coolers anymore? They must, right?"

"I doubt the water cooler industry has gone out of business," Flynn said, closing his locker with a bit more civility than Dev had. He felt both Teddy and Eileen's eyes on him like a brand, no doubt searching for the same hostility Dev had shown, but probably for different reasons. "What d'you figure, they were taken out by big vending machine?"

"Are you guys always like this?" Teddy wondered aloud, following the group when they filed out of the locker room and into the elevator, where Tara joined them with her computer gear. Normally they'd drive over to Logan Airport, but since time was a factor they were taking the helicopter instead. "Making up conspiracy theories for inanimate objects?"

"Gotta stay sane somehow," was Tara's reply, punching the button for the roof with her knuckle. She was wearing her back brace instead of using her wheelchair, and her face betrayed her discomfort. "Or at least pretend we are. Last thing any of us need are more visits to the government-sanctioned shrink."

"Amen to that," Dev muttered, his shoulder brushing against Flynn's even as his eyes stared straight ahead. "Now let's get this over with."

~***~

It was hard to find privacy on the Renegade jet to give Teddy a shovel talk, but like most of life's difficulties, Eileen found a way around it.

She waited until he got up to use the bathroom, then sauntered to the rear and waited for him to be done doing his business. As Teddy started to exit the lavatory, Eileen planted a hand on his chest and shoved him inside. He made a surprised sound and stumbled, but regained his balance when his back hit the wall behind him. His eyes went wide when Eileen crammed herself in with him and relocked the door, and he looked like he wanted to say something in protest but wasn't sure what.

"You should already know why I'm here, but in case you're particularly daft, I'll spell it out for you." Eileen stared him hard in the face, hands planted on her hips and her hair a wild tangle from the power nap she'd taken somewhere over Pennsylvania. They had about a half-hour left in their flight to Bozeman, where they'd have to make the rest of their journey by car. "I may not always make it obvious, but I care for the people on this plane a great deal." Her throat tightened without warning, but she managed to muster through without a voice crack. "And if anything—I mean *anything*—happens to Dev while you're with him, I'm holding you personally responsible."

Teddy blinked rapidly and swallowed audibly. "You're... not who I expected to do this. But here's the thing, I... Dev was my friend too, once upon a time. And he's the reason I'm not under

Aleksandr's control anymore. So while I can't guarantee that he isn't going to get hurt—it would be stupid to say that, given what we're up against—I *can* promise to do everything in my power to get him back to you alive."

Eileen looked at him for a long moment, then nodded. "That's what I wanted to hear. An honest answer." She started to leave the bathroom but turned back to Teddy, curious about something. "Why not me? Who did you think it would be?"

"Well, like you said, you don't make it obvious," Teddy started, then clarified, "How deeply you care about them, I mean." A sheepish shrug. "I figured it'd be Flynn." Something knowing flickered in his eyes. "He's in love with him, isn't he?"

"Horrendously so, yes," Eileen replied without hesitation. "I keep hoping that one of them will figure out their shit, but it hasn't happened yet." Her mind flickered briefly to thoughts of Lottie, but she put a mental kibosh on that before it could get out of hand. "I'm going back out there before someone gets the bright idea that *we're* a thing. But remember what I told you. He makes it back, or it's your head."

Teddy's chin dipped in a nod. "Yes ma'am."

~***~

Dev didn't like driving.

Actually, if he was being honest with himself, he kind of hated it. He *could* drive, of course—he was behind the wheel of the massive SUV that had been waiting for them at Bozeman Yellowstone International Airport, which was actually about eight miles north of the city in a town called Belgrade. While it was usually Flynn, Lottie, or a combination of both that did the driving, Dev was in charge this time around because he was the one who knew the area the best besides Teddy, and no one trusted him enough to let him drive. From Belgrade they had to go about an hour to the southwest, into a tiny town called Cardwell, where Tara and Eileen would get set up in a motel room to run comms. From there, Teddy would hogtie Dev and throw him into the back of a waiting panel van, while Lottie and Flynn hiked into the foothills of Hollowtop Mountain, where the Reborn lived.

"Still can't believe there's a motel out here," Dev heard himself say, eyes flicking away from the curvature of the road for a moment to look at Teddy in the rearview mirror. "When I left, all Cardwell had going for it was the Lewis and Clark campsite."

"That's pretty much all it has going for it now, too," Teddy replied, smiling a little, and some of the tension left Dev's shoulders; they'd get through this, even if it was going to be ugly. "Oh, and there's a gas station now. Big doings."

"I can't get over how this place *looks*," Tara said, the expansive farm fields and scrub brush outside reflected in the lenses of her glasses. She was in the middle row with Teddy and Eileen, and Flynn was in the passenger's seat, leaving Lottie as the sole occupant of the back. "It's not flat, but it isn't exactly mountainous either… what *is* it?"

"Hilly?" Lottie suggested. Dev couldn't see her very well with the angle, but from the sounds of things he guessed she was sharpening a knife. "I think the word you want is hilly."

"And empty," Flynn muttered. He hadn't purposefully made eye contact with Dev since the incident outside the office building, and as much as it was killing him not knowing what his partner was thinking, Dev couldn't find the courage to ask—plus it wasn't a conversation he wanted to have in front of the entire team. "Reminds me of parts of Texas that I'd rather not visit again."

"Too many sundown towns?" Tara guessed, and when Flynn hummed his agreement, she sighed. "Yeah, unfortunately that makes sense."

"What the bloody hell is a *sundown town*?" Eileen sounded as though she was equal parts curious and wary of the answer. "Is this one of those uniquely American things that will make me want to vomit?"

"Yep," Dev said, slowing down for a particularly hairy turn. According to the GPS and his memory, they'd be at the motel in a few minutes. "Basically, a sundown town is a place where they have rules intended to keep Black people and other minorities from living there. In the early twentieth century, these towns would allow Black people to work in an area but not reside there. By sundown, they had to get out of town or they'd be harassed, arrested, or worse. It was an open secret, and they still exist today."

"Some of them even have signs," Lottie added, her voice carrying an ache that only someone who had been targeted by bigots could feel. "'Whites only after dark', shit like that."

Eileen sighed harshly. "You lot are very lucky I have a strong constitution, or that vomit thing would be literal." Her tone changed as the motel got bigger on their side of the road, a neon cowboy jumping over a tumbleweed in perpetual stop-motion the main feature of the sign. "Is that where we'll be staying, then?"

"That's the kinda place that looks like it smells like a cat box, and I'm not even out of the car," Flynn commented, but when Dev glanced in his direction, his partner's eyes were on him, not the sketchy low-slung clapboard building. "Remember that one hotel we stayed at in Japan? It had the—"

"Do *not* remind me about the robot toilet," Dev interjected, feeling himself smile and noticing with relief that Flynn did the same. Maybe his colossal fuckup earlier hadn't done as much damage to their relationship as he'd previously thought. "That thing scared the shit out of me."

"Well at least you were in the right place for it," Teddy joked as they pulled to a stop in front of the motel's office. In the space next to them was a rust-spotted white panel van of generic make and model, the kind favored by burglars and kidnappers everywhere. "Is that our ride?"

"It sure is." Tara opened up the door on her side, squawking indignantly when Lottie used her as a handhold to climb over her seat and out. "If I had a nickel for every time you almost tore off one of my boobs like that…"

Lottie chuckled and held out her hand, taking Tara's computer bag for her so she could clamber out with her brace. "You'd have a lot of nickels, which would be weird since nobody uses coins anymore."

"Actually, I carry coins," Dev commented absently, killing the engine and getting out too. He waited to speak again until they were all outside the SUV. "They're useful for a lot of things—loosening a screw, testing your tire treads… or, you know, paying for stuff." He studied the van for a moment, then sighed and looked at Teddy. "Aleksandr isn't going to buy that you were able to subdue me without hurting me. I think somebody's going to have to rough me up a little. Not enough that I can't function if things get hairy, but enough to make it look real." No one said anything, and Dev couldn't help but raise an eyebrow. "Really? None of you have wanted to punch me at least once?"

"Oh, I used to want that very much," Lottie said dryly, arms folded over her chest, Tara's bag dangling from her elbow. "But only for like, five minutes after we broke up. Not anymore." She glanced at Flynn. "I'd argue that you and I know the most about beating people up, so it should be one of us."

Flynn looked up at the sky like it held the answer to the mystery of life; instead of letting him in on the secret, it started spitting snow. Blinking away the flakes, Flynn met Dev's gaze and jerked his head toward the back of the motel. "Come on, I'll do it. Just not out here."

Swallowing hard, Dev followed Flynn around the corner. They weren't out of earshot of the others, and in fact Dev could hear it when someone retrieved the keys for the van—probably from the wheel well, left behind by the tactical team that was on standby as a last resort—and opened its back doors. Eileen cracked a raunchy joke about the coil of rope and duct tape that they found inside, and while that normally would've made Dev laugh, in that moment he could barely comprehend what was going on around him.

"Hey," Flynn murmured, his hand settling warm and heavy on Dev's shoulder. "If you don't want me to do this, I can—"

"Just do it," Dev interjected tightly. He reached up to push Flynn's hand away, but instead of following through, his own hand rested awkwardly on Flynn's arm. That lasted for an instant before he took a step back, tilting his head up and to the left. "Don't break anything."

Something that Dev couldn't place flitted through Flynn's expression, taken over a moment later by grim determination. "Fine," he ground out, the same hand that had been touching Dev curling into a fist. "Here we go."

A right hook arced in Dev's direction, and he had to lock his knees to stifle the urge to dodge it. Flynn pulled the punch, but only a little, the *crack* of the contact loud against the wet asphalt and cold air. There was a rush of pain to Dev's jaw, skin flushing hot as it bruised, and as Flynn followed that up with a fist to his stomach, Dev made peace with the fact that this was probably going to be the last interaction he had with the person he loved most in the world. Because while he would do everything he could to survive the Reborn a second time, the chances that his luck would run out were much better. But if he could destroy them from the inside out, keep them from hurting anyone else… it would be enough.

I have come to bring fire to the earth, Dev thought, spitting blood into a nearby puddle after another blow, teeth wet with red and eyes manic, *and how I wish it were already blazing.*

Chapter Nineteen

The Chosen One couldn't stop trembling… because he didn't want to die.

And to that end, Dev had cornered Dani a week before the moment when he stood before the crucifix.

"I know you don't believe in this." When Dani had pinned Dev with a hard stare in the shadows behind the barn, the relatively isolated location and feeble animal noises acting as cover from any listening ears, Dev gestured around them with one hand. "All of this. Any of it. You didn't *want* to—" his voice cracked, but he forced himself to finish the thought "—to kill all those kids. That isn't what you signed up for."

Dani was quiet for a long moment, long enough that Dev feared he might have made a grave miscalculation. Just when he thought she might pull her gun and put a bullet in his head (completing the prophecy a little early, but Frederick could spin it), she sighed heavily. "You're right. I… I don't know what I was looking for when I came here, but this wasn't it."

"So what do we *do* about it?" Dev fixed her with an imploring look, hoping she had a thought or two to complement what he had come up with so far on his own. "Because I have an idea… but it's pretty crazy."

Dani snorted. "Kid, I don't know if you've noticed, but this whole place is crazy. I think the only way we're gonna get out of here is if we're a little insane ourselves."

With that in mind, they hatched their plan. On the face of things, it was fairly simple: Dev would arrive early to the chapel and crawl into the rafters when he heard the mob approaching. Dani would enter the chapel with Frederick and the others, but not before submitting an anonymous tip to the local sheriff's office about Minnie's murder; as much as Dev wanted justice for Teddy too, he had no proof that he had been killed, while he knew precisely where to find what was left of his mother. With any luck, the calvary would arrive before either Dev or Dani had to do anything rash, but if it came to it… Dev knew he needed to live, for Minnie, and Teddy, and all of the kids.

And he'd do whatever he had to in order to make that happen.

Chapter Twenty

Lottie had hiked into her fair share of unwelcoming territory when she was in the Army. It didn't matter if it was a snowy mountain pass during the day or a parched desert under the cover of night—*Rangers lead the way*, after all, and that *way* could be just about anywhere. So picking her way through a thick forest at the base of a mountain range, with nothing to go on but a static aerial map and Dev's vague directions, was no big deal. Even carrying a fifty-pound rucksack was normal, although she wasn't used to it holding a parabolic microphone that could pick up the sound of a moth farting from a thousand yards away—credit for that colorful description went to Flynn. And speaking of Flynn, he was precisely what wasn't normal about their current situation. Lottie had never met another human being that liked to talk as much as Flynn did, and he had been eerily, ominously mute ever since he'd beat Dev up behind the motel.

She counted ten more steps in her head, then gave up. "Okay, I can't take it anymore," she declared, glancing over at him before squinting up at the sun to ensure they were still traveling in the correct direction. "What the hell is wrong with you?"

Flynn frowned, carefully lifting a boot over a fallen branch without looking down at it. Moving in near-silence through any terrain was Special Forces 101, and Deltas had the market cornered on being like ghosts with machine guns. "What do you mean? I'm fine."

"Bull fuckin' shit you are," Lottie retorted, the edges of her worn-down Boston accent coming out with her annoyance. "I'm a lot of things, Walker, but stupid isn't one of them. I know something happened between you and Dev while I was calling for the cleanup team. What was it?"

Flynn eyed her for a second, then reached for his ear and turned off his comm—far from mission protocol, but clearly this wasn't something he wanted Tara or anybody else overhearing. He waited for her to do the same before he spoke again: "He kissed me."

Lottie would've been less surprised if Flynn had reached out and snapped her bra strap like they were in junior high. "Run that by me again?"

"I told you, he—" Flynn cut himself off, frustration and something else—sadness, maybe—pulling his face taut. "He kissed me. I don't know why, but… it happened."

"Flynn…" Lottie reached deep within herself for her sympathy, trying to blow an errant strand of hair away from her face. It didn't move an inch because of the beanie on her head and she frowned at it. "Look, okay… here's the thing. When it came to me and Dev, *I* showed interest in *him* first. *I* asked *him* out first. *I* kissed *him* first. If *he* kissed *you*… that's different. It means something. And even if it was a spur-of-the-moment action, it wasn't some random impulse. Clearly the idea had occurred before then."

"That… was kinda what I thought, actually. Hearing it from you… it makes a lotta sense," Flynn admitted, sighing. "And I realize this is probably awkward as hell for you to talk about, since… well, you know."

"Since Dev and I had a cataclysmic breakup? Yeah, I know all about that." Lottie's tone was wry, and she nudged Flynn lightly with her elbow to reinforce the fact that she was joking. "For whatever it's worth… a part of me knew Dev had feelings for someone else, even when we were together. It was one of the reasons we never really worked. I mean, I knew he was bisexual, obviously, but I wasn't sure who—" She cut off when Flynn tripped over a rock and nearly face planted into the dirt, her hand gripping his jacket to keep him upright. "Whoa, what the fuck? You okay?"

"Did you just say—" Flynn fell silent abruptly, then grabbed Lottie's arm and dropped into a crouch, forcing her to join him. He turned his comm back on, and Lottie did the same without being prompted. When Flynn spoke again, he was all business and very quiet: "Do you hear that?"

Lottie listened, pulse quickening, and she did, in fact, hear it: the faintest crunching of boots on snow and old leaves. Further analysis revealed it to be two pairs of boots, and the smell of cigarette smoke and murmured conversation joined the party a moment later. "Patrol," she muttered. "We must be closer than we thought."

"You are," Tara confirmed in their ears, blessedly not bringing up the fact that their comms had gone dark for several minutes. "According to my satellite feed, GPS puts you less than a quarter-mile from the edge of the compound."

The pair of guards passed them, close enough that the hair on the back of Lottie's neck stood up in warning, her right hand itching for the silenced pistol hidden inside her coat. Beyond the guards, she could just make out the pattern of a chain-link fence, topped with thick rolls of barbed wire; Teddy had warned them about that, which was why Flynn's rucksack contained bolt cutters. She waited to speak again until the footsteps faded, slowly rising from her crouch at the same time as Flynn. "We need to find a hiding spot. If they've got patrols out here, they're not messing around."

"No, they're not," Flynn agreed, glancing up at the sun just as Lottie had earlier. "We've got about three hours of daylight left, give or take. We'll watch 'em for a while, pick our time and place to infiltrate once dusk hits."

A beat of silence, then Eileen wondered over comms: "But... will Dev stay alive for that long?"

"He'll have to," Lottie said grimly, hiking her pack higher on her back. "If he survived these people once, he can do it again." She nudged Flynn and began moving backward. "Let's go set up the mics."

Flynn could barely tear his eyes away from the fence, but he nodded and followed her lead. "Yeah. Okay."

~***~

As someone who had been kidnapped for real on more than one occasion, Dev could attest to exactly how shitty it was. For some reason, he'd thought knowing he would be tied up and tossed into the back of a van before it happened would make it better somehow, but it really didn't. He still felt every bump and bang as the van's bald tires rolled down the long, narrow dirt path that led to the compound's entrance. That paired with his new bruises courtesy of Flynn left something to be desired as far as comfort was concerned, and while it was tempting to talk to Teddy as he drove, he knew they were both too nervous for that.

After what felt like an hour but was probably only a handful of minutes, the van jolted to a stop, making Dev curse quietly under his breath when his head smacked against a barely-carpeted wheel well. Teddy exited the van as Dev was reorienting himself with which way was up, and he got that done just in time for the back doors to be wrenched open by one of his least favorite people in the world.

"I was beginning to think I'd never see this day," Aleksandr Lichtenson said, looking Dev's form up and down with something that could only be described as glee. A feral-looking grin spread over his face, making the scar on his forehead—a souvenir from one of

Dani's bullets, on a night that felt like a lifetime ago now—twist in on itself like the world's fleshiest pretzel. He grabbed Dev by the ankles and yanked hard, so Dev all but flew out of the back of the van and landed hard on his bound arms, nearly wrenching his shoulders from their sockets and knocking the breath from his lungs. "Adam Devereux... the *Chosen One*, in all his glory." His steel-toed boot connected with Dev's ribs, then his thigh, the kicks as casual as steps to a dance. "Or... wait, what's the opposite of glory?" Another kick, this one dangerously close to Dev's head. "Come on, *genius*— tell me."

Dev gritted his molars together and met Aleksandr's gaze. "I'm pretty sure it's idiocy, he replied, baring his teeth and making a show of struggling against his bonds. He didn't have to put much effort into pretending, since he was without his knife and had no hope of getting free unless someone untied him. "And you'd know it like the back of your hand."

Aleksandr's face turned thunderous, and bent to grab Dev by the front of his dress shirt—it was the same one he wore in Bucharest, to lend authenticity to the idea that Teddy had nabbed him straight from the black market auction. It along with his pants and loafers were splattered with blood, and one of his jacket sleeves had been completely torn away (by Eileen in the motel parking lot, but nobody needed to know that). "You fucking—"

"Enough." Teddy's interjection was a single sharp word, but it was enough to make Aleksandr still, holding Dev in mid-air like a rag doll. Even the people Aleksandr had brought with him to inspect the van—two men, one woman, all holding AK-47s—turned their attention his way. "I may not know everything that goes on around here, but I'm smart enough to figure out that Father wants Adam alive and relatively unharmed. Would you like me to be the one to tell him that you allowed yourself to lose control and gave the Chosen One a brain injury, or do you want to do that yourself?"

"Fuck off, Vasquez," Aleksandr snarled, but he dropped Dev back into the snow-crusted dirt. "What the hell happened to your team? Why are you two days late?" He leaned to the side to look over Teddy's shoulder into the conspicuously empty van. "And where's the goddamn DMT?"

"Language," Teddy admonished, with the same cutting edge he'd used when he spoke to Dev inside the old church; if Dev didn't know any better, he would've assumed Teddy was still under the

Reborn's control. And that was good, since Aleksandr needed to believe that was the case in order for them to pass through the front gate without any extra bullets. "A lot's happened, but let's see if I can recap." He ticked off the salient points on the fingers of one hand as he spoke them aloud: "Team's dead, I'm late because smuggling a live person across the Atlantic is harder than you'd think it is, and the DMT got destroyed." For extra flair, he kicked Dev—not quite as hard as Aleksandr had, but it still smarted. "That about cover it?"

"Eat me," Dev groaned out, his ribcage feeling like it was doing its best to leave his body. "Actually, wait, I wouldn't put that past you fucking people. Don't do that."

Aleksandr ignored him, too busy goggling at Teddy like he'd just whipped his dick out unprompted. "The entire field team is dead? Because of *him*?"

"He has friends, you know," Teddy pointed out, hooking a thumb over his shoulder at the van. "Now, how about you let us in and we pay Father a visit?"

Aleksandr blew out a breath and dragged a hand over his jaw. The olive tinge of his camouflage gear made him look even paler and sickly, like he'd been out in the cold for far too long—which depending on exactly how militarized the Reborn had gotten could be a possibility. "Fine." He waved to his minions, who snapped to attention like toy soldiers. "Open the gate." Quick as a snake, he leaned down and grabbed the length of rope attached to Dev's feet, dragging him around the van rather than back to it. "But I'll be taking this, and you won't be joining us."

Dev's gut clenched with a spike of fear—that wasn't even *close* to the plan—but he forced it down and away, years of training taking over. Still, he couldn't help but ask: "So does that mean he's alive? My father?"

Aleksandr grunted, pulling him through the yawning mouth formed by the opened gate and into the abyss. "You'll have to see for yourself."

~***~

Tara sat at a pathetic excuse for a desk in a motel room that looked and smelled like it hadn't been remodeled since 1992, her fingers flying over the keys on her rig. It had taken her a while to get everything set up, but now that she had reliable internet and her second monitor, she was busy repositioning an NSA satellite over the Reborn compound and half-listening to Flynn and Lottie's quiet chatter over the comms. She was vaguely aware of Eileen pacing the room behind her, restless after shutting the blinds and barricading the door, but once Tara was in the zone it was difficult for anything to break her out of it.

Except for Eileen poking at her ear and turning off her comm without warning, evidently, because *that* nearly made Tara jump out of her skin. "Jesus Christ, Eileen! *What?*"

"I don't want to distract them," Eileen explained, switching off her comm too. "Besides, they did it to us earlier." She sat down in the office chair Tara wasn't using, expression intense with... something. "I want you to humor me. Did anyone ever do a follow up at Blakely Manor? You know, after Diana was undercover there and subsequently went out of her fucking gourd?"

"I'd like to see you describe it that way to her face," Tara remarked, but her interest was piqued. She closed out of the satellite controls and pulled up a few databases. "But to answer your question, no, I don't think anybody did. What exactly do you want me to look for?"

"Anything." Eileen scooted closer to be able to look at Tara's monitors while she typed. "Was the place shut down? Did ownership change hands after Anton Codreanu got arrested?" She shrugged her shoulders. "Call it a hunch. Completely unfounded, mind you, but I had to say something."

Tara put in some search parameters, and almost immediately got a hit. She read a few lines, then read them again to make sure her brain was interpreting what her eyes saw correctly. "Holy *shit*." She flicked open images of documents, Anton Codreanu's mugshot, and anything else that seemed relevant. "Okay, so nearly all of Codreanu's assets were seized when he got arrested, first by BPD and then by the FBI. They let Sebastian keep the townhouse in Back Bay and the restaurant, because otherwise he would've been homeless with no way to support himself. But all of his shell corporations were dissolved, including the one that owned Blakely Manor. Mikael Ivanov's Russian bruisers—the Pack—they all split, including his sister the so-called doctor. That left the place more than understaffed and the patients in a bad way."

"I'm sensing a *but*, and it has nothing to do with my fantastic ass," Eileen said, rolling her hand in the universal signal for keep going. "Then what happened? I can't process all this bollocks as fast as you can."

"It looks like once the Feds got what they needed for evidence, they allowed some of Anton's assets to be auctioned off." Tara typed a bit more, closed some tabs on her rig and opened new ones. "And in came a different shell corporation, this one with ties that are pretty difficult to trace… but I suspect it's Russian. A different kind of Russian, though… like Valeriya's kind."

"And what does DMT do again?" Eileen pressed, a manic shade of brilliance flaring in her eyes. "The same thing they were trying to do with the Rapture at Blakely Manor—mind control."

"Diana wouldn't have been a good candidate for that, not with her… history," Tara said slowly. While tech was more her forte than science, she knew enough to guess that someone with a past pattern of disassociation wouldn't respond to Rapture *or* DMT in the way that an individual without that issue would. "So what are you thinking? The Spectres bought Blakely out from under the Pack, then continued their mind control aspirations, but with a different drug?"

"One that has a better chance of actually rewiring someone's brain, rather than just fucking them up temporarily." Eileen pulled her phone from the back pocket of her jeans. "They probably tried out Rapture again on Teddy, and when that didn't work they switched tactics. We need to get somebody over to Blakely. If there's even a chance that we're right—"

"Call Kaja," was Tara's response, focus zeroing back in on her rig. Her fingers started up their drumbeat, code marching along in time with her pulse. "I'll crack open this shell corp and see if we're right about what's inside."

~***~

Chapter Twenty-One

As soon as he heard the oncoming mass of fanatics heading for the chapel, Dev set his plan into motion.

He went to the area behind the dais, which was swathed in shadows thanks to the prayer candles that kept the area where his father preached perpetually bathed in an orange glow. He felt around in the dark until he found the rung of a ladder and wasted no time climbing to the top; ostensibly the ladder existed so that one of the handier followers could check in on the electrical wiring, but today it had a different purpose. He used it to reach the chapel's angular rafters, standing on the top rung and using his upper body strength to clamber higher, until he could lie down on a beam and observe what was happening down below.

"The time has finally come," Frederick declared as he pushed in the doors to the chapel, his flock filling the void behind him. He wore a simple black turtleneck with matching pants, never one for a frock or any other formal attire. At his right hand was Aleksandr, carrying a hammer in one hand and a box of nails in the other. His forehead had a large, deep gash across the middle that was stuck together with black sutures. He matched Frederick's steps until they reached the dais where the crucifix hung, stopping short of joining him on the elevated platform. "Tonight, the Chosen One will embark on a journey that will propel us all to everlasting life in the face of unspeakable evil." He placed his hands flat on the altar, leaning against it as he looked several members of the congregation directly in the eye; among them was Dani, Dev noted with some relief. "What comes next will not be easy, but it is what must be done." He nodded at a pair of men who stood near the crank mechanism at the side of the dais. "Lower it." It took both of them to move the heavy wooden cross, even with the pulley's assistance, but soon enough it was flat on the dais, in front of the altar. "Now, where is the Chosen One?"

"He's not coming." Dani's voice rang through the chapel like a gunshot, visibly startling the gathered crowd. They all turned to look at her almost simultaneously, but to her credit, she didn't flinch. "And if the rest of you were smart, you'd run before Frederick decides one of *you* will be the Chosen One instead."

Despite the fact that it was completely illogical, Dev feared that the ensuing silence was so intense that someone would hear his heart beating. He held his breath, gripping the wood beneath his prone form with white knuckles. In that instant, nobody moved or seemed to know what to do or say; it was a little bit like watching one of those old Christian cartoons Minnie used to put on for the kids, the compound's singular VHS player whirring in time with the static from the tube television.

It was Frederick who popped the silence like a balloon, face gone tight and white with his quiet brand of rage. "Danielle... have I wronged you?" He used one hand to gesture around at the congregation. "Have *we* wronged you? Because the only thing I can think of that would justify such heresy twisting your tongue is some sort of personal slight." He straightened up from his place at the altar and stepped around it, until he stood right on the edge of the dais, towering over her. "Please, my child, do tell us the sin we have committed to endure your righteous indignation."

"You know damn right well what you've done," Dani snapped, a fire in her eyes and hands clenched into fists at her sides. "Just like I know you don't believe a single word of what you preach. You just want power, and this is the easiest way for you to get it."

Before Frederick could speak, Aleksandr lashed out with the hammer held in his right hand. It hit Dani square in the abdomen, a sickening wheeze leaving her as she doubled over in pain, knees cracking against the wooden floor. "Blasphemy." Aleksandr hissed the single word like it was a curse, his arm rising to poise the hammer over the back of Dani's head. "What would you have me do with her, Father?"

Dev's vision zeroed in on the handgun tucked into the back of Frederick's waistband as his father considered Aleksandr's question. "Well, she certainly is not fit to join us in the eternal life that the Chosen One's sacrifice will grant us." He started to reach for the gun. "I will—"

Dev dropped down from the rafters and onto the altar, the shock of the landing rattling the bones of his legs. "You're not going to do anything," he said with far more confidence than he felt, barely resisting the urge to flinch when his father whipped around to face him, the rest of the congregation watching the scene playing out before them with wide, shocked eyes. "According to you, *I'm* the Chosen One, right? If that's the case, why are we forced to follow *your* rules?" A murmur rippled through the crowd, and while Dev couldn't parse out any words, he could tell what he said had an effect. "Dani's right. If I wasn't around, he would've chosen somebody else, and—"

He was cut off when Frederick backhanded him, similarly to the way he had the day Teddy vanished from existence. "That is *enough*," his father growled, grabbing Dev by the collar to keep him from falling down or backing up; with Dev standing on the altar, they were the same height. "I do not know how this heretic managed to fill your head with egotism and lies, but you…"

Frederick didn't actually trail off, but his voice became an incoherent drone as Dev's world narrowed to focus on reaching around his father for the gun in his waistband. While the action of moving his arm, grasping the weapon, and bringing it up between them only took a millisecond, for Dev it felt like an entire lifetime passed around him. The gun was heavier somehow than the ones he'd learned to shoot at targets, even though he was sure the number of bullets inside was comparable. He felt every notch and groove of the grip dig into his palm, the smooth curve of the trigger fitting perfectly into the nook of his index finger.

It was only when the gun appeared between them that Frederick began to react. His eyes went huge and he used his grip on Dev's shirt to try and push him away, his free hand rising to attempt to move the gun. But by that point, it was far too late—Dev's finger had already applied pressure to the trigger, and with a burst of fire and a roaring snap, the bullet hit Frederick in the chest. For a single moment he looked to be in shock, and then he stumbled backward, tumbling off the dais and into the horrified panic of the crowd.

Chapter Twenty-Two

Blakely Manor sat tall and foreboding on several acres of forested land, a sprawling building made of stone that was divided into several wings for the inpatient treatment of various mental disorders. High arches rose like eyebrows above reinforced doors and barred windows, and the central building that housed the main entrance and the common area was the oldest portion. It was purchased by Doctor Donald Blakely's family after the Vietnam War, and originally converted into a nonprofit asylum for veterans with post-traumatic stress disorder. Until Anton Codreanu's arrest, it had been funded entirely by private donors and run by his shell corporation, Morningstar Holdings.

From what Tara had told Kaja over the phone, it sounded like the Spectres had made the government an offer for the property that they couldn't refuse… but the question was *why*. The manor had previously been operated by the Pack, who were busy doing sick experiments on people with Rapture, but Kaja doubted the Spectres' only motive was to show up their rivals. Eileen's theory about the DMT and Rapture being connected somehow would only hold water if this little field trip could link the Spectres to the Reborn, which at this point didn't seem very likely.

"So what's the plan?" David asked from behind the wheel of their Renegade-issue SUV, which they'd parked almost directly across the road from the gates guarding Blakely Manor's long, tree-lined driveway. "Guns blazing or ninja style?"

"The fact that you're still alive is nothing short of astounding," Scarlett said dryly, strapped into the backseat with Diana on her left and Wolfe on her right. "They don't build spies like they used to, I guess."

"Hey, he didn't pick that up in spy school. Half-assing your way into a situation and then using your full ass to get out is Special Forces one-oh-one." Wolfe's words were lighthearted, but his focus was on the imposing fence surrounding the Blakely property. "Besides, you and I bullshitted our way into this place once before— I'm sure we can do it again."

"I do not think it will be as simple as bullshitting this time," Diana commented. If Kaja didn't know her as well as she did, she never would've guessed that she was facing down a place where she was tortured; the only tell she had was the barest hint of tension around her mouth. "Eileen's conspiracy theory seems like exactly that, but even if she is half right and the *Prizraki* are now in control of the manor, they are not going to let us walk in the front door just because we ask nicely."

They all mulled that over for a moment, and then Kaja remembered something. "There's a blanket in the back," she said slowly, peering through the passenger's window at the gate and fence. "It looks like the only cameras are at the gate, and they face the driveway. If we can't go through the gate without them knowing we're coming, we could throw the blanket on top of the fence to cover the spikes and climb over that way."

"I like that idea much better than whatever he's cooking up in here," Scarlett declared, leaning forward to tap David on the side of his skull with her knuckles and snickering when he swatted at her and missed. "Let's go try this before we collectively decide to do something even dumber."

Kaja frowned as they all piled out of the SUV, following Wolfe as he loped around to the back to open the lift gate. "You know that you two don't need to come with us, right? I understand that you want to help, but you don't work for Renegade—hell, you don't even work for the government. I can't ask you to stick your necks out like this."

"You aren't asking," Wolfe pointed out. He retrieved the folded blanket, shook it out, and promptly sneezed three times in a row thanks to the dust cloud that arose from it. "Holy *fuck*. Anyway, you haven't asked us to do anything. We volunteered. When we needed help a few months ago, you all stepped up with no questions or complaints. It's only fair that we return the favor." He leaned in close for a smile and a conspiratorial whisper, all boyish charm— exactly like his father. "I'm pretty sure that's what they call *friendship*."

Kaja shook her head, shoving him lightly before checking the load in her pistol. "Smartass. I don't know how Sebastian puts up with you."

"I can tell you from experience that it is not an easy task," Diana said wryly, opening up the driver's door and sliding behind the wheel. They needed someone there in case a hasty exit was necessary, and Kaja wasn't about to demand that Diana accompany them back into a place that had caused her so much pain. "And we will not examine the fact that I went from dating Jim to dating his father. The CIA shrink has enough fun with me without that little detail."

"Hey, forget you two putting up with him—what about *me*?" Scarlett managed to appear genuinely miffed, save for the glimmer of affection in her eyes when she looked at Wolfe. Their relationship reminded Kaja a bit of hers with her brother, minus the natural conflict that came with one sibling being a spy and the other a police detective. "*I'm* the one who suffers the wrath of Jimmy's ass when we eat Taco Bell at three in the morning on a stakeout, not Bash. I deserve compensation."

"Sounds like you should take that up with Taco Bell," David remarked, also checking his weapon before glancing around at them all. "Ready?"

There were nods and murmurs of ascent, and the group sans Diana trekked across the road and between the trees as a unit, all trained in one fashion or another to keep their steps silent in the snowy underbrush. Wolfe and David were the tallest, so it was them that threw the blanket upward, so it draped over the spikes that lined the top of the fence. Then it was a waiting game as each of them took their turn climbing over, landing on the other side with varying degrees of success. Kaja couldn't help but snicker when David nearly face planted into the ground, rolling her eyes when he gave her a dirty look; the obstacle courses at the Farm had done much worse to both of them, but watching someone you knew could be graceful and deadly wipe out would never not be funny.

They moved through the woods cautiously, instinctively expecting a patrol or dogs, but they shouldn't have worried—they didn't see a single soul on the approach to the manor. As the structure came into view, Kaja spotted a handful of vehicles in its circular driveway. They were all utilitarian SUVs with Massachusetts plates, not unlike the one Diana had stayed with, and matching cars almost always meant *gang activity* if they didn't mean *government nonsense* (sometimes those two things were hard to tell apart, even for Kaja). She moved off to the left with David after he exchanged hand signals with Wolfe, gun held along her leg and eyes trained on Blakely's many barred windows.

"Seems pretty dead," David whispered as they ducked between the cars to cross the driveway. A glance told Kaja he was tense, mouth pulled down in a frown. "I don't know what I expected, but it wasn't this."

"If they're doing something in there, it won't be where the patients are," Kaja surmised, recalling the blueprints they'd looked at on the ride over from the city. "I think there's offices in this wing, toward the back." She stopped abruptly at the corner of the building, pressing her shoulder to the stone and straining her ears. She'd heard *something*, for a half-second. "Hey, what was that?"

David paused too, his frown only growing deeper. "Sounds like somebody talking on the phone... maybe an old landline? Sometimes they'd echo like that if the cords got chewed on by animals." He glanced around them, then tapped Kaja's arm to get her attention. When she looked over, she spotted a tangle of phone lines and electrical cords bolted to the exterior wall, most of which looked as though the local mouse population had been having a field day with them. "You know, like that. Must be afraid of taps on cell phones." They crept forward, past several windows that were blocked off by heavy curtains, and the dull murmur of conversation grew louder. A pair of windows before the manor's next turn looked in on an office, opulent with woodwork and stained glass. "Is that Russian?"

Kaja hushed him, fearful that the old building's probable lack of insultation might give them away. She leaned out, just a bit, and caught a glimpse of blonde hair and impeccable posture, followed by a familiar voice. "Valeriya," she whispered, a sinking feeling gripping her chest and pulling steadily downward. She hadn't wanted Eileen to be right, but realistically there were only so many places the Reborn could've gotten the fund necessary to rebuild their compound and recruit new members. "Your Russian is better than mine—what is she saying?"

David listened for a moment, head cocked. "She says whoever she's talking to is being foolish," he said slowly, following a beat behind each new word Valeriya spoke. "And that outsourcing their hard work on the… something she calls the Destroyer, to those freaks in Montana… is a mistake." He gripped Kaja's shoulder, blinking a few times. "That it's a mistake, *Father*. She's talking to Grigoriy Sidorov."

Before Kaja could formulate a response to that revelation, she was shocked—not only by the news that Sidorov had a personal interest in whatever the Destroyer was, but by the merciless force of a stun baton hitting her between her shoulder blades. She fell like a rock with electricity arcing through her body, and the last thing she

saw before her eyes rolled back in her head was the same thing

happening to David.

~***~

Whatever Dev had expected to see as he was dragged through

the compound by Aleksandr, it certainly wasn't what he got. The

ramshackle buildings and lean-to shelters of his youth had been

replaced with honest-to-god houses, not for one family but for all of

them, and the burned husk of the chapel had been reconstructed to

look more like a traditional church. A group of teenagers surrounded

a stone well, pumping out water and rolling it in large drums toward

what looked to be a mess hall and a bath house. Younger children

appeared to be receiving some sort of lesson in farming from a few

of the women, tending raised bends full of lettuce, radishes, and

various herbs. There was a healthy mix of genders and races, and

labor appeared to be split equally among everyone. It was all

surprisingly peaceful, if one could overlook the fence that cut

through the tree line and the guards with weapons of war.

Something must've showed on Dev's face, because Aleksandr

stopped walking abruptly and took out a knife. "Not what you expected?" He leaned down and neatly sliced through the rope around Dev's ankles, putting his blade back in his boot afterward. "Figured we were still a bunch of animals rolling in our own shit?"

"Not sure about you, but I stopped doing that when I was about seven," Dev replied with a grunt, rolling on his side and then his front, pushing himself up with his bound arms to get to his feet. He shook his hair out of his eyes, glancing around once more. "It's... different. Better. DMT trade must be paying pretty well." He screwed his face up when Aleksandr snorted. "What? You can't expect me to believe that all this is the product of my father's preaching."

"It isn't," Aleksandr acknowledged. He tied the excess rope around Dev's bound wrists, forming a sort of makeshift leash that he could use to pull him along. "And you can hold in any of your other burning questions for another five minutes." His expression darkened, a tinge of resentment to it. "I'm not the one who gets to decide what you know."

People were staring at them now, whispering behind their hands and taking steps back if it looked like their paths were going to cross. Another set of older children—middle school aged, probably—were running drills around an agility course built from logs and stones, and even they stopped to watch Dev get led around like a dog. He had a feeling that every single one of these people knew who he was, and that they were all a little too interested in his fate. He kept his eyes on the path in front of him, chin raised in a picture of defiance—he needed to act like he was there against his will.

After about a half-mile of walking, they reached an intersection with a wide, groomed dirt ribbon that appeared to be a fire road. It ran all the way through the back of the compound and out via a secondary guarded gate, making it a convenient emergency exit in case there were ever another raid by the sheriff's office or the Feds. But that wasn't the part that made Dev stop in his tracks, only to be jerked forward a few more feet by Aleksandr's grip on the rope. No, he paused because the structure that sat at the crossroads was nothing short of a mansion by comparison to everything else around. It was bigger than all the other buildings save the church, with a wide front porch and arched windows, and made the bare-bones home he grew up in look like a hovel.

"Impressive, isn't it?" Aleksandr should've sounded smug, but instead his tone was tainted. By envy, maybe, but there was something else present there too. It almost sounded like sadness, which wasn't an emotion Dev was aware Aleksandr was capable of feeling. He extracted the knife from his boot again, flipping it once in his hand before pointing the blade at Dev. "If I untie your wrists, are you going to do something stupid? Because I may not be able to kill you, but that doesn't mean I won't defend myself."

Dev stared at him for a moment, then held out his bound hands. "Untying me seems like a bad idea, strategically speaking. The last time I was in a room with my father and my hands weren't tied, I shot him."

"I remember," Aleksandr said dryly, slicing through the rope. This time he didn't put the knife away, but held it down along his thigh—a threat and a promise, all rolled into one. "And so does he. I'll be going in there with you."

"Delightful." Dev resisted the urge to rub at his chafed wrists, sore from rope burn and prickling just like the scar on his back. They mounted a short staircase to the porch, where Dev paused, unsure. "Do I knock, or...?"

"He's expecting you," was all Aleksandr said, less than helpfully. His mouth compressed into a tight line. "Behave yourself."

Dev tried the doorknob, pushing inward when he found it to be unlocked. He supposed when you were beloved enough to have people come back to your cult after a raid left it decimated by fire and piled high with dead bodies, you didn't really need to be preoccupied with basic safety measures. He found himself facing a staircase inside a tiled entryway, each row of marble just slightly askew, marking the work as amateurish. A kitchen was off to his left, and he could see the beginnings of a living room to his right. While the house was rigged to a propane-powered generator—as were many of the structures they'd passed on their journey—the interior was washed in the shadows of the late afternoon in winter, no lights to be found save for the orange glow of a fire coming from the living room.

Heart pounding a staccato in his chest, Dev forced one foot in front of the other until he was fully in the living area, which was set up with a couch, a recliner, and what could only be described as a shitload of medical supplies. There were carts lined up against one wall, full of tubing, syringes, and several things he didn't recognize. An IV pole stood sentry next to the recliner, but the hooks at the top were empty. And in the recliner itself, looking pale, withered, and about thirty years older instead of fifteen, was Frederick Devereux.

His eyes were sunken into his gaunt face, but when they landed on Dev, they were the same vivid shade of blue. "Adam. You came."

"Not by my own volition," Dev replied, hearing the words but not understanding they were coming from his mouth. The whole situation was so improbable that he felt like he was participating in some kind of play, or maybe he was the protagonist of a novel. Somehow, he'd expected his father to be the same enigmatic, effortlessly charming man he was before Dev tried to kill him; because surely there was no logical way one bullet—even at close range—caused all of *this*. "But I would've made it here eventually. You're not dead."

A raspy chuckle, which trailed off into a cough. "Here to finish me off, then?" When Aleksandr took a step forward, Frederick held up a hand. "Not necessary. If he wants to kill me, let him. I'd say he's earned it."

For a split second, the mission and its importance flew out of Dev's head, and he was very, *very* tempted. He had no weapons, of course, but it would've been so easy to just… close the distance between himself and the chair, grab Frederick by the head, and give one good *twist*—

No.

He wasn't the type of person who could hurt, let alone kill, another human being if they were defenseless. That was at his core, and part of the reason he had become an EOD tech in the Army was to *stop* those kinds of killings. Plus, there were a lot of other things riding on his behavior than just his own vendetta. And as much as a part of him wanted nothing more than to see Frederick's haggard face go slack with death, he wanted to stop whatever the Reborn were doing with the DMT a whole lot more.

"Alright then," Frederick continued, evidently satisfied that Dev wasn't going to give into his more primal urges… at least not yet. He put both hands on the armrests of the recliner and pushed himself to his feet, waving off Aleksandr when he moved to try and help him. "None of that." Standing up, he and Dev were about the same height; it was disconcerting, since the last time they saw each other, that hadn't been the case. "Come on. There's something I want you to see."

"*Father*." Aleksandr sounded like he'd barely kept himself from shouting the word, and when Dev glanced at him, he looked equal parts annoyed and perturbed. "Are you *sure* that's a good idea?"

"Here's what I'm sure of," Frederick replied, bringing an absent hand up to rub at his chest through the thermal shirt he wore. The first few buttons were undone, showing the edges of a starburst scar, from the bullet that Dev had thought drilled through his heart… along with what he recognized after a half-second delay as a chemotherapy port. "Everything in this world happens for a reason. If God had wanted me to die the night Adam shot me, I would have. But He didn't, and I didn't, and I believe I have just enough time left on this earth to try and make amends." For a moment, his expression hardened. "Plus, the Reborn need a leader to guide them after I'm gone. And we both know that's not *you*, is it, Aleksandr?"

Redness flared in Aleksandr's pale face, but he didn't protest. Instead, he looked down at his boots for a moment, then turned and headed for the door. Evidently, he intended to accompany them wherever they were going, because he stopped to wait for them on the porch. Meanwhile, Frederick looked at Dev for a long moment before taking slow, measured steps in the same direction.

That didn't leave Dev much of a choice but to follow his father.

~***~

"You know, for religious fanatics, these guys are pretty boring," Lottie said to Flynn, pitching her voice low so as to not be overheard. They were sitting with their backs against a mighty pine tree that had to be at least three hundred years old, their parabolic microphones pointed toward the circuitous route the guards took around the outside of the Reborn compound. "All they talk about is the usual shit—fucking, fighting, and in the case of that one dude, fungus."

"Don't remind me." Flynn shuddered dramatically, disrupting the dusting of snow that had accumulated on his coat in the time they'd been still. "I didn't think it was possible to wanna puke just from a description of somebody's toe jam, but I guess I was wrong." He tapped the comm in his ear, frowning when all either of them continued to hear was static. "You don't think Tara and Eileen got made somehow, do you?"

"I sure as hell hope not," Lottie replied, squinting up into the dusky sky. "No cell service out here, so they're the only connection we've got to HQ. Plus, *if* they got caught, it would be by fuckers from the Reborn, and that... would be *very* ugly." She didn't like to contemplate the idea of Eileen—smart-mouthed, cocky but not in an off-putting way, gorgeous Eileen—at the mercy of people like the ones Dev grew up with. "Let's assume they're busy."

Before Flynn could respond—and most likely to wonder what they could be busy with that would be more important than the mission at hand—their comms crackled to life, and Tara's voice filtered through: "Guys? You there?"

"We're here," Flynn confirmed, sitting up a little straighter. "What's wrong?"

Quickly, Tara filled them in on Eileen's theory regarding Blakely Manor's role in the DMT quandary, and Lottie had to admit that it made some sense. "But here's the problem," Tara continued once she paused to take a breath. "I've lost contact with Kaja's comm, and her cell is turned off. I'm trying to turn it on remotely, but I think there's something out there blocking service. David and Diana went with her, so did Wolfe and Scarlett, and I can't reach any of them—

not even Diana, and she stayed in the car. I was texting with her until about ten minutes ago, when she stopped responding."

"*Fuck*, this is bad." Lottie was always one to say what the group was collectively thinking out loud. She squeezed her gloved hands together so hard the leather squeaked. "I can't believe I'm suggesting this, but should we call the cops? Staties, maybe?"

"Charlotte, rule one of doing illegal or extralegal things for a living is that you never, *ever* involve the police, even if they have a cute nickname," Eileen said, and while she tried to sound like her usual chipper, upper-crust self, it fell flat. "I'm afraid I've cocked up rather brutally here, everyone." Quieter: "I didn't want to be right."

"Everyone who went out there is resourceful as hell," Flynn said, clearly aiming for optimism. He was a natural optimist, unlike Lottie and Dev, but even he seemed to be struggling. "They'll find a way out of whatever mess they're in. Besides, callin' in the cavalry could just get them in more trouble."

"You're right," Tara agreed, letting out a harsh sigh. "I guess we have to wait, at least for a while. God, I'm not a good waiter."

Lottie snorted. "I don't think any of us—" She cut herself off, goosebumps rising on her skin and a chill running up her spine. She tilted her head and put a hand on Flynn's shoulder, rising slowly and noiselessly from her seated position. *Someone's here*, her hindbrain whispered, the oldest part of her crawling out of the darkness to play. *You can't see them, but they see you.*

Just as she looked at Flynn to confirm he felt the change in the air around them too, the softest *whoosh* of sound reached her ears and pain blossomed in the side of her neck. She tried to raise a hand to the spot, but her arm flopped back down to her side, the world warping in front of her like a funhouse mirror. "Tranquilizer," she slurred, watching as Flynn staggered a step forward before landing on his knees in the snow, then falling face first into the brush. A dart stuck out from the skin directly over his jugular. "*Shit.*"

Lottie dropped like a puppet with its strings cut, bouncing off Flynn's shoulder in a way that would've been painful had she had any feeling left in her body. The last thing she saw was two pairs of combat boots approaching their position, and then she floated off into a dreamless sleep.

~***~

Chapter Twenty-Three

Dev ran.

He would continue running for a good portion of his life, but at the time, all he knew was that he had to get away from the flashing lights and the swarming cultists and the way Dani had looked at him with wild eyes, drew her gun, and screamed at him to *go, Adam, RUN!*

The woods enveloped him like they were embracing an old friend, but he didn't pause behind a tree or hide in the open pit graves that housed their desiccated farm animals. Instead, he kept running, getting scratched by stray limbs and tripped up by obstacles he couldn't fully make out. It was similar to the day when Dani had shot her gun in the air and he and the other children had run for their collective lives, except now he was alone. No Minnie. No Teddy. Not even Dani.

He heard the word in time with his wild heartbeat: *Alone. Alone. Alone.*

Dev burst through the tree line and on to the emergency road that he had only caught glimpses of while learning to hunt deer or forage for mushrooms. It was crowded with vehicles equipped with flashing lights, which blinded him almost immediately, their oscillating colors migraine-inducing after being in near-total darkness. Then there was shouting, and men and women in uniform with their weapons drawn, pointing at him, telling him to *put your hands up, put your goddamn hands up right the fuck now*, and he did, falling to his knees in the dirt from a combination of exhaustion and fear. The running was over for the moment, but Dev knew in his bones—even as he was getting patted down and half-dragged to what he vaguely recognized from old books as an ambulance—that it would start again, probably sooner than he imagined.

And now there would be no one to save him but himself.

Chapter Twenty-Four

Kaja dragged in a ragged breath as she was shocked awake by a tidal wave of ice-cold water being thrown over her whole body. She had been stripped down to her dress and tights, no coat or snow boots, and she knew before she opened her eyes that her weapons were gone. She was tied to a wooden chair, thick coils of rope wound around her wrists and ankles, and as she shook a dripping curtain of hair away from her face, she spotted David a few feet away, in much the same predicament. He was also coughing up cold water and cussing, and missing his outer layer of clothing as well as his weapons.

"Oh good, you're finally awake," a woman with a thick Russian accent said, and it took Kaja a half-second to recognize her as Doctor Elena Ivanova, sister to Mikael Ivanov and the mastermind behind Rapture, also known as the party drug from hell. She was relatively unremarkable in appearance, with mousy brown hair and a face like a hatchet, but Kaja knew from everything she'd read that the good doctor was just as cunning and cruel as her brother. "I was starting to think the stun guns worked a bit too well."

"Fuck you, crazy bitch," was David's response to that, causing Kaja to groan. The last time they'd been kidnapped together (weird that it had happened twice), he'd chosen the role of Bad Victim without consulting her first, which led to him getting smacked around a bunch while Kaja tried to find a way out of their predicament. This time he looked at Kaja incredulously, really hamming it up. "What? You *don't* think she's a cu—"

Ivanova took two quick steps in David's direction and punched him square in the face, the *crunch* of his cartilage audible in the room. "That is not a nice word," she chided, wagging her finger as she backed away again, avoiding the fountain of blood David tried to spit in her direction. "And here I was told you were not that kind of man, David Wolfe. That you are more like your son." A smirk. "Well, one of them, anyway. The one that killed those he could justify because they were in a uniform, rather than the one who killed for pleasure."

Kaja was busy surreptitiously testing the strength of her bonds, but she saw the moment David's anger went from manufactured to genuine as Ivanova brought up Wolfe and David's other son, Josh— the late serial killer known as the Mass Art Murderer. When he spoke again, his voice was hard and frosty: "What do you want from us?"

"What I want is quite simple," Ivanova replied genially, beginning to pace the room between the two hulking orderlies she had brought with her; each of them hung on to now-empty buckets that had previously been full of water. "I have two questions for you. Whoever answers them first in a truthful manner will walk out of here alive and relatively unharmed. The person that does not... well, let me say that what we will do to you will not hold a candle to what we did to the pretty spy with the ugly mind that came here looking for trouble." She meant Diana, obviously, and was doing her damnedest to rile David up. "Now, to my questions. The first one is: who stole the formula for Rapture? It was taken from this place last year."

"How the hell would we know that?" David drew Ivanova's attention back to him right as she was about to move toward Kaja, who was now trying to rock her chair in an attempt to break it. "And why would we care? I'm CIA, and she heads up an organization that doesn't exist on paper. Do you really think either of us give a damn about your crappy club drug gone apeshit?"

"No, I do not," Ivanova snapped, her hands slamming down on the backrest behind David's head, on either side of him, hard enough to make him flinch. "But you know what I *do* think? I *think* your son had something to do with it. Him and that blonde bitch, and Codreanu's faggot son." She took in a deep breath through her nose and stepped away again, turning toward an instrument cart that was nestled against the tile wall. In fact, the more Kaja thought about it, the more she realized the room they were in looked like some sort of operating suite, complete with a drain in the floor. "But, given the fact that you were a *very* absent father, perhaps he does not tell you secrets, hmm?"

David glanced at Kaja, who shook her head as subtly as she could; no way to get free, not without help. That caused him to sigh, flexing his arms against his own bonds, much to the chagrin of the orderlies; for a guy David's age, he was in incredible shape. "Yeah, yeah, I'm not gonna win any dad of the year awards. What's your second question?"

"My second question is for you," Ivanova said as she turned back toward them, zeroing in on Kaja. Something metallic glimmered in her right hand—a scalpel, maybe? "Did you tell your team that it was *you* who initiated the transfer of funds to YK4 as payment for their thievery of the DMT, and not some nameless Russian gangsters? Or did you want their simple minds to be comforted by the idea that everything just *happened* to fall into place that would allow Adam Devereux to solve the mystery of his father… and for *you* to find out what the Reborn are plotting with that scumbag, Sidorov?"

Kaja went very still. "Go to hell," she spat, but it must've been a half-second too late, because David was staring at her with wide eyes. She didn't deny Ivanova's accusation because she couldn't. The words she said next sounded like they came from someone else: "I hope Sidorov deepens his foothold here and skins you and your brother alive. You both deserve it for the things you've done."

Ivanova's expression darkened and she stalked forward, scalpel raised in one hand while the other grabbed Kaja by the jaw. "*Suka*," she growled, squeezing Kaja's bones together so hard that something in her face popped. The tip of the scalpel hovered dangerously close to her left pupil. "I will cut out your miserable eyes and watch you bleed to death, you fucking—"

A deafening noise echoed through the room, causing everyone to flinch violently. It took Kaja a few seconds to place what it was: a fire alarm.

She smiled.

And bit down on Ivanova's hand as hard as she could.

The doctor shrieked in pain and dropped the scalpel reflectively, boxing Kaja on the ear to try and get her to let go. One of the orderlies stepped forward to help her while the other made for the door, either to check on the reason for the alarm or to get help. He opened it and promptly got his head blown off his shoulders by Diana, the barrel of her gun a yawning black hole. His corpse hit the floor like a felled tree and she stepped over it, her pistol barking twice more as she shot the other orderly in the chest. Center mass, dead before he hit the ground... and then she set her sights on Ivanova.

"*You*," Diana growled out, more venom in her voice than Kaja could recall hearing in recent memory—not since Diana was much younger and just being taught the ways of proper spy craft (or as David called it: How Not to Always be an Assassin 101). She aimed her gun at Ivanova's head, her face gone blank and cold. "I cannot wait for your brother to come here and find your rotting corpse." She didn't give Ivanova a chance to respond before she pulled the trigger. The doctor's brain matter splattered into Kaja's lap as she fell to the floor, lifeless as a discarded toy. "What a cunt."

David let out a strangled laugh. "Now, now, that's a bad word." He wriggled. "Can you get us out of these?"

"Yes, and we have to hurry," Diana replied, stowing her gun in the holster at the small of her back. She traded it for a wicked-looking dagger that she extracted from the top of her right boot. "I left Wolfe and Scarlett upstairs—somehow they got in here and one of them pulled the fire alarm, but that brought the other orderlies out to play." As if on cue, more noises drifted in through the open door; the yelling and thudding that usually accompanied a fight. She cut David free first, then Kaja, frowning when she saw the blood dripping from Kaja's chin. "You are okay, yes?"

"Not mine," Kaja said, bending to spit Ivanova's blood on the floor before she stood on shaky legs. She found she couldn't meet David's eye. "Let's get out of here before the cops show up."

"Yeah," David agreed, his gaze a brand on the back of her neck as he followed her and Diana to the door. "Let's do that."

~***~

Just when Eileen thought all hope might be lost: a spark.

It came in the form of her phone vibrating off the edge of the bed and on to the floor, startling both her and Tara out of their respective depressive catatonia. Eileen scrambled for the device and dropped it once, swearing loudly before recovering it and swiping to answer the call and put it on speaker. "Kaja? Are you alright?"

"More or less," was their boss's answer. Eileen felt some of the tension drain from her body... but that didn't last long. "You were right, Eileen. And you were wrong." A sigh. "I need to tell you something—the whole team, actually. What's their status?"

"Not good," Tara said, rubbing a hand over her face. "We lost contact with Lottie and Flynn about twenty minutes ago. I found more information on a shell corp connected to Aleksandr Lichtenson—it was the organization that purchased Blakely Manor. Then I started looking to see if I could figure out who paid off YK4, but I kept running into dead ends."

"There's a reason for that." Kaja's tone was tight and grim, and in the background of the call Eileen could make out low conversation and the sound of an engine; Kaja was in a vehicle, probably on her way back to headquarters. "I was the one who paid YK4 to steal the DMT and bring it to the auction in Hungary. Lichtenson's shell corp had previously made shady purchases of drugs at similar events overseas, and I thought I could bait the Reborn into showing their faces."

Eileen stared first at her phone, then at Tara, whose expression mirrored her own disbelief. For someone who nearly always knew what to say, Eileen was amazed to find that she was rendered speechless for several seconds. "*What*? So... so you sent us after the DMT *knowing* Flynn and Dev wouldn't be able to stop it from getting nicked?"

Kaja made a noise that was the equivalent of a verbal shrug. "I was fairly certain. There were some variables I couldn't predict, obviously, but it was no more dangerous than any other mission I've sent them on in the past."

"But *why*?" Tara pressed, her elbows on her knees and her head in her hands. "Why would you do that?"

"Precisely because of what we just discovered at Blakely Manor," Kaja replied. "The Reborn are in bed with power-hungry people who have little self-control and even fewer morals. They've been on the intelligence community's radar for a long time, even before that stupid docudrama came out. Just because it wasn't known whether Frederick survived the raid or not didn't make them any less of a threat. Plus, this is personal for Dev—he needs closure, one way or another."

Eileen took a moment to process that, acutely aware of the room tilting around her like she was sloshed. She shut her eyes and took a deep breath in through her nose, letting it out slowly. "What power-hungry people are you talking about? Who are the Reborn working with—was I right, is it the Spectres?"

"Not just the Spectres, but Valeriya herself," Kaja confirmed, and while Eileen had half-expected to hear her theory become reality, that didn't mean she enjoyed it. "David and I overheard her talking to her father on a landline right before we got jumped. It sounds like he was the one who brought the Reborn into things, and she disagreed with his decision."

"Dissention in the ranks, huh? Interesting." Tara checked her computer again and frowned, biting the inside of her cheek. "Still nothing on comms from Lottie and Flynn. And without them, we have no way of communicating with Dev or Teddy."

"Wait," Kaja urged, but something in Eileen rankled at that. Where did she get off, telling them what to do after manipulating this entire situation? "Lottie and Flynn are both perfectly capable of getting out of a less than ideal situation. The tactical team is on standby, but we can't go barging in there without—"

"No." Eileen's interjection was firm as she got to her feet, Tara rising too, albeit much more slowly. She squeezed the phone in her hand so hard her knuckles whitened, the case creaking under the pressure. "They're either in there alone, and they've got no idea that you used them, or they're dead. You're right, we can't send in the tac team—but we can't stay here and do nothing either."

"Eileen, *stand down*." Kaja's voice got stringent enough that the hum of background conversation on her end of the call went silent. "That is a direct order."

Eileen stared down at the phone screen again for a long moment, and then swiped over the button to hang up. The device began to vibrate with another call almost instantaneously but she ignored it, shoving it under one of the pillows on the bed. She grabbed her coat, shrugging into the shearling and pulling a black beanie down over her flaming hair. "Fuck that, I'm going to find them." She looked at Tara. "You don't have to come with me."

"Like you said, fuck that." Tara shoved her rig back into her backpack and exchanged it for a prescription bottle. She swallowed a pill dry, then yanked on her own coat. "Let's get out of here before Kaja sics the tac team on us."

~***~

Despite the evidence to the contrary, there was a part of Dev that thought Frederick and Aleksandr might be taking him someplace more isolated just so they could kill him—they'd certainly put more distance between the common area of the compound and themselves. But the more he examined that possibility, the easier it was to discard; if they wanted him dead, they'd capitalize on the moment and do it in front of everyone. So he kept his head high and his eyes focused on Frederick's back, a part of him in a permanent state of disbelief. His father was alive, but he was dying, and in his peripherals Dev could've sworn he saw blurry shapes and indistinct faces, like the shadows or spirits of his childhood competition come home to roost.

"This is it," Frederick declared as they came upon a large swath of ground, perhaps several yards in diameter, that had been cleared of snow and other debris. Sticking out of the dirt in the center of the space was a domed hatch, sort of like the ones Dev had seen on submarines during a brief stint in San Diego. It even had an old-fashioned crank wheel on top, which Aleksandr moved to start turning without direction from Frederick. "Aleksandr will go first, then you, then me."

Dev nodded mutely, eyes darting over to the tree line. Looking directly at it he didn't see any ghosts, of course, but his heart held the faintest hope that he'd catch a glimpse of Flynn or Lottie, even as his head told him that was foolish. He knew they were out there, not a doubt in his mind about it, but their whole purpose was to observe until Dev needed extraction; then they had a code word that would hopefully be picked up on their parabolic mics. If not... well, Dev had done his fair share of screaming in the past, so wailing for help was always an option.

With a grunt and a final shove of the wheel, Aleksandr opened the hatch and began descending a ladder. Dev followed him as instructed, noting that while he had expected a dark and damp space beneath the earth, that wasn't the case. The space he climbed down into was the size of a large closet, with walls made of bedrock and a concrete floor. A fluorescent light hung overhead, and the only thing inside the room besides the ladder was a large, hermetically sealed door—he recognized it for what it was because they had very similar doors in the laboratory at Project Renegade. This one was sealed by a biometric lock that required both a palm and retina scan in order to open from the outside.

It was Aleksandr who stepped forward to scan his hand and eye, and that made Dev blurt out a question to Frederick that had been on his mind since he stepped into the house: "What's wrong with you?"

Frederick looked at him for a moment, then focused on the door, hands clasped behind his back. "Cancer," he replied, succinct in a way that he never was when Dev was a child. "Pancreatic, to be precise. When I began to show symptoms, the nurse here insisted I seek Western medicine, but it was too late. It's spread everywhere— my liver, my colon, and it's begun chipping away at my bones." A thin smile. "The only reason I'm alive is the grace of God and a cocktail of extremely strong, extremely costly drugs."

Dev frowned. "So… that's what this is?" He gestured at the secure door as its tumblers slid back and it swung inward, revealing more concrete floor and exploded rock walls, which appeared to go on for a short distance before bending around a corner. "This bunker… it's not for the end times, is it?" Frederick's silence and Aleksandr's glare spoke volumes, so Dev pressed, "Is it for research? To try and find a cure for your cancer?"

"Not exactly," Frederick hedged, motioning for Dev to lead the way even though he didn't know where he was going. Aleksandr fell in behind him, and Frederick brought up the rear. Behind them, the door automatically swung closed, locks snapping shut with all the finality of a tomb sealing. "What we're doing… curing cancer would be a side effect. A bonus, if you will. Our purpose is much grander."

"Grander… than curing cancer?" Dev asked slowly, glancing around as he walked. He was less than comfortable with having Aleksandr's gaze boring into the back of his skull, but it wasn't like he had a choice in the matter. Where the bunker's corridor bent he followed, coming into a large open space that housed rows of bunk beds, similar to what he remembered from every Army barracks he ever slept in. It was decorated about as nicely as an Army barracks too, which was to say not at all. Beyond the room was another corridor, this one branching off in two different directions. "What could be grander than that? It's killing you, and it kills millions of people every year."

"Survival," Frederick replied, and now that Dev knew to listen for it, he heard a slight hitch to his breathing that came in time with the steps he took. "*Survival*, Adam, has always been the point. You escaped into the outside world, lived in it for years now—you fought for this miserable, sinful country and almost died for it. Someday, very soon, it and the other powers that be are going to blow each other to smithereens. And since you left, I've come to realize the only way we can hope to persevere is not by simply saying we're better than them… but by *becoming* better than them."

Dread was a living thing, reaching up from the pit of Dev's stomach to bury its claws in his throat. Whatever Frederick was talking about, it was enough to put that maniacal fire back in his voice—the one that used to whip the congregation into a frenzy every Sunday. "What do you mean?"

"Keep walking and we'll show you," Aleksandr snapped, shoving Dev between his shoulder blades so he stumbled into the right-hand fork of the corridor. A quick glance told him the other direction led to a kitchen and perhaps some kind of communal living area. "This way."

"What is this?" Dev couldn't disguise his shock as the stone walls abruptly turned to shiny white sheetrock, the floor shifting to linoleum. There was another door dead ahead—also locked from the outside and showing a glimpse of a laboratory-like setting through a small window—but all this one took to open was the tap of a keycard, provided by Aleksandr. He shoved Dev through the door first, and he quickly took in rows of metal exam tables and chairs, all outfitted with stations full of medical equipment... and restraints. "What the fuck are you *doing* in here?"

"Like I said, we're gonna show you." Aleksandr shoved Dev again, harder this time, so that he stumbled and wound up falling into one of the unforgiving chairs, which was similar to something one might see at the dentist. Unlike the dentist, however, this chair had wrist and ankle cuffs that Aleksandr wasted no time snapping into place, as well as a strap that went across Dev's forehead, keeping him painfully upright. "I should get you a mouth guard— wouldn't want you breaking any of those pearly whites."

Dev tried and failed to brute force his way out of the restraints, panic lighting up the base of his brain. He turned wide eyes on his father, mouth gone dry and body leeching sweat. "Let me go."

"Why would you want me to do that?" Frederick seemed genuinely puzzled, and then appeared to have a realization. "Of course—I haven't actually explained anything. You know Aleksandr, he does like to get right to the point." He took a seat on a nearby rolling stool, leaning on the neighboring exam table to keep himself upright. "Long story short, we're conducting research on behalf of a very wealthy benefactor. As you might remember from your childhood, our residents come from all walks of life, including the fields of science and medicine. And as you've probably figured out, dimethyltryptamine plays a large role in our work, but its effects are... less than ideal, in its native state." He took the rubber mouth guard that Aleksandr handed to him and turned it over in his fingers as he talked. "Our goal is to refine the effects of DMT into something greater. Currently, we're experimenting with a combination of drugs that has a... decaying effect on the memory, acting as a reset button of sorts in some folks. That aspect was effective on dear Theodore, but it doesn't work on everyone." He shrugged. "More refinement is necessary before it could be given to someone like me who's already ill, or before the effects on the memory would be permanent. I hear our Russian friends are working on that end of things... but either way, we've decided to call it *Perditor*. I'm sure you remember your Latin, don't you?"

"Destroyer," Dev whispered, eyes flicking away from Frederick for a moment to watch Aleksandr set up an IV pole with a fresh bag of saline. Despite the mighty yank he gave with his arm, he couldn't stop Aleksandr from inserting the IV catheter into the crook of his elbow. He saw now with frightening clarity exactly what was going to happen to him. "What does it do?"

"Haven't you been listening?" Aleksandr snapped, unlatching something behind Dev's chair—it sounded like a metal case. When he came into Dev's sightline again, he was flicking the bubbles out of a syringe filled with a pale green liquid. Apparently satisfied, he inserted the needle into the IV line's access port and pushed down the plunger, smiling all the while. "It makes you stronger, faster— but you know what? It doesn't matter. You're about to find out anyway."

~***~

Chapter Twenty-Five

Dev ran, but he couldn't run forever.

He lived on the fringes of society from the ages of twelve to seventeen, traveling all over the United States with little more than a backpack and a knife to his name (not a gun, *never* a gun). He quickly learned what types of people were helpful, as well as the ones that weren't, and how to select an easy mark. The ones that were dangerous he avoided when could and hurt when he couldn't, but was careful not to kill them—a body was much more reliable a memory, at least as far as a court of law was concerned. He added to his survival skills, combining the ones he already knew to form new ones, such as pick-pocketing and burglary. He got caught a few times, of course, but he was able to squeak out of it—literally in one case, when he'd slipped his skinny body between the bars of his holding cell.

One day, however, the stash of luck he'd scraped together ran out. He selected the wrong mark in a little town in Tennessee, got too greedy, and stuck his foot in a bear trap. The man who caught him was well within his rights to blow Dev's head off with his double-barreled shotgun, but instead he called the county sheriff. As it happened, Dev had taken *just* enough in valuables from the man's home to elevate his laundry list of charges from state to federal. With that type of scrutiny came questions, the kind about the Reborn and the murder of his father, derived from former members squealing to the law in an ever-growing circle that bled from the direction of Bozeman. And in a stifling hot courtroom in Memphis to the backing drone of ceiling fans and yawning lawyers, Adam Devereux was given a choice.

Go to jail, or join the Army.

He chose the latter.

~***~

Chapter Twenty-Six

Flynn woke up with a pounding in his head and a mouth that tasted like the inside of somebody's ass. Not exactly new territory for him, but not his favorite thing to revisit either. When he pried his crusty eyelids apart he was greeted by the sight of Lottie's back, clad in a long-sleeved black tactical shirt; both of them had been stripped of their outerwear, including their boots and socks, as well as all of their weapons. They were lying on a concrete floor, and when Flynn rolled from his side to his back, he discovered that the ceiling above him was held up by support beams not unlike those found in a mine. Three of the walls around them were bedrock, save for one, which was made up of iron bars—a holding cell, and a small one at that, since the whole space was barely wider than Flynn was tall.

"Fuck," Lottie groaned, rolling over too, slinging an arm over her eyes to block the nagging fluorescent lights. "I feel like somebody sat on me. And by somebody, I mean... a car or something, not a person."

"You feel like you got run over, I think is what you mean." Flynn sat up slowly, every muscle in his body protesting at once. He carefully dragged himself backward until he found something to lean against—a cot, which their captors hadn't bothered to utilize for one of their unconscious bodies. "And you would know, since you've gotten hit by like three cars."

"Four," Lottie corrected, following Flynn's lead and scraping herself over to lean on the cot. "Although I don't really count the Mini-Cooper. That was like getting smacked with a newspaper."

"See, then it's three." Flynn did a careful once-over of himself, and other than his head hurting something awful and a sore on his neck, he wasn't in terrible shape. "Seriously, though, you okay?"

"I'll make it," Lottie replied. She glanced around slowly, probably trying not to barf, and then focused on Flynn. "Where the hell are we?"

"Some kind of bunker, would be my guess," Flynn said, now taking the several precautions necessary to stand. He used the cot for balance as he got his feet underneath him, then offered a hand up to Lottie once he was sure he wasn't going to fall down again. "You know, I knew these people were fuckin' nutjobs, but I didn't think they were the bunker-building type of nutjobs."

"That is a special type of nutjob," Lottie agreed once she was standing too, peering beyond the bars to what looked like a kitchen. "This… is not where I would expect a holding cell to be."

"My guess is they only had so much time to build, or a very tight materials budget." Flynn grabbed a bar in both hands and tugged experimentally—solid like the rocks around them, didn't move an inch. "Damn. They bought the good shit, at least."

"I don't remember Dev saying anything about a bunker whenever he talked about the Reborn." Lottie was frowning, pressing herself against the bars to see as far as she could. "Did he mention it to you?"

"He mentioned a lotta things." Dev used to give Flynn bits and pieces of his past as they laid awake together just outside their barracks in Afghanistan, backs in the dirt and eyes on the endless stars. Flynn couldn't sleep because being back in the Sandbox reminded him of the first time he was there, and Dev… well, Dev didn't sleep much at all. Once he started hearing what Dev had been through, Flynn didn't have to be a genius like him to figure out why he was an insomniac. "End of days, death, destruction, the whole nine yards. But no, he never said shit about a bunker. Which probably means it wasn't here when he was."

Lottie opened her mouth to speak, but froze as a hair-raising scream pierced the air.

Flynn would've known that sound anywhere.

It chilled him to his bones, then lit a fire inside him comparable to the heat of the sun. The last time he'd had cause to hear it was when he and Dev had been captured and tortured by an Al Qaeda splinter group. He knew exactly how much pain it took to get Dev to make a noise like that, and once the shock of hearing it again wore off, Flynn was ready and willing to kill an army to get to him.

He threw himself into the bars, rattling them in place. "Hey!" He had no idea if there was anyone guarding them, but they were about to find out. "*Hey*! What the fuck is going on out there?!"

Lottie didn't try to stop him, nor did she join in; instead, she flattened herself against the wall nearest the cell door's hinges, where anyone approaching would have a difficult time seeing her. It was a good move, since a second later a bedraggled-looking man in camouflage came into the kitchen. He had a pistol in a holster around his leg but didn't draw it, which was a mistake on his part—he might've stood half a chance if he'd made a different choice.

Flynn didn't bother with pleasantries, sticking both arms out through the bars and grabbing the guard by the front of his flak jacket. He yanked him forward and smashed him face-first into the bars until he fell unconscious, then held his limp body upright while Lottie snatched the keys off his belt as well as his gun. She handed Flynn the gun and flipped through the keys quickly, selecting the one that looked most likely to fit the lock in their cell door. A turn and they were free, albeit with no precise idea where they were or how many enemies were around.

"Just like old times, huh?" Flynn asked as he checked the load and magazine in the Glock 17 he held. While Flynn and Lottie had never served together on their respective tours of the Middle East, they both knew what it was like to be in the shit as Special Forces. "All we're missing is some pointy-headed douchebag from D.C. screaming in our ears."

Lottie slotted the sharp ends of the keys between her fingers so they stuck out like claws and shot him a slightly manic look paired with a smile that was all teeth. "I don't know about you, but I prefer this version."

That was all the go-ahead Flynn needed to sidestep their downed guard and start looking for Dev.

~***~

Tara was pissed off.

She was pissed off that they lost contact with everyone, she was pissed off that Kaja had gone behind their backs even if her intentions were somewhat good, and most of all, she was pissed off that she couldn't fucking walk right to save her goddamn life. She'd dry-swallowed another painkiller once she and Eileen were in the SUV, but she didn't dare to take anything more and now that they'd ditched their ride to walk the rest of the way to the Reborn compound, her spine felt like a snap glow stick trapped in a recalcitrant five-year-old's fist.

"I can hear you growling to yourself," Eileen said, pitching her voice low as they picked their way through the dense forest. They were using an honest-to-god paper map of the area that the motel gave out for free to find their way, marked with an X to signify where the compound was according to satellite. They both carried flashlights with duct tape wrapped around most of the front, so that only a sliver of light could escape for them to see where they were putting their feet. "And as much as I appreciate your effort to scare off the local bear population by asserting your dominance, I'm rather afraid any people that are around will hear you too."

"I don't give a shit," Tara muttered, but she forced down her frustration and refocused on the task at hand. She also stopped growling and swept her muted flashlight around quickly. There, a metallic gleam: a fence, tall and topped with barbed wire. "Looks like we found it. But how do we get in?"

"I actually have an idea about that." Eileen folded up the map and stuffed it in her back pocket, trading it for the utility knife that Dev usually carried. He'd had to leave it behind and Tara hadn't seen Eileen snatch it up, but that didn't mean anything since Eileen's whole shtick was that she could literally steal candy from a baby. Now she flicked through the various tools contained in the body of the knife until she found what she was looking for: a pair of wire cutters, albeit fairly small ones. "Keep watch for me?"

Tara nodded in the relative darkness, then rolled her eyes at herself when she realized Eileen couldn't see that. "Sure, no problem." She drew her gun and held it down along her thigh, moving her eyes in quadrants through the trees like Flynn had taught her—*a sniper sees life in fractions, but I hate math*, he'd said a long time ago, and while the statement was meant to be humorous, there had been an undercurrent of trauma there that was impossible to shake. "Why do you think she did it?"

"Hmm?" Eileen forced her way through the first hexagon of wire, twisting as she went to mitigate sharp ends that might snag on their clothes as they went through the hole she was creating. "Who did what now?"

"Kaja," Tara said, trying to keep the terseness she felt out of her voice. As the team's tech whiz, she was most often the one that worked side-by-side with their boss in the loft at headquarters. The news that Kaja had orchestrated at least part of the mission they were on now sat in her belly like a stone. "I keep thinking about it, and even if she had good intentions—wanting to find the Reborn, letting Dev get his closure... she still betrayed our trust."

With a grunt of effort, Eileen tore the fence in earnest, cutting through enough wires until she made a section that could be bent down toward the ground. "I know. But right now, all that matters is that we get everybody back in one piece, yeah? We can deal with Kaja and any ill feelings we have later on." She used her boot to hold down the cut section of fencing, crouching down to squeeze through the gap. "We're family, and that's what family does. Or so I've been told."

"I wonder what I missed, I guess," Tara said, following Eileen through the hole and swearing quietly when her fingertips grazed a sharp piece of metal, drawing blood. "And whether I would've missed it from anybody else who was trying to sabotage us. Finding out there was a mole from the Reborn working at Renegade was bad enough. Add in our boss going behind our backs... it just sucks."

"It does," Eileen agreed, putting away Dev's utility knife as they began picking their way through the trees, toward a vague source of light that looked like it might be a barn. They were near the place the Reborn kept their animals, then. "But here's a more pressing question: should we try and find dear Theodore? I'm sure they separated him from Dev, and he may be useful for navigating around this place."

"Can we trust him?" Tara asked, and not just because her trust was in short supply as of that moment. "We have no way of knowing if whatever they programmed into him is totally gone, or if he was just faking being normal again to get Dev here."

"I spoke with him before we touched down in Bozeman," Eileen told her, which was... not what Tara expected her to say. "I made it explicitly clear what I would do to him if he was planning on betraying us, or if he let anything beyond superficial harm happen to Dev." She paused, tilting her head. "Do you hear that?"

Tara listened hard, and her ears picked up distant sounds that she couldn't place at first, but then they snapped together like puzzle pieces. "Somebody's getting the shit beat out of them." There was a loud cry of pain, blubbered out in garbled Spanish. "Correction, *Teddy's* getting the shit beat out of him."

"It's times like this when I ask myself, WWDD?" When Tara stared at Eileen blankly, the redhead shrugged and clarified: "What Would Dev Do?"

Tara sighed. "He'd help. Come on."

~***~

Before Aleksandr shot the Reborn's DMT cocktail into Dev's arm, he thought he knew what pain was. After all, he was practically skinned alive at the ripe old age of twelve, and he was no stranger to torture. But this… this was different.

Time had no meaning anymore. He was a child, a teenager, and an adult all at the same time, strands of himself warped and woven together like the world's worst kind of rope candy. It felt as though each beat of his heart was not only circulating the poison in his veins, it was tearing him apart from the inside out. He was dimly aware of someone screaming, a throat-rending, never-ending wail, and it took him far too long to realize it was him.

Vaguely, he recognized voices—Aleksandr and his father, but also other voices, ones that were nice to him but in that moment were struck through with anger and fear. He couldn't remember how to open his eyes, but he managed to crack his lids enough to make out the shapes of Lottie and Flynn being manhandled by armored goons. They were both swearing and struggling, but the reality was that they were simply outnumbered. The last thing Dev made out before he began to seize was twin white coats sliding IVs into the arms of his friends, and then he was dragged under the spell of Destroyer and hurled into the abyss.

~***~

Chapter Twenty-Seven

Dev thought the Army wasn't so bad.

Well, only if you didn't mind getting shot at multiple times a day, roasting in the blazing sun, and having sand trapped in places sand should *never* be. But compared to growing up with the Reborn and then struggling to survive on his own, basic training and his first few weeks as an infantry grunt were a goddamn cakewalk. He hated the fact that he had to carry a gun, but his first assignment being lead dishwasher for the mess hall meant he hadn't seen too much action.

Until one fateful day when chaos erupted out by the tables, long after midday chow had ended. Dev dropped the wet plate in his hands and ran out front in time to see four men in bloodied fatigues carrying an even bloodier man between them, choking and gasping as he clutched at a wound to his chest. His white armband displayed a red cross, marking him as a medic, and Dev knew for a fact that the base medic was occupied with puking and shitting his guts out in the latrine after eating some bad tuna.

"What the fuck happened?" Dev asked, rushing over to the nearest relatively clean-looking table and clearing any detritus with his arm. "Put him down here, carefully."

"Sniper," the tallest of the men said, his shock of reddish-blond hair standing out against pale skin pinked by sunburn. His name patch read WOLFE, and Dev recognized the emblem on his sleeve—a Ranger. "I saw the flash but he was down before any of us could react. I think he got it in his lung."

"Shit." Dev's mind raced, and then he sprinted for the large first aid kit mounted on the wall next to the defibrillator. "Any of you have a pen?" He came back to the table, pawing through the kit for the single-use scalpel. When he got four shaking heads, he growled in frustration. "Whoever runs the fastest, go get one from the PX!" He pulled his utility knife from his pocket and flicked open the blade as the oldest of the group booked it out of the mess, slicing through what was left of the wounded man's uniform. He saw the name SHEFFIELD for an instant before he cut it in half. The entry wound was ugly to say the least, a yawning void with ragged edges, and when Dev felt around underneath his patient, there was no sign of an exit wound. "Good, okay, I can work with this."

"You a medic?" another of the soldiers asked; Dev vaguely recognized him, his brain placing him as an MP a second later. He must've been on the gate when they came in with the injured man. "Shouldn't you be wearing a band?"

Dev snorted. "Yeah, like it did this guy any good." He grabbed a small bottle of rubbing alcohol and dumped it unceremoniously on Sheffield's chest. The poor guy tried to scream but couldn't get enough air to do it, letting out a pathetic wheeze instead. "I'm just the dishwasher."

The older soldier returned to the mess in time to hear that—his name patch read WALKER—along with the base commander and a woman Dev recognized as an EOD technician or a bomb nerd, as they were called by enlisted men and officers alike. "I ain't never seen a dishwasher perform a miracle before, but there's no time like the present," Walker drawled as he handed over the pen Dev requested. He had to be at least fifteen years older than the men he came in with, but only wore a sergeant's stripes alongside a Delta Force crest. Interesting. "What're you gonna do with that?"

Dev felt his mouth flatten into a grim line. "I'm going to perform an emergency tracheotomy." He took the pen apart quickly, discarding everything except the outer plastic barrel, which he shoved in Wolfe's direction. "Pour rubbing alcohol through that. Don't touch anything you don't have to."

While Wolfe did that, Dev ripped open the packaging that surrounded the sterile scalpel. He slapped a portion of the thin crinkly plastic over the bullet wound, letting the blood act as glue to create a seal. The soldiers other than Wolfe and Walker had backed off, so Dev said to Walker, "You need to hold him down by the shoulders, *hard*. He's not going to like this."

"I don't think I'd like getting my chest cut open on a mess hall table either," their BC said, startling everyone. When Dev glanced over at him—not for permission, more to gauge his reaction—he nodded. "Go for it. He'll die if you don't."

Dev took in a deep breath—a luxury Sheffield couldn't afford—and sliced through the skin and muscle between two of Sheffield's ribs, making a cut that was only about an inch long. As predicted, the injured man tried to come up off the table, blue lips and all, but thankfully Walker was strong enough to restrain him. Putting the scalpel aside, Dev grabbed the pen barrel from Wolfe and jammed one end into the incision. Blood spurted out of the hollow tube for a beat too long, and Dev wondered if it was too late… but then, Sheffield took a gasping breath. And another, and more after that.

"Oh my god," Wolfe said, half in awe and half in disbelief. "You did it." He shook Dev by the shoulder, gripping his shirt to keep Dev upright when his knees went a little weak with relief. "You fucking *did it*!"

"Chopper's on its way to fly him to Landstuhl," the bomb nerd— JANSEN, her name patch read—informed them. She stood with her arms crossed over her chest, an intrigued gleam in her hazel eyes. Her brown hair was pulled back into a regulation bun so severe that it looked like it hurt. "What's your name, soldier?"

Dev wiped the blood on his hands off on his shirtfront and met her gaze. "Private Second Class Adam Devereux, ma'am."

"Well, Private Second Class Adam Devereux," Jansen said slowly, inclining her head, "you're quick on your feet, dexterous as hell, and way too smart to be washing dishes." She smiled at him. "How would you like to learn to disarm a bomb?"

~***~

Chapter Twenty-Eight

Eileen liked to think of herself as a lover, not a fighter. Or at the very least, a grifter and a con artist, but not someone who deliberately initiated physical conflict. She had found through previous experience that getting into an altercation with another individual or a group usually just ended in perfectly avoidable bloodshed that tended to attract attention from the wrong people, such as the police or the Feds.

There were no cops in the Reborn compound, and evidently there were no rules about literally kicking a man while he was down, either. Teddy was bleeding into the snow-crusted dirt and there were four armed people—three men and one woman—alternating between striking him with their boots and the butts of their rifles. He had rolled into the fetal position to protect himself but it didn't matter, steel toes continuing to make squelching contact with flesh and bone.

"I'll take the two on the left, you get the ones on the right," Eileen whispered to Tara, rotating her gun in her hand so she could wield it like a bludgeon. The other woman did the same, the matte black of her handgun incongruous with her manicure. "No shots, yeah? We want to keep this quiet."

Tara nodded and they split up, both bent low to the ground and moving as quietly as possible. Eileen had to stifle a wince as she listened to one of Teddy's ribs splinter before she could reach him, and then there was no time to feel sympathy because she was straightening up and smacking one of the goons in the back of the head as hard as she could. The second one barely had time to react as his friend crumpled to the ground gushing blood from his scalp, and was blindsided when the butt of Eileen's gun connected with his temple. She didn't look at Tara or the other two guards, intent on not fucking up her own plan, but she didn't need to worry; when she turned toward Teddy, the guards Tara had been assigned to take out were sprawled nearby, unconscious.

"Theodore, now's not the time to die," Eileen said, crouching down next to Teddy and putting her hand on his shoulder. He flinched away from her touch for a second before relaxing into it, realizing she wasn't someone there to hurt him. "I take it they didn't buy your story about breaking away on your own to kidnap Dev?"

"Not even a little bit," was Teddy's groaned response, rolling slowly on his back before turning his head to spit red into the dirt. One of his eyes was blackened and already swollen shut, but when he focused on Eileen with the other one, it was filled with a fiery anger. "Where's Dev?"

"We were hoping you'd know," Tara admitted, pain flickering across her face as she reached down to help Eileen get Teddy to his feet. Her nostrils flared as she took a deep breath, clearly trying to keep from cursing. "We lost contact with Flynn and Lottie a while ago, and since we don't know our way around here, we thought maybe you could help us find him. Or them. Whichever we stumble on first."

"There isn't a plan anymore." Eileen figured it was best to rip off the metaphorical band-aid. "As it turns out, the only reason we're here at all and you're not doing your best impression of the Manchurian candidate is because Kaja set up the DMT heist."

"*What?*" Teddy staggered in between the two women for a moment, until they got him to a tree he could lean against. "Jesus. *Fuck.* Okay, let me think." He raised a hand to rub his face, then seemed to decide that was a bad idea. "Aleksandr dragged Dev off to see Fath—*Frederick*, and he's been spending a lot of time at his house. It's on the outskirts of the compound, but I know the way from here."

"You aren't too concussed to be leading us around?" Tara asked, but instead of the skepticism Eileen expected to see on her face, there was only concern. Concern for *Teddy*. Oh, so it was like *that*, was it? "Also, if it comes down to it… are you going to be able to hurt these people? I'm sure you've lived with some of them for your whole life."

"Trust me, after that little stunt? I won't have a problem." Teddy's tone was grim, and he pushed himself off the tree so he could grab an AK-47 from one of the fallen guards. "Let's go."

They went.

It wasn't a long walk, nor was it a particularly complicated one. But as they approached Frederick's residence, it became clear that no one was inside. There was no light whatsoever coming through the windows, and Eileen's finely-honed instinct for burglary told her the place was empty. A quick search of the interior confirmed it, and almost implied that Frederick was ill, perhaps severely, which was something Teddy appeared to be unaware of before that moment.

"What the hell is happening?" he asked, seemingly to himself, his stolen gun slung over his shoulder, one hand cradling his broken rib. "Where could they have gone?"

"Again, kind of hoping you'd have an idea about that," Eileen said, chewing on the inside of her lip. Their circumstances were less than ideal, and getting progressively worse by the minute. "If they were going to execute him or something, I'm sure we would've heard a commotion by now."

"Okay, let's think," Tara said, squeezing her eyes shut. "Eileen's right—if Dev's head was on the chopping block, Frederick's entire flock would come running. So if that's not happening... what is?"

Teddy went very still. "There's... there's a bunker," he said slowly, like he was testing out the plausibility of the words as they left his mouth. "I wasn't supposed to know about it, but... I was chasing down a defector one day and stumbled across the construction site. They were putting in biometrics, blast doors... heavy-duty Cold War type stuff." His brow creased, dried blood flaking off his skin. "I don't think we could force our way *in*... but we might be able to make everyone inside come *out*."

"Color me intrigued." Eileen glanced around briefly, looking for some reassurance that they were alone, but the isolated darkness of the compound offered no solace. Any minute now, they could be attacked. "How would we do that?"

"I think it's powered by propane, like a lot of the stuff around here." Teddy scratched at the blood on his forehead, frowning at it like it offended him. "If we could figure out a way to sabotage the tanks, get the generators to turn off... the lack of electricity would make them come topside, right?"

"I've got no idea," Tara said, looking to Eileen, who tilted her head in silent agreement. "But it's the only plan we've got. So let's do it."

~***~

When Lottie woke up, she immediately turned her head to one side and vomited up everything she'd ever eaten. Or at least it felt that way, given the amount of stomach acid that burned her throat on its way up. Her whole body felt sore, like she'd run a marathon while she was unconscious, and she had sweated through her clothes. She had vague memories of getting outnumbered by Reborn thugs and dragged into a room that looked like something out of a bad medical horror movie, then… nothing, not after a syringe was shoved deep into a vein. Gasping, she rolled away from the puddle of sick and on to her front, then pushed herself to her feet.

The world was tilted and wobbling around her, but she tried her best to take in her surroundings. She was still in the bunker—that much was obvious from the low ceiling and the narrow room—but this was a different space, not the holding cell and not the mad scientist's laboratory she and Flynn had been dragged into, where Dev had been screaming in agony and thrashing all over the place. Her ears rang even now with how loud his cries had been, and since her own throat felt like sandpaper, she guessed she had done some screaming of her own. This room contained nothing but an observation window set into one wall, with what she assumed was a locked door next to it.

Sensing a presence behind her, she turned quickly (*very* bad for her equilibrium) and thrust a fist into the face of her attacker, but it was caught and she was quickly yanked into a headlock. That lasted for all of a second, because her "attacker" turned out to be Flynn, who looked and sounded just as shitty as Lottie felt. "What the hell happened?" he slurred out, letting her go and leaning against the nearest wall for support. "Christ, I feel like my head's gonna explode."

Lottie caught movement in her peripheral vision, and when it resolved into—improbably, impossibly—Dev aiming a *handgun* at them, she swallowed more vomit. "It still might—*duck!*"

She and Flynn hit the floor at the same time that three bullets slammed into the wall behind them, the noise deafening in the small space. "Dev! What the fuck are you doing?!" Flynn yelled, and had to roll away from a vicious kick for his trouble, more bullets pounding into the space he'd occupied a second before. At Lottie, he hollered, "What's wrong with him?"

"I don't know!" was Lottie's response as she scrambled up and tackled Dev from the side while his focus was still on Flynn. He let out a grunt as his body impacted the floor, but appeared to be otherwise unaffected, trying to swing his gun hand around to aim at her even as she pushed at his arm and all but shrieked in his face: "Dev? *Dev!*"

"They must've given him somethin' like what they dosed Teddy with," Flynn realized aloud, scrambling over to pin Dev's arm to the floor and wrench the gun from his fingers. "But why didn't it do this to us?" The grip left a reddened checkerboard pattern in its wake, and Flynn earned a slug to the jaw for his trouble. "*Fuck!*"

Lottie realized a second too late what was going to happen and reeled back when Dev slammed his forehead into her nose in a brutal headbutt. She felt and heard the cartilage snap like a wet toothpick, blood streaming down her face in a thick warm river. The pain arrived an instant later, causing her to let out a guttural noise as she crawled away from Dev and in the direction the gun went. Flynn was up on his feet now and was grappling with Dev, clearly trying not to hurt him even though Dev wasn't affording him the same kindness, and Lottie now knew it would take something a bit more shocking than a fistfight to break Dev out of the spell he was under.

She closed her fingers around the gun's grip and rolled to her back, aiming through blurred vision at the two struggling men. "Dev, *stop!*"

What happened next took place so quickly that at first it didn't make sense in Lottie's brain. Dev clawed and shoved at Flynn, hitting him in the gut hard enough to double him over, then began advancing toward Lottie, blank eyes zeroed in on the weapon in her hand but seemingly unbothered by it. He was a threat as much as he was her friend, and in that instant the training the Army had drilled into her took over. She could barely see, was filled with pain and desperation, and she would realize later that while she thought she was aiming at Dev's shoulder, she had in fact been pointing the gun at his heart. Her index finger moved from resting on the trigger guard to sitting on top of the trigger itself, and it only took the slightest twitch to pull it.

The gun jumped, jerking her arm back, and she tasted nothing but copper as she watched Flynn twist around and push Dev out of the way of the oncoming bullet. They both toppled to the floor, with Dev's head making a sickening sound as it smacked the concrete. A groan came with it, and a moment later he was throwing up just like Lottie had, then crawling over to her. "Lottie?" he asked, horror in his voice. "Oh my god… what did I do?" His hands went to his hair, digging in and pulling hard. "What did I *do*?"

"Wasn't you," Lottie rasped, forcing herself to sit up even though her head felt like it was going to explode. She spat out a stream of blood and saliva, dropping the gun and putting what she hoped was a reassuring hand on his shoulder. "Not you." She focused beyond Dev to Flynn, and her whole body went cold. "Oh no."

Dev looked too, going rigid in her grasp when he saw the slowly spreading pool of blood, emanating from the giant hole that had been punched through Flynn's chest. The noise he made wasn't human as he wrenched himself away from her and toward his partner, and Lottie was helpless to do anything but follow, equal amounts of terror and guilt clawing at her insides.

She made it two steps before the lights went out.

~***~

Flynn knew he was dying.

He'd come close many times before, from shrapnel to snake bites and everything in between, but this one… this one was going to stick. He could feel the life draining out of him even as Dev's frantic hands clamped down over the wound to his chest, pressing so hard his ribs ground together. He couldn't see anything in the sudden blackness, but he knew it was Dev, everything about him intimately familiar—his breathing, the strength of his fingers, the way his voice cracked on Flynn's name as he tried to tell him he was going to be alright.

"Think this is gonna be the first time you're wrong, hoss," Flynn managed to grind out as red emergency lights flickered on around them, the door to their room unlocking and swinging open— probably some kind of safety precaution, in case of fire or flood or any number of other issues. He tried to move his arm, wanted to at least pat Dev on the shoulder, but he couldn't. In fact, he couldn't feel much of anything below where Dev's hands were trying in vain to keep his blood inside his body. "I'm not getting out of here. But you two are."

"*No*," Lottie protested with a whimper, landing on her knees next to Dev and adding her hands to the pile. "Flynn, I… I'm s-so sorry. It was—"

"An accident, I know that," Flynn interjected. He looked into Lottie's ruined face and chose his next words deliberately. "This is not your fault, you hear me? It's the fault of these fucking psychopaths and their goddamn obsession with power." He glanced at Dev, whose eyes were darting around in the way that they did when his brain was working as fast as possible to come up with a solution to the problem… except there wasn't one. "Listen to me,

Lottie... you've gotta get him out of here. He's not gonna go on his own, you have to make him leave."

"I'm not leaving," Dev said, right on cue, nearly drowned out by the chaos happening in the bunker at large. White coats and soldiers alike were scrambling to get out, carrying armfuls of specimens and chemicals and god knew what else. Something was happening beyond a simple power outage, and whatever it was had to be damn serious for these people to be running around like chickens without heads. "Flynn, I *won't*." Quieter, choked: "I can't."

"You have to." Flynn felt like the world was slowing down around him, when in reality it was him that couldn't keep up. Blackness began creeping in at the edges of his vision. "Dev... if I can't move, I can't run. And if I can't run..." He swallowed against the emotions clogging his throat. "Anyway. Take care of Rambo. Hell, take my place, if you want. What I didn't leave to my family, I left to you." Tears burned his eyes even as his vision continued to narrow. Words were hard to find, but he found the ones that he thought mattered: "It was always you, Dev."

Dev made a choked sound, and then Lottie was on her feet and grabbing him under the arms, pulling him up and back. "We have to go," she said gruffly, the blood on her face thinned by tears. She tightened her grip on Dev and dragged him toward the door as he began to thrash. "Don't fight me, Dev. Please."

"*No!*" Dev was actively trying to get away now, throwing elbows and even a backward headbutt, but Lottie was nothing if not tough. She held on, even though it looked like she wanted to throw up again. "Flynn, no—*no!*"

It was only fitting that the last things Flynn would hear and see were Dev. He would've died for him a million times before, so what was one more when it really counted? As Flynn's vision faded away, he watched Lottie force Dev out the door and pull it shut behind her, sealing him inside. And when the darkness took him, he embraced it like an old friend. Like he would've embraced Dev, had he gotten the chance.

~***~

Chapter Twenty-Nine

Normally, EOD training took 51 weeks to complete. Dev did it in half that time, got promoted to specialist, and was given his first assignment soon afterward. He wound up back at the same base where he'd washed dishes what felt like a lifetime ago, and Jansen almost seemed sad to be dropping him off. Like a mother bringing her son to school, only Jansen was just about the least maternal person Dev had ever met, and until the military, Dev had never encountered traditional learning.

"Gonna miss you, kid," she said, giving him a crisp salute. That was highly unusual since she outranked him, but Dev returned the gesture nonetheless; secretly, he was touched that her regard for him was so high. "Go give 'em hell out there, yeah?"

"I'll do my best," Dev promised, and with a perfunctory wave, off he went.

It took him no time at all to remember the base layout, and he found the barracks with ease. Locating his bunk was as simple as finding his last name scribbled on a piece of paper taped to the end of a bunk bed, and when he saw the name WALKER written right below it, he had to wonder…

"Hey, it *is* you!" Walker exclaimed, much more jovial than he had been on the day he, Dev, and Wolfe had worked together to save Sheffield's life. "I thought so when I saw the name taped up there. Made it through bomb nerd training, huh?"

"Apparently I beat a record," Dev replied, taking the hand that Walker offered him to shake. He resolved then and there to not think about how large the other man's hands were, calloused from years with firearms. Don't Ask Don't Tell was a fickle beast, and Dev had no desire to make any more enemies than they already collectively had. "I think Jansen was almost sad to see me go. Almost."

"Well, I think I can speak for everybody when I say that we're glad you're back." Walker's expression quickly turned grim. "There's been an uptick in IED deaths as of late, and from what I heard, the last bomb tech that got deployed from here lost both his arms." A pause. "I'm probably not selling you on the job, huh?"

Dev snorted. "Don't worry, I know what I signed up for." He tossed his bag into their shared foot locker. "But what I'd *really* like to know is why a badass Delta Force operator like you is hanging around here terrorizing newbies."

"Badass, huh? Good to know you respect your elders." Flynn managed to keep a straight face for all of three seconds after saying that before he chuckled and shook his head. "Actually, we're gonna be working together. I'm your overwatch."

Dev raised his eyebrows. "No offense... but isn't that kind of like scut work for you?"

"Let's just say I pissed off the wrong piece of brass, and they think this is their way of getting back at me," Flynn said, motioning with his head for Dev to follow him out of the barracks. Once they were outside and moving toward the mess, he asked, "So, what's all this I hear about you growin' up in a cult?"

"We're not there yet, big guy," Dev said, allowing himself the tiniest smile. "But if you keep me alive for the next six months or so, we can circle back."

~***~

Chapter Thirty

When asked about it later during debrief, Dev couldn't remember the period of time between when Lottie hauled him out of the room where they left Flynn, and when he'd climbed the ladder that led out of the bunker. All he knew for certain was that they were the last two people to leave, because there had been nobody in front of or behind them as they made their way to the surface. The hatch above them was open to the night sky and the frigid air, and since Lottie had pushed Dev ahead of her—no doubt afraid he would try and double-back to Flynn—he reached the top first.

He was promptly grabbed by the collar of his coat and tossed into the nearest snowbank by Aleksandr. "We were starting to wonder if you'd croaked down there after all," he said conversationally, striding over to kick Dev in the stomach hard enough to make him see spots. A glance past Aleksandr revealed Frederick standing near the fire road with a few of his armed goons, watching everything that was taking place. "But since you didn't, I'm going to enjoy this."

"Oh no you're not, asshole!" Launching herself off the top of the ladder, Lottie tackled Aleksandr from behind, both of them landing hard on the damp ground. She punched him a couple times in the side of the head before he rolled her off, and when she reached for the gun tucked into the back of her waistband (the gun that had doomed Flynn), Aleksandr jumped to his feet and stomped hard on her shoulder. Something *cracked* and Lottie howled, punching ineffectively at his legs. "*Fuck!*"

Dev forced himself to his feet too, grabbing Aleksandr by the shoulders and spinning him off balance so he could deck him hard, a wild haymaker that had zero precision involved but broke his nose all the same. Unfortunately, Aleksandr flailed out the hand that didn't rush to clutch his face and in it was his knife, which Dev didn't see until it was buried in his gut. He sucked in a deep breath, eyes widening almost comically as his hands moved on autopilot to steady the intrusion. That didn't do him much good, however, because Aleksandr shoved him to the ground again, straddling his thighs and hitting him again and again and again.

"*Savior*, my ass!" Aleksandr yelled through blood and snot, doing his level best to pulverize Dev's face. The snow around them was stained scarlet and smelled like copper, and through the agony raking his body, Dev heard the distant sound of an engine; all their efforts would mean nothing if Frederick got away, if those people in the bunker were allowed to continue their research. "You can't even save *yourself*!"

There was a loud *bang*, and the beating ceased.

"Maybe he doesn't *need* to save himself, prick," Eileen said, kicking Aleksandr's dead body aside. She'd shot him in the back, severing his spine and blowing up his heart, and Dev found he didn't give a shit. "Shit, he did a number on you."

"Lottie," Dev gasped, spitting a mouthful of blood and at least one tooth into the snow. "Check… on Lottie."

"Teddy's got her, and don't worry, Tara's ringing up the cavalry." Eileen put her hands under Dev's arms and pulled hard, until he was at least in a sitting position. The world around him tilted and whirled together, spinning like the worst kind of carnival ride. "Where's Flynn?"

The question had no sooner left Eileen's lips than a deep, ominous rumble sounded beneath them, followed by an explosion so powerful it shot a column of debris and flames up into the air through the bunker's access point. Anyone who was standing got thrown to the ground, but as soon as he could Dev was crawling toward the destruction of the bunker, and even though his hearing was gone he tore his throat raw as he screamed Flynn's name. That single utterance turned into a litany of broken wails, and Dev barely felt the pain from the knife wound, his chest cracked open by despair.

An arm wrapped around him and yanked him away from the caved-in ruin of the bunker, smoldering and unstable as it was. It belonged to Lottie, and through vision warped by tears he saw her sobbing openly, her other arm hanging limp and useless at her side. After what could've been minutes or hours, they were joined by Eileen, Teddy, and Tara, all of them staring at the wreckage like they expected Flynn to emerge any moment, a triumphant if unlikely hero. Instead, a black column of smoke billowed into the bruise-dark dawn, the crumbled remnants of the bunker a reflection of Dev's broken heart.

~***~

When word reached Project Renegade that Flynn Walker was dead, Kaja sat down hard in one of the loft's leather chairs and didn't get back up again. The crackle of static filled her mind, and when she closed her eyes to try and gather herself, she felt a tear roll down her cheek. A part of her couldn't believe that one simple step she'd taken had led them down this road, but another more jaded, shrewd part said in her brother's righteous police detective voice, *the road to hell is paved with good intentions* and *you should've known better*.

Sabene was still on their feet, saying something to Tara that ended with: "Keep us posted." Then they muted the comm line and swiped at the tablet in their hands. "The plane's fueled and ready to go on the airstrip. If there aren't any delays, they should be back here before noon for debrief." They looked at Kaja with eyes full of sympathy. "I'm sorry, ma'am. I didn't know Agent Walker well, but he was clearly well-loved around here." They cleared their throat. "The tactical team evacuated as many members of the Reborn as they could find, and they'll be given medical attention if necessary before they're questioned. Aleksandr Lichtenstein is dead thanks to Agent Stanley, but Frederick Devereux is in the wind."

Kaja didn't say anything for a long moment, and she startled a bit when David spoke for her, a hand landing on her shoulder; she had forgotten that he was there, along with Diana, Wolfe, and

Scarlett. "Could you give us a minute, Sabene?" He addressed the group at large: "Actually, could Kaja and I please have the room?"

Sabene nodded, setting the tablet down and smoothing their hands over their slacks. "Sure, of course. I'll be downstairs." They nodded toward the others, and as a unit the four of them shuffled toward the stairs like a row of shellshocked tin soldiers, faces pale and gaunt with grief.

David waited until they were gone to sit down on the coffee table in front of Kaja, deliberately putting himself in her line of sight. He sought out eye contact, and there was nothing but sincerity on his face when he said, "Kaja... I'm so sorry."

"It's my fault." Her voice rung hollow to her own ears, and there was a pressure deep in her chest that felt like it was going to break her ribs. "David... Flynn's dead because of me."

"You didn't know any of this was going to happen," David argued, and Kaja appreciated it, she did, but it didn't change how she felt or the reality of the situation. "And while I might not agree with your decision, I'm also not the one who's had to watch Dev hunt for answers about his father for years."

"That's the worst part." Kaja stared down at her hands, which were clenched into fists in her lap. "After all that, Frederick got away. *Again.*"

"Not for long. From the sounds of things, he needs medical treatment—the kind that's expensive. I'm sure you can come up with a way to track him down through that." David grabbed her hands and forced her fingers to relax. "Losing Flynn is tragic. But I believe you can right your wrongs."

"If I'm here to do it," Kaja said grimly, forcing herself to sit up straight. What was done was done, as callous as that sounded; the only way she could deal with it was to move forward. "My guess is, someone from higher up will come calling about this fucked up mission, and I plan to tell them the truth, so…" She shrugged. "If I lose my job… well, I don't think it makes much difference. I haven't spoken to them yet, but I know I've lost the team." She stood up and pulled her phone from her dress pocket. "Thank you, David. Now if you'll excuse me, I have a funeral to plan."

~***~

The plane ride home from Bozeman was hell.

It was a cliche way to describe something unpleasant, but Tara could think of no other word that was fitting. She sat in a seat next to Teddy, who'd had nowhere else to go at the end of everything except back to Boston with them. He'd proved to be a loyal, valuable asset, and Tara had the feeling that he might even be approved to join their team. They had a vacancy now, and that single thought opened up a yawning chasm of grief inside her chest.

Dev was practically comatose with his eyes open, covered in blood from head to toe, most of it his own but some of it belonging to both Flynn and Aleksandr. Tara could've sworn she saw him get stabbed right before Eileen had killed Aleksandr, but there was no knife sticking out of him and he wasn't actively bleeding, so maybe she had interpreted something wrong in the chaos. Next to him was Lottie, who had her right arm cradled in her lap and a mess of clotted blood on her face. Her dark eyes looked empty, mouth drawn down in a permanent frown, and while Tara didn't know exactly what had happened down in the bunker, she suspected it was much worse than anything she had thought of already.

"We'll have to tell his family," Eileen said, and it was the first time anyone had spoken since they boarded the plane. Her voice was rough from crying, and even as she talked, more tears slipped down her freckled cheeks. "They'll… they'll want to know why there isn't a body to bury."

If Tara had thought Eileen sounded bad, her voice was nothing compared to the way Dev's rang hollow and raspy: "I'll do it. Just… not now."

"But what about Frederick?" Tara heard herself ask, almost unaware it was her who spoke up until Dev's eyes, bright and intense with sorrow, snapped to her. "We have to—"

"*Not*," Dev said slowly, a seething anger creeping into his words, something barely controlled about the way he was leaning toward her, like a rabid animal straining against a leash. "*Now*."

For the first time since she'd known any of her coworkers, Tara felt genuine fear. Not fear of Dev, but fear of what a loss as great as Flynn's was going to do to their team, their *family*. She snapped her mouth shut and saw Eileen do the same, and everything went as quiet as the grave once more.

~***~

Chapter Thirty-One

Six months turned into the remainder of Dev's tour, and while Dev had never taken kindly to the idea of working with a partner—it reminded him too much of Teddy, and losing him was a wound that would never fully close—he had to admit, there were benefits attached. Like not worrying about getting his head blown off while he was trying to defuse a bomb, because he knew Flynn had his back from a perch with his sleek and deadly M24 sniper rifle. Or knowing that he would always have access to food even if he took two minutes longer in the shower, because Flynn would take an extra tray and stare down anyone who tried to give him shit about it. Or that he'd make new friends through Flynn, including Jim Wolfe, whose unfortunate fate they learned one day after a double shift clearing IEDs off a critical throughway.

"You guys hear what happened to those Rangers last night?" a private, green and bubbling with excitement at the idea of combat, asked Dev and Flynn right as they walked into mess. "Everybody's talking about it."

"We were a little busy last night," Flynn drawled, and Dev's traitorous stomach swooped but that was *not* what he meant, not in the slightest, and Dev tried to write off the feeling as hunger. "Why?"

"A whole unit got obliterated," the private said, sobering only slightly as the words tripped out of his mouth. "Some of their infantry backup is still kicking, but only one of the Rangers made it out, they flew him to Germany already. I heard one of the MPs say it looked like half his body got run through a wood chipper."

"Poor fucker." Flynn shook his head sadly, speaking for both of them; Dev didn't mind, since he shared the sentiment and also didn't exactly have a knack for small talk. Sometimes he contemplated how amazing it was that he knew how to hold any type of conversation without killing someone. "Anybody I'd know? I was Delta before this gig."

"A sergeant named Wolfe," the private replied, right before getting waved down by some of his buddies. He scurried away, calling over his shoulder, "Gotta go, fellas. Do yourselves a favor and don't eat the beans!"

Dev swallowed hard, looking at Flynn who seemed just as shocked as he felt. "*Shit*. Poor Wolfe. Do you think he'll…?"

"I don't know," Flynn murmured, rubbing a hand over his mouth. When he met Dev's gaze, his dark eyes were full of pain. "But Wolfe's one of the good ones, and a tough bastard on top of it. I hope he pulls through." He clapped his hand down on Dev's shoulder, squeezing firmly. "Stop thinkin' so hard. I ain't gonna let that happen to you." He snorted. "Hell, of the two of us I'm probably the one that'll get blown up."

"I wouldn't that happen," Dev said quietly, watching his partner even as he turned to collect a tray from mess. He felt the conviction of those words deep in his bones, and murmured the next ones to himself: "No matter what."

~***~

Chapter Thirty-Two

When Lottie, Dev, and Teddy were escorted into the triage room on Project Renegade's second floor, Lottie took one look at Kaja and punched her in the face.

It was with her non-dominant hand, since her right shoulder was still fucked up, but the *crack* of her knuckles against Kaja's jaw was satisfying all the same. The other woman stumbled backward clutching her face, and the fact that she didn't retaliate was telling. Instead, she met Lottie's gaze and spat blood on the floor, probably from her molars cutting the inside of her cheek. It was easier, Lottie imagined, for Kaja to look at her than it would've been to look at Dev, who was eerily silent. They all knew exactly the kind of violence he was capable of when provoked, and Lottie couldn't think of a bigger provocation than Flynn being fucking *dead*.

"You know what you did." When Dev finally spoke, he still sounded as hollow as he had on the plane, but now there was an undercurrent of exhaustion to the words. "You don't need me to tell you why it was wrong. And while any of us could die on any mission on any given day, those missions usually don't have your fingerprints on them before our plane even lands." He took in a shaking breath and let it out slowly. "Consider this my resignation."

"Dev—" Kaja started to speak, then thought better of it. She nodded instead, and left the room without another word.

Since there was only one exam room, they had to take turns on the table, allowing a government-subsided doctor to look them over, patch up any injuries, and in the case of Lottie and Dev, take their blood to see what sorts of chemicals they were exposed to while they were in the bunker. Lottie wasn't shy about her body—she was covered in tattoos from the neck down and had been a Ranger, for Christ's sake—and had no problem taking off her shirt in front of Teddy and Dev so the doctor could set her shoulder. She hardly felt it when the doc pushed her shoulder back into place, and wouldn't think that was strange until later, when her and Dev's test results came back and all of Renegade's medical personnel lost their collective shit.

"What am I gonna do after this?" Teddy wondered aloud, looking a little better now that he had an ice pack for his face and proper bandages for his wounds. He'd lost some of the chalky cast to his skin, at least. "I don't have anywhere to go."

"You can come stay with me." Once, Lottie thought Dev might've been excited at the prospect of being roommates with his old friend. Now it seemed like none of them would be excited about anything again. Grief could do that to you. "My landlord is cool, she won't mind. I... I'm going to be spending time at Flynn's, though."

"Of course," Teddy murmured. He hesitated for a second before draping an arm around Dev's shoulders, hugging him from the side. "I'm so sorry, *hermano*."

Dev's eyes closed, a pained line appearing between his brows. "Yeah. Me too."

"Dev," Lottie said, her voice feeling thick in her throat. He didn't open his eyes to look at her, but she knew he was listening. "M'sorry." Her eyes welled with involuntary tears, and she did nothing to stop them. "I... you know I didn't mean to shoot him. You know that, right? You *have* to know that."

"I know." Dev's fingers were so twisted together in his lap that they looked like they might never come undone. "You... love him too." He made a pained sound. "*Loved* him. You were just trying to stop *me* from—*fuck*, I need to go." He shook off Teddy's arm and stood, glaring at the nurse who tried to block his path. "I wasn't kidding earlier when I told Director Kamienski that I quit. You can't keep me here." Either because of Dev's words or the look on his face, the RN stepped aside, and Dev glanced back at Lottie and Teddy briefly. "I'll be at Flynn's. Somebody's gotta feed Rambo."

Teddy tipped his head forward in acknowledgement before letting it drop back against the wall behind his chair, eyes falling shut. Lottie raised a hand to wave before Dev disappeared down the hall; much like not feeling the pain from her shoulder being set, the significance of her knuckles not being bruised from hitting Kaja wouldn't sink in until later.

~***~

Dev wasn't sure how he made it from Project Renegade to Flynn's house in one piece. The route was as deeply ingrained in him as the one to and from Aoife's, sure, but that didn't account for asshole drivers, other pedestrians, and the unpredictable miasma that was the MBTA. That meant when he stepped off the Green Line at Union Square in Somerville and found himself whole and alive, he was surprised, if in a distant and disaffected sort of way.

The logical part of his brain—which was *always* whirring away no matter what the rest of him was doing or feeling—was more than a bit puzzled by the fact that he was unhurt, and it had fuck all to do with his sense of direction. It kept picking apart everything that happened in the moments that led up to the bunker explosion, and reminding him that he had, in fact, been stabbed in the gut by Aleksandr. But yet when he pulled up the hem of his (filthy, stained with Flynn's blood) shirt, he saw only a faint pink line where the knife had gone in, like it'd happened months ago instead of only hours prior. That meant something big and bad, but at this point Dev couldn't find it within himself to give a shit.

Flynn owned a house on Vinal Street, between Spring Hill and the Inner Belt, directly across the road from a combination athletic field and dog park. The whole reason he'd traded his apartment in Charlestown for something more spacious was because of Rambo, who now enjoyed not only proximity to the dog park, but her own fenced-in yard, tiny as it was. The house was a classic New England Colonial, with an exposed brick foundation, sage green siding, and a bright red front door; the garage where Flynn stored his 4Runner was tucked behind the house, along with the aforementioned postage stamp of grass.

Dev stood on the sidewalk in front of the house for several minutes, staring up at its darkened windows with his hands shoved deep into the pockets of his coat. As he was studying it, he realized that Rambo, the 4Runner, and the house and its contents were the only things left of Flynn; his wallet and dog tags would've been destroyed along with him, if not by the explosion then by the fire raging afterward. His only hope (wasn't that an ugly word, *hope*) was that Flynn had lost enough blood that he died before feeling the lack of oxygen from the gas leak or the searing lick of flames along his skin. Imagining his friend, his partner, his… *whatever* they were, it didn't matter now, suffering like that, was too much for even someone as battle-tested as Dev to think about.

Taking in a deep, shaking breath of bitterly cold air, Dev mounted the steps up to the front porch and pulled his keys out of his pocket. He flipped to the right one without conscious thought, remembering to jiggle the knob as he unlocked the door so it didn't get stuck. Then he was inside and flipping on the lights to reveal the living room, with Rambo jumping up from her bed under the picture window to greet him. She was a beast of a dog in the looks department, but Dev knew she had a heart of gold... just like her owner. Or her owner *used* to.

"C'mere, girl," Dev choked out, dropping to his knees on the cold entryway tile and not feeling it at all. He elbowed the door shut right before Rambo got to him, licking his face and wagging her whole butt in the way that only a Rottweiler could. He scratched behind her ears and rubbed her big head, then wrapped his arms around her and just hung on. He buried his face in her short fur, eyes burning even though he thought he was all out of tears. "M'sorry, Rams. I'm so sorry." The dog made a confused whining sound and nuzzled at his shoulder, which only made him cry more. "I'm sorry I couldn't save him."

He let himself sit there for a minute, two, maybe ten or twenty or an hour—the concept of time was strange and nebulous, like everything else about a world without Flynn in it. Dimly he was aware of his phone buzzing in the pocket of his jeans with text messages and calls, and when it got to be too annoying, he simply yanked the device out of its resting place and hurled it across the house. It hit the bifold doors in front of the laundry closet with a satisfying *crack* and fell to the floor in pieces, blessedly going silent and still.

Letting his head fall back against the door, Dev counted the swirls of plaster in the old home's ceiling, pressing one hand to his chest. It *hurt*, like someone was digging around in there with their hand and yanking at his heart. Flynn was… gone, Frederick was in the wind, Kaja had broken his trust, and he'd left his job and his friends behind as a result. He'd have to call Flynn's family, find out about arrangements for a funeral, all while trying to keep the abyss of the loss from swallowing him whole.

For the first time in a long time, Dev felt well and truly alone.

~***~

Right after the field team arrived at Project Renegade, Eileen had broken away from the group and stalked through the parking garage to her car. She drove a nondescript Toyota Corolla, bland as oatmeal right down to the color; much of her life was spent looking for easy marks, and those with flashy, expensive cars were often tops on the list. Before Eileen lost sight of her, Tara had almost looked like she wanted to stop her from leaving, but if she had tried, Eileen would've gritted out something she would've regretted later and gone anyway. Even her concern for Lottie couldn't tamp down the fiery anger stoked inside her, black little heart nothing more than a burning coal.

She had one thing on her mind: Smack the shit out of Valeriya Sidorova until she admitted her gang's involvement in the production of Destroyer, or die trying.

The drive from Renegade in South Boston to Valeriya's tea room in Brookline should've taken about a half-hour, maybe a few minutes either side of that depending on traffic since it was after rush hour. Eileen made it in fifteen minutes exactly, her hands white-knuckled on the wheel and her mind processing exactly nothing of her surroundings. She drove using muscle memory alone, and she was surprised that she didn't accidentally switch to the other side of the road, as if she were back in the UK. As it was, she parked the wrong way in a parallel spot and left her engine running, in case she needed to make a speedy getaway.

It wasn't until she was yanking on the locked door of the tea room that she realized something was wrong. The lights were off and the blinds were down, which wasn't totally unexpected—it was early in the morning, and Eileen doubted very much that most people thought *Russian tea room* when they wanted breakfast. Especially not in Greater Boston, where chances were good that you'd find two Dunkins across the street from each other and both would have drive-thru lines into the street at this time of day. But no, the issue before her was much bigger, right in front of her in the form of a giant paper sign that read: **PERMANENTLY CLOSED**

"What the *fuck*?" Eileen asked herself aloud, banging a fist on the glass of the door in frustration.

A homeless man groaned from the doorway of the cell phone repair store that occupied the next unit, rolling over on his blanket. He peered at her from under a faded New England Patriots beanie, wrapped up in an equally battered LL Bean coat. "You lookin' for those Russians?"

"Unfortunately, yes," Eileen said, resisting the very strong urge to find a loose brick to hurl through the window of the former tea room. She focused instead on the homeless man, noting that one of his legs was much stiffer than the other. "Where did you serve, sir?"

He snorted. "Think I'm still a little young for *sir*. But to answer your question, Afghanistan."

She came closer, motioning to the leg that was clearly artificial. "And did that happen over there, or was that a present when you came home?"

"I like you," the homeless man declared, sitting up to lean against the shop door. He had the faintest southern drawl, and it made Eileen's heart ache for Flynn, even if this man's was less Texas and more bayou. "You're very direct. And observant. Lost the leg after I got home, believe it or not. Car accident."

"I'm sorry," Eileen offered sincerely, folding her arms over her chest to keep away the early morning chill. The Starbucks down the block was starting to get crowded, cars honking at each other as they fought for parking space. She debated how to approach her next question, and in a rare moment for her, she opted for the truth: "I'm looking for the Russians because I work for the government."

A wry smile. "Kinda figured that. Direct and observant often come with spook attached." He offered her a gloved hand to shake. "Jason Sheffield."

"Eileen Stanley," she said, taking his hand and tilting her head to one side. The name sounded familiar, but she couldn't recall why.

"The Russian I want is a woman. Blonde hair, eyes like ice chips, a killer figure—"

"Valeriya." It was a statement, not a question. "She was here yesterday night, bitchin' up a storm. My Russian ain't real good, but I heard something along the lines of, 'if you can't do something right, you have to do it yourself'." Jason's brow furrowed. "And then she mentioned Montana, which I thought was random. Then something about going to see her father."

"Believe it or not, Montana isn't quite as random as you'd think." Exhaustion felt like a physical weight on Eileen's shoulders, and she tried and failed to remember the last time she slept. "Thank you for telling me where I need to go next." She hesitated, one hand drifting toward her crossbody bag. "Do you need money? Or is there some other way I can help you?"

It was Jason's turn to hesitate. "Do you... would you be willin' to leverage your... *connections* to help me find someone?"

"That depends on who it is and why you want to find them," Eileen replied, intrigued by his choice of request. "You seem like a nice enough fellow, but I'm not going to be responsible for any type of harassment."

"Don't worry, I'm not tryin' to get back in my ex's good graces or anything like that." Jason grimaced and rubbed his chest, as if afflicted by a sudden pain—or a memory. "I'm looking for an old Army buddy, name of Jim Wolfe. He's one of the people who saved my life, way back when. Noticed he's kinda famous nowadays, what with being a detective and his brother turning out to be… deranged. Anyway, I could use his help with something personal, but I'm not sure how to get in touch without it becoming a public spectacle. Plus, I figured unless I see him in person, he might not believe it's me."

Eileen felt herself smile. "Now *that's* something I can help with. Let me give you his address."

~***~

Chapter Thirty-Two

Somewhere in between getting tortured together in the desert (successfully dismantling an Al Qaeda cell from the inside out in the process) and being discharged from the Army, Dev and Flynn wound up on the radar of a CIA agent by the name of Diana Johnson. They both clocked her watching them one bright, sunny morning in Washington DC, as they were leaving the hotel they'd stayed at during their final military debriefs. Flynn knew of Diana since his break from the Army was in fact a stint with the CIA, and what he told Dev made him instantly wary. She sounded an awful lot like him: reared in a less than traditional or pleasant environment and shaped into a weapon, then tossed headfirst into the wider world and expected to behave normally.

"She's lettin' us see her," Flynn declared once they were in their rental car and on the way to Ronald Reagan. Since Dev didn't have anywhere else to go, Flynn was bound and determined to give him a tour of Texas, which as far as Dev knew would include meeting his entire extended family, learning how to ride a horse, and drinking his body weight in sweet tea. "Johnson's the spookiest of spooks—if she wanted to observe and report without us knowin', we wouldn't."

Dev raised an eyebrow and resisted the urge to scratch at the sunburn peeling across his nose. "I'm sorry, are you saying she's better at stalking people than you *and* me?" A mischievous smile stole across his face as he added casually, "Because her being better than *you* I could see, but *me*? Come on."

Flynn spluttered, starting up the car—and then jumped above ten feet in the air when Diana rapped on the driver's window with her nails. Nails, Dev noted, that were short but filed to points and covered in a light pink polish that seemed incongruous with the rest of her. "Jesus, woman!" Flynn exclaimed, rolling down his window. "Are you tryin' to get shot?"

Diana shrugged her shoulders, tossing aside a lock of jet-black hair. "You both saw me. I made sure of that. Decided to take my chances." She spoke in the clipped way Eastern Europeans often did, sliding into the backseat of their sedan like she belonged there. "We need to talk, gentlemen."

Dev's eyebrow, which he'd never bothered to lower, climbed higher on his forehead. "We do?" He feigned confusion, and couldn't help but grin when it made Diana roll her eyes. "Whatever do you mean?"

"What I *mean* is, I am here to offer you a job." Diana raised a hand to silence Flynn. "*Not* a CIA job, Agent Walker." She smirked, winking at Dev. "You don't need to worry about me corrupting this one *too* badly."

"I'll be the judge of that," Flynn muttered, then put the car in gear and started driving, out of the parking lot and heading for I-66, which would take them across the Theodore Roosevelt Bridge and into Virginia. It was past rush hour, so they didn't immediately get caught in a standstill. "We've got a flight to Dallas that leaves in four hours. You've got until I turn this rental in at the airport to make your pitch."

"I will not need that long," Diana said, sounding self-assured but not smug. She fixed her attention on Dev, crossing her legs and sitting forward a little. "So, Adam Devereux. I have heard many things about you. Some of them are quite… contradictory. That you acted selfishly and without remorse, up until the day you were—what's the phrase?" She snapped her fingers. "*Strong-armed* into joining the Army. There you turned over a new leaf, decided to defuse bombs in order to help others." Her head tilted, expression unreadable. "Which one is the real you?"

A shudder crawled down Dev's spine and he tried his damnedest not to let it show. He hadn't been so clearly read by someone who didn't know him personally in… well, actually, he was pretty sure it'd never happened before now. "Depends on the day," he replied, mirroring her blank expression. "What are you getting at?"

"The job I'm offering requires a lack of self-preservation and the ability to think on your feet. You seem to have both of those in spades, and I already know Agent Walker is the same way." Diana didn't flinch when someone honked at them as Flynn changed lanes so he could exit for the airport. "My partner and I have been tasked with assembling a team of like-minded individuals to take on missions that even the CIA cannot or will not touch, for one reason or another. We have a couple of other recruits to interview, but things are coming along. Are you interested?" She jerked her chin at the back of Flynn's head. "Or would you rather tip cows with him for the rest of your life?"

"Hey, we know how to do more than tip cows in Texas," Flynn protested, glancing at Dev. "It's up to you, hoss. I've done the whole spy song and dance already, but I told you back in the shit—I go where you go."

Dev couldn't lie to himself: he was intrigued. Intrigued by the idea of working behind the scenes instead of on the front lines, by being a part of a bigger team than just him and Flynn and maybe the occasional bomb dog. He also knew that if he didn't have something to do now that he wasn't with the military, he'd probably end up right back in a jail cell in under a year. "We're still going to Texas," he decided aloud, "for two weeks. But after that… we'll talk. Where should we meet you?"

"God, not here," Diana said with such disgust that Dev couldn't help but laugh. "I hate DC. Besides, my partner would like to be closer to his family… we're thinking about setting up shop in Boston." They were off the highway and headed into the airport complex now, moving along at a crawl behind a chain of cars. She nodded at Dev and reached for her door handle. "Two weeks. I'll be in touch."

Once she exited the car she disappeared behind an SUV the size of a small boat, and Dev looked to Flynn for guidance. "Was that the right move? Or should I have blown her off?"

Flynn considered that for a moment, tapping his thumb against the steering wheel. "You know as well as I do that neither of us are very good at sittin' around doing nothing for real long. And that's what we're staring down the barrel of right now. So... I think you made the right call." He glanced at Dev and smiled. "Plus, you managed to convince her you hadn't already been corrupted."

"That happened a long time ago," Dev said, feeling lighter than he had since his boots first touched American soil. "It's what I do with it that matters. And I think I can do some good."

"Then that's good enough for me." Flynn reached over and squeezed his shoulder, pulling into the rental return area. "Now, let's go tip a damn cow or two."

~***~

Epilogue

Valeriya Sidorova waited in the trees on the outskirts of the compound that had once belonged to the Reborn with her men, until the personnel from various alphabet soup government agencies packed up their investigation. The clock in her head, which had never once led her astray, told her it took just about 72 hours from start to finish. And when the last sounds of helicopter rotors and tires crunching on gravel faded out, she stood straight and tall while leading the way to the crater in the ground.

Some of the rubble had been moved around both with heavy machinery and by hand, so it wasn't too hard for Valeriya to pick a path downward. She held a handgun with a flashlight attachment out in front of her, partially for the light it provided and also because she'd been briefed on the potential side effects of Destroyer and she had no desire to be ripped in half by a deranged science experiment armed with superior strength and speed. The bullets in her magazine were hollow points, and she carried two extra mags in her coat pockets—a girl could never be too careful.

Valeriya directed her men with hand signals to search the flanks

of the ruined bunker while she walked deeper alone. She was the

only child of a Russian crime lord, and had been trained since birth

to trust no one but herself to watch her back. Her instincts were

sharp, her knives sharper, and she preferred to work alone wherever

possible. She'd even offered to come to this hovel outside of

Bozeman sans the men, but that idea had been swiftly shot down by

her father.

Her boot hit a slick patch and she slipped a little; if it weren't for

her ballet conditioning, she would've fallen on her ass. "Fuck me,"

she muttered, looking down to see what could only be described as a

lake of blood. It had had ample time to dry, but with the temperature

it had frozen instead, a thin layer of ice cracking when she put her

foot on it. "Damn, these were new shoes."

A scraping sound reached her ears and she froze.

It hadn't come from her men; they were too far away. There was

the possibility that it was a fluke. The incidental shifting of rubble,

perhaps, or an animal that found itself trapped in the wreckage…

except it happened a second time, when Valeriya was actively

listening for it. The noise was coming from somewhere off to her right, and with her finger inside the trigger guard, she ducked under a crumpled doorway and into what remained of an observation room.

Several large chunks of concrete and rebar were piled in the middle of the space, and the simple action of stepping into the space kicked up a cloud of dust that Valeriya sincerely hoped wasn't made from asbestos. She heard yet another scrape, and soon found its source: a bloodied hand, sticking out between two pieces of rubble and clawing weakly at the outside world. She stood and watched until it went still, then grabbed the edge of one of the chunks of and pushed it aside.

Valeriya sucked in a harsh breath through her nose when she laid eyes upon Flynn Walker, battered and broken but very much alive.

She swore again, this time in Russian, dropping into a crouch to inspect him further. He looked to have passed out, from exhaustion or pain or maybe both, and it seemed that a bullet had torn clean through his body at some point. Using the muzzle of her gun to peel blood-soaked fabric away from skin, she noted that the wound was closed and beginning to scar, all on its own. That meant he'd already received a dose of Destroyer, and it was working as intended.

"I am so sorry," she whispered, pushing back to her feet and wiping a forbidden tear from her cheek. She knew her father's plans, knew he would see Flynn as the perfect test subject for the next phase, but she also knew she couldn't get him out of the bunker alone without being asked questions she couldn't answer. She warred with herself for a long moment, debating putting a bullet in Flynn's head and ending his misery before it could truly begin… but even she wasn't that cold. Instead, she raised her voice, and like a nail in a coffin called out, "I need help! Someone is alive down here!"

THE END

Acknowledgements

Well, we made it back here again! Another book in the can means another acknowledgements section, and as always, I only have a vague idea of what I want to say. If you've kept up with me at all in the 2 years since *Wounded* came out, you'll know that *Project Renegade* isn't just a spinoff novel from the Wolfe & Vaughn Mysteries—it was my graduate school thesis project! Fun fact: I conceptualized and began outlining *Project Renegade* in between *Scar Tissue* and *Wounded*, but I wanted to finish the Mass Art Murderer story arc before I published anything else. As it turns out, that was the right call for a number of reasons, not the least of which being that this "standalone" book is what earned me my MFA.

As far as thanking people is concerned, I have to give my first one to Mom and Dad. Thanks for putting up with my insanity for my entire life but particularly over these past 2 years when this project consumed my brain. Love you.

Jenn, Michelle, and Sam, you guys already know how much I appreciate your support and friendship, but I'm going to tell you again here just because.

To Katie, Aimee, Lavender, Sarah, Loch, Sam, and the rest of my Tumblr fam: THANK YOU as always for being awesome.

I probably forgot somebody I wanted to mention, so presume that if we've ever interacted at all I appreciate the hell out of you.

If you like the cover of this book, it was created by Mindbomb Design on 99designs!

Last but certainly not least, I want to give a huge shout-out to my Kickstarter backers! Without them this project would not have been possible. In no particular order, thank you to: Giovanni, Enzo, and Brizeida Rivera, Shelby Bolstridge, Phoebe Miller, Aimee Schwintz, Rae Samsun, Sabrina Ramjan, Emily Magnon, and Michelle & Albert Lee.

About the Author

Samantha Simard holds a Master of Fine Arts from Southern New Hampshire University and graduated *magna cum laude* with a Bachelor's in English & Creative Writing from SNHU. She possesses a deep love of books and has been writing stories since she learned to read, and in addition to writing books she currently works as a marketing copywriter. When she isn't crafting a blog or working on her next novel, her hobbies include video games, caring for her houseplants, and playing with her cats. You can visit her website or follow her on social media to tell her she needs to write more.

Website: samanthasimard.com

Facebook: @thesammykinz

Instagram: @the_sammykinz

Threads: @the_sammykinz

TikTok: @the_sammykinz

Substack: Samantha Simard

Ko-Fi: sammykinz

www.ingramcontent.com/pod-product-compliance
Lightning Source LLC
Chambersburg PA
CBHW050920250626
47155CB00001B/309